SHADE'S CHILDREN

GARTH
NIX

HarperCollins *Children's Books*

To my family and friends

First published in Great Britain by HarperCollins *Children's Books* 2004
This edition published 2006
HarperCollins Children's Books is an imprint of
HarperCollins Publishers Ltd
77-85 Fulham Palace Road, Hammersmith, London, W6 8JB

www.harpercollinschildrensbooks.co.uk

3 5 7 9 8 6 4 2

Copyright © Garth Nix 1997

ISBN13: 978 0 00 717498 0
ISBN10: 0 00 717498 5

Garth Nix asserts the moral right to be
identified as the author of the work.

Printed and bound in Great Britain by
Clays Ltd, St Ives plc

VIDEO ARCHIVE
INTERVIEW 1759 • ELLA

A razor blade gave me freedom from the Dorms. A small rectangle of steel, incredibly sharp on two sides. It came wrapped in paper, with the words NOT FOR USE BY CHILDREN printed on the side.

I was eleven years old then. Eight years ago, which means I am probably the oldest human alive. Five years past the time when the Overlords would have wrenched my brain out of my skull and used it in one of their creatures.

Actually, I guess Shade is the oldest human around. If you can call him a human.

Shade would say that it wasn't the razor blade that gave me freedom. It was what I did with it. The object is irrelevant; my action is the important part.

But the blade still seems important to me. It was the first useful object I ever conjured – or created, or whatever it is I do. I remember when I first realised what a razor blade was, staring at that faded page of newspaper I found. The newspaper that had lain in a wall cavity for forty, maybe fifty years, long before the Overlords decided to use the building as a Dormitory.

And there, in black-turned-grey on white-turned-yellow, an advertisement for razor blades with a picture perfect for me to put in my head.

It took three months of practice for me to build that picture into something real, a hard, sharp object to hold in my hand. Then one day, it wasn't just a thought. It was there in my hand. Real. Sharp.

Sharp enough to cut the tracer out of my wrist. To make escape a possibility...

Well, I did it. Only one in ten thousand get out of the Dormitories, according to Shade. Most can't find anything to cut the tracer out or don't have the wits to disable it in some other way.

Even when they do find something sharp, most don't have the guts to slice open their own wrist, to reach in and pull the capsule out from where it nestles between veins and bone.

Even now, when I look at the scar, I wonder how... But it's done now. I've been free for eight years...

I don't know why Shade wants to record this. I mean, who's going to see it? Who cares how I got out of the Dorms?

Of course, I really do know why Shade records. And who's going to see this video.

I've been here with Shade for three years. But he's been around for nearly fifteen – ever since the Change. There's been a lot of children in this place since then.

I've seen their videos, but I'll never see them. You sit in the dark, watching their faces as they talk through their brief lives, and all the time you wonder what got them in the end. Was it a Winger striking out of the sky? Trackers on their heels till they dropped and the

6

Myrmidons came? A Ferret uncoiling in some dark hole where they'd hoped to hide?

Now you're watching me... and you're wondering... what got her?

CHAPTER ONE

Gold-Eye crouched in a corner under two birdshit-caked blankets, watching the fog streaming through the windows. Sixteen grey waterfalls of wet air cascading in slow motion. One for each of the windows in the railway carriage.

But the fog had only a small part of his attention, something his eyes looked at while he strained his ears trying to work out what was happening outside. The carriage was his third hide-out that day, and the Trackers had been all too quick to find the other two.

They were out there now, whistling in the mist; whistling the high-pitched, repetitive notes that meant they'd lost their prey. Temporarily...

Gold-Eye shivered and ran his finger along the sharpened steel spike resting across his drawn-up knees. Cold steel was the only thing that could kill the Overlords' creatures – some of the weaker ones, anyway, like Trackers. Not Myrmidons...

As if on cue, a deeper, booming noise cut through the Trackers' whistles. Myrmidon battle sound. Either the force behind the Trackers was massing to sweep the area, or they'd encountered the forces of a rival Overlord.

No, that would be too much to ask for – and the whistles were changing too, showing that the Trackers had found a trail... His trail...

With that thought Gold-Eye's Change Vision suddenly gripped him, showing him a picture of the unpleasantly close future, the soon-to-be-now.

Doors slid open at each end of the carriage, forced apart by metal-gauntleted hands four times the size of Gold-Eye's own. Fog no longer fell in lazy swirls, but danced and spiralled crazily as huge shapes lumbered in, moving to the pile of blankets...

Gold-Eye didn't wait to see more. He came out of the vision and took the escape route he'd planned months before, when he'd first found the carriage. Lifting a trapdoor in the floor, he dropped down, down to the cold steel rails.

Back in the carriage, the doors shrieked as they were forced open, and Gold-Eye both heard and felt the drumbeat of Myrmidon hobnails on the steel floor above his head.

Ignoring the new grazes on his well-scabbed knees, he began to crawl across the concrete ties, keeping well under the train. The Trackers would wait for the Myrmidons now, and Myrmidons were often slow to grasp what had happened. He probably had three or four minutes to make his escape.

The train was a long one, slowly rusting in place between Central and Redtree stations. Like all the others, it was completely intact, if a little time-worn. It had just stopped where it was, all those years ago.

Not that Gold-Eye knew it as a form of transport. It was just part of the fixed landscape to him, one of the many hiding places he moved among. Gold-Eye didn't have memories of a different time, except for the hazy recollection of life in the Dorms – and his escape with two older children. Both of them long since taken...

At the end of the train, he got down on his belly under the locomotive, steel spike clutched in his fist, white knuckles showing through the ingrained dirt.

Peep, peep, peep, peep, peep, peep...

The Trackers were on the move again, spreading out to search. It sounded like a trio on each side of the train, coming towards him.

Gold-Eye pictured them in his head, trying to get his Change Vision to show him exactly where they were.

But the Change Vision came and went when it chose, and couldn't be controlled. This time it didn't show him anything – but a memory arose unbidden, a super-fast slide show of Trackers flashing through his mind.

Thin, spindly stick-humans that looked like half-melted plastic soldiers. Bright, bulbous eyes, too large for their almost-human eye sockets. Long pointed noses that were almost all red-flared nostril...

They could smell a human out with those noses, Gold-Eye knew. No matter where he hid.

That thought was foremost as Gold-Eye listened again. But he couldn't work out where the Trackers were, so he edged forward till he was almost out from under the train and could get his knees and feet up like a sprinter on the starting blocks. It was about thirty yards to the embankment wall. If he could cross that open space and get up it, the Trackers would go past to look for an easier way up – and Myrmidons were very slow climbers.

At this time of day that left only Wingers to worry about, and they would be roosting in City Tower, avoiding the fog.

Then the Trackers whistled again, giving their found signal – and Myrmidons boomed in answer, frighteningly close.

With that boom, Gold-Eye shot out like a rabbit, jinking and zigzagging over the railway lines, frantic with a terrible realisation.

The Myrmidons had crept through the train!

He could hear their boots crashing on to the gravel around the tracks as the huge creatures jumped down from the lead carriage, the bass shouts of their battle cries joining the frenzied whistles of the Trackers.

Heart pounding, face white with sudden exertion, Gold-Eye hit the embankment at speed, reaching head height before he even needed to take his first hold. Then, as his feet scrabbled to take him higher, he reached out... and slipped.

The fog had laid a film of moisture on the old stones of the embankment and in his panic Gold-Eye had run to one of the hardest spots to climb. His fingers couldn't find any cracks between the stones...

Slipping, his feet touched bottom and he added his own wail of despair to the awful noise of the creatures behind him.

Soon the Myrmidons would surround him, silver nets shooting out to catch him in their sticky tracery. Then a Winger would come to take him away. Back to the Dorms. Or if he was old enough... straight to the Meat Factory.

As Gold-Eye thought of that, bile filled his mouth. Then he turned to face the Myrmidons and hefted his steel spike.

"Kill me!" he screamed at the tall shapes approaching through the fog. "Kill me!"

The Myrmidons stopped ten yards away. Seven of them – a full maniple. Seven-foot-tall, barrel-chested monsters with long arms ending in spade-shaped hands. Six-fingered hands, with thick, oversized thumbs.

These Myrmidons wore gold and green metal-cloth armour that was all spikes and flanges, heavily decorated with battle charms and medals, sparkling even through the fog. Crested helmets enclosed their heads and black glass visors hid their faces.

If they had faces. They certainly had mouths, but they were silent, now that their target was trapped. The Trackers were quiet too, clustering in their trios behind the line of Myrmidons. Their work was done.

I'll make them kill me, Gold-Eye thought desperately as the Myrmidons – toying with him now – raised their net guns. He tensed himself, ready to lunge, hoping to strike one behind the knee, to irritate it enough that it would kill unthinking...

"Hey, you! Shut your eyes and *duck*!"

It was so long since Gold-Eye had heard a human voice that he almost didn't understand, till a fizzing, sparking object sailed past his head and bounced towards the Myrmidons.

He ducked, curling himself into the embankment, face pressed against the wet stone. For a second nothing happened save the massed growl of the Myrmidons' surprise.

Then there was a brilliant flash, smacking his eyes with red even through closed eyelids, and his bare neck with sudden heat.

At the same time something hit his back and he flinched.

"Grab the rope!" called the voice again. "Hurry up! The flash will only hold them for a few seconds."

A rope! Gold-Eye uncurled and saw the knotted end hanging above him. His eye followed the rope up the embankment, up to the fog-wreathed figures on the road above the railway.

Humans. Three of them. All older and larger than he.

For a moment he hesitated, glancing back at the blindly groping Myrmidons. Then he started to climb.

VIDEO ARCHIVE
INTERVIEW 1802 • DRUM

Shade made me do this. He's watching now, flapping his arms like a Winger.

I suppose that means I should say something.

<BREAK. VIDEO INTERVIEW RESUMED IN 27 SECONDS.
INTERVIEWEE HIGHLY UN-COOPERATIVE.>

How did I get out of the Dorms?

I just read that. he held up a sign. Or made one, I suppose. Being a hologram.

<SILENCE. 27 SECONDS.
NO BREAK IN VIDEO INTERVIEW.>

OK. I am going to talk.

The Overlords took me out of the Dorms when I was eight.

<SILENCE. 14 SECONDS.
NO BREAK IN VIDEO INTERVIEW.>

That is how I got out of the Dorms.

<BREAK. VIDEO INTERVIEW RESUMED
IN 3 MINUTES 12 SECONDS.>

I was taken to the Training Grounds. That's where the big, strong kids go. Lots of exercise, food... and the drugs. Steroids. Shade explained those to me... what they do... what they've done to me... Then when you're fourteen, they don't just take your brain, they destring your muscles too. Muscles to put in Myrmidons...

<BREAK. VIDEO INTERVIEW RESUMED
IN 8 MINUTES 10 SECONDS.>

The tracer? That was easy to get rid of.

I moved it out. If I can see something or I know where it is and how big, I can... think... it somewhere else.

When it was gone, I strangled the Watchward and left. I was thirteen and ten months old. Sixty days to go.

<SILENCE. 48 SECONDS.
NO BREAK IN VIDEO INTERVIEW.>

When? Three years? Five?

<SILENCE. 36 SECONDS.
NO BREAK IN VIDEO INTERVIEW.>

I don't count my birthdays. Not since then.

<BREAK. VIDEO INTERVIEW RESUMED
IN 2 MINUTES.>

I don't want to say any more.

<BLACK.>

CHAPTER TWO

There was no time for discussion at the top of the embankment. Gold-Eye was pulled up and over the edge, without apparent effort, by an extremely large, heavily muscled man. Or perhaps a boy – for his face was round and hairless, totally at odds with his mammoth physique.

The other two were women – or rather a young woman and a girl. It took a second for Gold-Eye to realise they were female, since all three of his rescuers had close-cropped hair and wore baggy green coveralls cinched at the waist with wide leather belts festooned with pouches and equipment. Long, broad-bladed swords hung in scabbards at their hips and they all wore heavy black boots.

They looked organised and Gold-Eye felt suddenly alien in his strange collection of mismatched clothing, with his matted hair showing the dirt of many weeks. He hadn't really been clean since the harsh washing rituals of the Dorms.

"Come on!" shouted the woman, grabbing him by the shoulder and starting to run. Gold-Eye stiffened, resisting, then lurched forward as the strong man almost picked him up by one arm. It was either run or have his arm ripped off.

"I run!" blurted Gold-Eye, picking up the pace. Immediately the others released him and he almost fell again before matching their stride.

"I'm Ella," said the woman, speaking in short bursts as they ran. "That's Drum."

"And I'm Ninde."

The girl was small, maybe only as old as Gold-Eye. Fifteen or thereabouts. Ella was much older, older than anyone Gold-Eye had ever seen, except in pictures. She looked as old as the women on the posters that were slowly peeling off the walls and billboards around the city.

Drum was harder to place, with a face as young as Gold-Eye's on a body that was easily twice as massive. And he hadn't said a word.

"The lane!" Ella called out, and the four of them suddenly changed direction, plunging down steps into a narrow alley where the fog lay even thicker, soaking up the light.

Halfway along they stopped so suddenly that Gold-Eye would have crashed into Ninde if Drum hadn't held him with one enormous hand.

"Ninde?" asked Ella, her breath making the fog eddy around her face.

Ninde closed her eyes and her forehead wrinkled. A second later she started chewing slowly on the knuckle of her forefinger, then more quickly, till Gold-Eye thought she was actually going to break the flesh.

"There are Trackers in Rose Street." Eyes still closed, she mumbled the words out over her knuckle. "But they have no orders. There is a Winger above the fog, taking messages west. I can't hear anything else thinking clearly."

"Thanks," said Ella. "We'll take a quick rest before moving on."

She looked at Gold-Eye properly then and her expression changed, the way it always did when anyone saw his eyes. They weren't normal human eyes at all, blue or brown or green irises against the white. His pupils and irises were gold, bright gold – and he knew this meant that these people would leave him right away. Or worse...

"Interesting eyes," Ella said calmly. "Shade will want to see you! Must have been born right at the time of the Change. What's your name?"

Gold-Eye frowned. He hadn't spoken to anyone for a long time, or even thought in words. But at least she hadn't hit him or tried to poke his eyes out with a knife, the way other people had.

"Come on," said the one called Ninde. "Out with it."

Gold-Eye looked at her, startled. All these questions made it hard for him.

"Your name," explained Ella, talking more slowly. "Tell us your name."

"Gold-Eye," he muttered. There had been another name in the Dormitory, but no one had ever used it. He pointed at his eyes. "Gold-Eye. Because gold eyes."

"Makes sense," said Ninde. "I wonder what Ninde means? I'll have to ask Shade."

"Enough chat," said Ella. "Let's move. We'll take the Ten West Tunnel at the back of Nancel Street."

"Have we got time?"

Ninde's eyes flicked up anxiously, as if to pierce the fog. Gold-Eye knew that look, the calculation of how long it would be till darkness. But the fog hid the sun, so there was no way of knowing when the Trackers and Myrmidons would go in and the Ferrets emerge from their dormant day...

Ella glanced at something metallic on her wrist. A watch, Gold-Eye suddenly remembered, long-ago classes in the Dorm coming back to him. Big hand for hours, little for minutes – or the easy ones just with numbers.

The big man – Drum – was also looking at his watch. He nodded but made a sign with his hand, large fingers scrabbling like a spider over broken ground.

"Just enough, if we hurry," translated Ninde. "Come on, Gold-Eye!"

Then they were off again, jogging rather than running, emerging on to the road, keeping to the middle between the lines of stopped cars. The fog seemed to run with them, layers breaking and reforming, twining in and around the cars, around their legs and pumping arms.

At a crossroad, the fog gained colour from the traffic lights, one of the few sets Gold-Eye had seen that still worked, inexorably changing from red to green to amber and back to red again above the silent cars.

As the lights turned green, washing the fog and their faces with sickly colour, Ella froze. The others stopped too, except for Gold-Eye, whose momentum carried him an extra step. His footfall sounded loud in the sudden silence.

"What?" he whispered. Ninde covered his mouth with her hand and he could say no more, struck by the strangeness of someone else's skin against his mouth. Her hand smelled of soap...

Then the lights flashed amber and Ella suddenly leaped forward, with Drum close behind her, their swords out, now streaking lines of red through the mists. Gold-Eye saw their reflections multiplied in the glass windows of the cars... many glaring red Ellas... many scarlet Drums... and then he saw the Trackers who were crouched behind a loaded truck.

"Shaaaaaaaade!" screamed Ella, and then she was standing over the lead Tracker and the blade screamed too as it cut through the air and into the Tracker's neck, shearing through leather gorget and the gold service braids of a Senior Tracker.

It crumpled, head half off, but the bulbous eyes still stared, still followed Ella, as if even now it would report her to some Myrmidon Master or Overlord.

Gold-Eye stared too, unable to believe what he was

seeing. People attacking creatures? You fought when you had to and tried to escape, but you never won.

Movement caught his eye again and he wished it hadn't, as Drum's sword came down and a Tracker's head flew through the air and bounced off a car roof. The headless body staggered back and started to crawl away, feeling the ground with pallid, spider-like fingers.

Drum ignored it. Swivelling on his left heel, he cut the remaining Tracker down with his sword. It crumpled where it fell and bright-blue fluid, too thick to be blood, bubbled out from the stump of its neck.

Then it was all over – and the traffic lights turned green again.

"An old one," said Ninde conversationally, removing her hand from Gold-Eye's mouth. "They can go for hours without a head when they're fresh. Mind you, they only crawl home – and I bet they don't get fixed up. Just used for spare bits and pieces..."

"Ninde!" shouted Ella, striding back, cleaning her sword at the same time with a strip of cloth. "Bring Gold-Eye! There'll be Myrmidons here any minute."

Gold-Eye didn't need urging, but as they started down the street again, he stopped and jammed his heels into the tar. Suddenly he saw Myrmidons. Two full maniples of them, all clad in deep-blue armour, a Myrmidon Master at their head. The Master was taller than the others, and his armour had spikes and ripples that moved over his shoulders and arms...

Ninde tugged at Gold-Eye's hand and the vision faded.

"No!" he yelped as she dragged at him, using his free hand to point ahead. "Myrmidons!"

"There's no one there!" exclaimed Ella, looking back angrily. "Drum…"

"There will be!" Gold-Eye spat urgently as Drum advanced on him. "I see them in the soon-to-be-now."

"You what?" exclaimed Ella. "Damn. OK, Ninde, see if you can pick anything up."

Ninde let go of Gold-Eye and started sucking on a knuckle. But this time her eyes flashed open in fright and she let go immediately.

"Two maniples… and a Master. They're already on Nance Street. The Master knows we're – ahh – look!"

The detached head of the Tracker was still staring at them. Its long tongue came out and lashed the road, slowly manoeuvring around so its bulbous eyes would have a better view.

"It has a mind-call," said Ninde, sucking back on her knuckle. "A new one, stuck in its head, not the sort on the neck-chain."

"Right!" called Ella, her voice much calmer than Ninde's. "Follow me! Drum, take care of that!"

Drum nodded and broke into a trot down the street. As he passed the head, he expertly kicked it up and away over the line of cars, not bothering to look to see where it went.

A second later Ella overtook him and suddenly turned left into a much narrower road, where there were few cars and little room between them and the tall buildings on either side.

They were about a block away before they heard the massed roar of the Myrmidons and the frightened bleating of more Trackers.

Another block later, after more twists and turns, Ella stopped to try the door in a relatively small building – only five floors high, not breaking through the fog into the sun like the others around it.

The door opened and she led them into a chill, dark foyer. Ninde and Gold-Eye stumbled in; then Drum closed the door, shutting out the fog and the distant noise of the Overlord's hunting creatures.

"Rest for a few minutes," ordered Ella. "Then we'd better figure out how to get back home. I guess it's too late for the Ten West Tunnel – and Nine West is too dry."

"Ferrets will be stirring now."

The voice was so high and whispery that it took Gold-Eye a second to realise it was Drum who had spoken.

"Yeah," answered Ella. "I think we'd better hole up here for the night. But not on the ground level. Let's find the stairs."

She reached into one of the belt's pouches and drew out a round ball smaller than her fist. She squeezed the ball and it suddenly shed a soft, golden light.

Myrmidon witchlight, thought Gold-Eye. On the extremely rare occasions that Myrmidons walked after dusk, they carried tree branches hung with small globes. Myrmidons must have died for Ella to hold that light...

His amazement must have shown, for Ella came and stood over him, the light held high in her hand. Tall and dangerous she looked, her stubbled blonde scalp gleaming in the light. Gold-Eye felt an almost overpowering urge to bow, as he had done on the Sad Birthdays at the Dorm, when the Overlords came...

"Yeah, we killed a Myrmidon," Ella said softly, and there was a light in her eyes that was no reflection. "Drum held it, just for a moment, and I—"

"Ella," interrupted the strange, reedy voice of Drum. "He is only a youngster..."

"That's all any of us are," Ella said, but the light was gone from her eyes and with it the sudden fear that had come over Gold-Eye. He realised then that he'd ducked his head. Hiding his eyes from the knife, or the hot wire...

"Myrmidons can be killed," Ella continued. "So can Ferrets, and Wingers. And Trackers. As you have seen."

"And Overlords?" whispered Gold-Eye, looking up again. This time is was Ella who lowered her eyes.

"One day..." She said. "We will find out. But now let's find the stairs."

"I've found them," called Ninde from one of the dark corners. "The fire escape, anyway. But the door's locked."

"Ninde!" exclaimed Ella, moving quickly to the door, the witchlight held high. "I've told you a hundred times. There could be a Ferret..."

"There will be many in a few minutes," whispered Drum, moving his bulk between Ninde and Ella to grip the handle of the fire door. He didn't try to force it, but just ran his hand over it as if feeling the smoothness of the metal. There was a click from inside the door and it swung open.

Far away across the city, a fire alarm sounded in a security company's control centre. No humans were there to see it, but a vaguely human thing sat in the master chair, watching the panels. It noted the address, then used the device around its neck to notify its master.

VIDEO ARCHIVE
INTERVIEW 1871 ● NINDE

'I'm Ninde. I've been waiting for ages to do this video, but Shade won't let anyone record anything till they've been here for three months. He says it takes that long for us to get our thoughts together and sometimes even to remember who we are and where we came from.

Of course, I had no problems remembering any of that. I think it's just laziness when you get people... like Nik when he came here... who've forgotten how to talk and wash and everything. You just have to practise thinking every day.

Oh, I'm supposed to say how I got out of the Dorms. That's what this first video is always about. "How I got out of the Dorms."

You'd think Shade would let us talk about something more interesting. I've watched heaps of these videos and really everyone just does whatever they can do with whatever they have, whether it's finding something useful or using a Change Talent. Of course, hardly anyone has a really useful and powerful Talent like mine...

Which is lucky, because I'd hate to have had to cut my tracer out like Ella did, because her scar is really ugly and it must have bled heaps. Ella doesn't care about blood, but I don't like it. It's so unfair that we women have to bleed once a month anyway. You shouldn't have to cut yourself open as well.

I am getting to the point, Shade. I was going to say that since I reached puberty... did I say that right? *Pew-berty*. Stupid word. We never said that in the Dorms. We just called it bleeding and hoped it wouldn't come too much before thirteen at least. I mean it's bad enough having your brain ripped out at fourteen without having to have babies first. Of course, some people used to say the girls that got taken away for breeding got an extension to sixteen... or even eighteen...

It is connected and I am getting to the point. When I reached puberty, somehow I started hearing what the creatures were thinking. Which is not much for most of them, but the Myrmidon Master who was in charge of my Dorm used to think a lot. And one of the things he thought when I was listening was about deactivating the Tracer when you get taken away on your Sad Birthday.

So I learned where the Tracer Key was, and then I sneaked in one night and used it. That was a bit hard, but I did know where everyone was, and I'd overhead the Master thinking about the access codes for the doors and gates...

The only thing was, I hadn't heard him thinking about an alarm that's connected to the Key, so when it went off, I had to leave a bit more suddenly than I expected.

So that's how I got out of the Dorm. Straight after that, I was—

<VIDEO INTERVIEW HALTED BY SHADE.
THIS SESSION NOT RESUMED.>

CHAPTER THREE

"Wake up!"

Gold-Eye woke, panicked for a second by the feel of something pressed against his mouth. Then he realised it was Ella's hand and relaxed. A few feet away, Drum shook Ninde awake, two enormous fingers sealing her mouth.

"Ferrets have broken through on the ground floor," Ella whispered, just loud enough for everyone to hear. "We've barricaded the stair door, but they'll probably swarm up the elevator shaft as soon as they can get into it. We have to move up to the roof."

A loud crash echoing up from below punctuated her words, followed by a hiss as if steam was venting from a boiler.

"One just fell in the elevator shaft," said Ninde sleepily, red knuckle in her mouth. "It's not hurt, though. Just angry. There are four more on the ground floor."

"Will they climb up?" asked Ella.

Ferrets hated heights and would never go beyond the first or second floor – unless forced to by a superior.

"Yes!" exclaimed Ninde, her sleepiness vanishing in an instant. "They know we're here and they have orders to search the whole building, right to the top."

"Even the roof?" asked Drum. He had his sword out and was honing the edge with a pocket stone, almost as if the Ferrets were seconds away rather than minutes.

"I think so…" faltered Ninde. "There is a very strong compulsion on them. It must have come from an Overlord, not just a Myrmidon Master."

"Shit!" exclaimed Ella. She raised the witchlight higher, looking around at the dusty desks that surrounded them, searching for something useful among the blank computer screens and neatly ordered piles of meaningless paper. "We should have picked a taller building."

Gold-Eye followed her gaze, wondering what she was looking for. He'd seen many rooms like this and they rarely had anything worthwhile in them. Clothes sometimes, and sweet food wrapped in shiny metal cloth. But nothing of any real use.

"Power cords," Ella said suddenly, pointing at the thin grey cables that ran behind some of the desks, connecting computers and lights to plugs in the wall. "Drum, Ninde, find the longest cords you can – cut them away from the computers if you have to. Just make sure you unplug them first. There could still be power here."

Drum and Ninde moved quickly to the task, and Gold-Eye moved to help also. But Ella stopped him with a quickly upraised palm.

"Gold-Eye. Can you see anything in the... what was it... soon-to-be-now?"

Gold-Eye shook his head. "It comes. I not happen it."

"You can't control it," Ella said, mouth showing her disappointment. "Pity. It could have been useful. Just help get the cords then."

Still a bit sleepy, Gold-Eye went over to Ninde and watched her pull the plugs out of the wall and then out of the machines, sawing with her sword if they wouldn't come out. Since he had only his sharp-pointed spike, Gold-Eye assisted her by holding the cord taut to make it easier to cut.

They were sawing through one of the last cords when Ella suddenly thrust herself between them and pushed them towards the fire stair that led to the roof.

At the same time a crash reverberated through the room, accompanied by a furious hissing.

"Up the steps! Go! Go!" shouted Ella, turning back to the lower fire door, where Drum was frantically heaving a desk up against the shattered door. Half off its hinges, it was being further forced open by something large and sinuous, like a long, black-furred worm. Halfway along its length, paws like overlarge human hands were ripping chunks of wood and cement filler off the side of the door as easily as if they were pulling petals from a rotting daisy.

31

Drum held the desk against the door with one hand while extending the other, open-palmed, to Ella. She put one of the sawed-off cords in his hand, careful to keep the exposed wires forward. Then she ducked down and plugged it in – and Drum thrust it around the desk and into the Ferret.

Sparks blazed across the rippling flesh of the Ferret, the golden glow of the witchlight lost in a sudden blue-white glare. The creature shrieked with pain, spraying foul-smelling spit from its fanged mouth. Then it was gone, retreating back down the stairs.

Drum pushed the desk back, forcing the door into its frame, and cautiously looped the still-sparking cable around the door handle, which hung by a single screw from the ruined door.

"Might work again," he said as he headed for the roof stairs. But Ella didn't answer, letting him get ahead while she circled back every few steps to watch for a sudden rush from the Ferrets below.

A steel trapdoor opened on to the roof from the top of the stairs. As soon as Ella came through it, Drum slammed it shut with a deafening crash of metal on metal and slid the bolts home.

The roof was flat save for an air-conditioning unit that perched like a hunchback in one corner. That provided a bit of a windbreak, but it was still cold. A wind had come up to clear the fog, and the sky was clear, lit with stars and the reflected glow from those parts of the city where the streetlights still worked. The Overlords maintained power and light in much of the city, shutting it on and off from time to time for no apparent reason.

Part of their games, perhaps, in the same way that they controlled the weather. Bringing in fog from the sea; raising winds; shunting storms from one side of the city to the other, all for use as backdrops in the battles they played out with their creatures.

When those creatures weren't employed hunting escapees from the Dorms...

"We've got a few minutes," said Ella quietly. Only Drum noticed the telltale shiver of apprehension in her left hand.

"First we need to get these cords tied together into a rope long enough to reach across the street."

"What!" exclaimed Ninde, looking out over the roof at the adjacent skyscraper, its dark bulk towering over their current building. "I am... not going to climb across a five-floor drop on an electric cord!"

"That or the Ferrets," said Ella firmly. "So start tying. Sheepshanks, I think. Gold-Eye, do you know any knots?"

Gold-Eye shook his head. The automated schools in the Dorms had taught him reading, writing and arithmetic, for the Overlords liked a reasonably agile brain as raw material for their creatures. But he'd forgotten a lot of that in the struggle to survive – and knots had never been part of the curriculum.

"OK, see if you can find something like a brick or pipe to throw – we'll have to smash a window for Drum to send the rope through."

Gold-Eye grinned to show he understood and started to look about for anything useful. A pile of half-seen stuff in the shadows under the air-conditioning unit looked interesting, so he headed over to make a closer inspection.

As he passed the trapdoor, it shook, bolts rattling. Then it began to bow outward and the steam-hiss of an angry Ferret came through. But the trapdoor and bolts were solid steel and they held – for the moment.

"Hurry up!" said Drum as Gold-Eye passed. His eyes were on the trapdoor, sword held at the ready.

Gold-Eye shuddered and sprinted the remaining few yards. In the starlight he could see several pieces of steel pipe that would make good window breakers.

If anyone could throw them across the gap, he thought, as he dragged one back to where Ella and Ninde were almost finished tying the rope together. He hoped they knew their knots. It was a long way to the ground.

"Good work!" said Ella, taking the pipe and hefting it easily in one hand. Then she walked right up to the edge of the building, the toes of her boots meeting the edge of emptiness that marked the five-story drop to the street.

The building across from them was all glass and steel, stretching up at least twenty more floors.

Lots and lots of glass. Floor-to-ceiling windows, the blinds still drawn back to catch sunlight that wasn't there.

Ella looked at the window immediately opposite for a moment, imagining how it might have been. With the lights on and people bustling behind the glass, clutching papers, talking on the phone...

Her parents had both worked in buildings like this. She had dim memories of going up in the elevators, of looking out through a window just like that one...

The bolts on the trapdoor suddenly screamed in protest. Gold-Eye and Ninde both let out strangled, frightened yells... and Ella threw the pipe as hard as she could towards the window.

It flew true, glittering with reflected stars, smashing through the window in a blaze of shards. Clouds of smaller splinters followed the big shards down, strange snow falling from starlight into shadow.

"Drum!" shouted Ella, holding out one end of the rope. "Think it across!"

"Throw it first," said Drum, that clear, almost angelic voice still seeming out of place in his great body. "It's much easier."

Even before he finished speaking, Ella was throwing the end of the rope, hurling a loop of it out towards the gaping hole where there once had been a window.

Halfway across, the rope end suddenly faltered and hung suspended, like a snake waiting to strike. Then it lunged forward through the hold, to lash about in the room beyond.

Gold-Eye could no longer see it, so he watched Drum instead and saw the sweat burst out on his smooth face, beads glittering, running together to form rivulets that soaked his shoulders, turning green cloth to black.

His hands were twitching too, fingers crossing and circling in a strange arabesque – and Gold-Eye realised that Drum's hands were mimicking what his mind was doing. Tying the rope to something in the room across the street.

"It's secure," he said finally, hands falling flat to his sides. He looked terribly weary, as if he'd just run for miles with something fearful at his heels.

"Thanks," said Ella, but it was an automatic, perfunctory expression. She was already tying the rope at their end to a sturdy antenna mounting and checking the tension. Unfortunately, the makeshift rope seemed to have a tendency to stretch.

"We'll have to go hand over hand," she explained. "But use your feet as well for safety. Then, at the end, you'll have to swing down into the room. Be careful to aim for the centre of the hole. And remember to swing forward… or it'll be a very long drop. Ninde, you go first."

"I will not!"

"Shut up and get your hands on the rope," commanded Ella. "Can't you hear those Ferrets? They'll be through—"

Even as she spoke, the trapdoor sounded with a sickening boom and one of the restraining bolts screeched, stretched… and let go.

Held only in one corner, the trapdoor buckled inexorably upward to show the white teeth and red eyes

36

of the Ferret blow, brilliant against the darkness of the steps. Drum stepped towards it, thrusting with his sword, and it ducked back down, the trapdoor falling shut behind it.

Without another word, Ninde launched herself on to the rope, twining her legs around it and pulling herself along with her hands.

"Like a rat on a hawser," muttered Ella, but she seemed to be saying it to herself. So Gold-Eye didn't ask her what a hawser was. He already know about rats.

"Gold-Eye! You're next!"

Gold-Eye knew better than to argue. He'd seen what Ferrets could do to people. Did do to people.

Thinking about that got him halfway across before he even realised that the rope was swaying, the knots stretching, the ground swimming into focus so far below.

Then he made the mistake of stopping and looking down.

For a split second the idea of a possible fall seemed almost attractive. It would be an easy end, better than having his blood slowly drunk in some dark Ferret nest till there was just enough to keep his brain alive for use in the Meat Factory.

Then the rope jerked and the sudden fear of a real fall gave him the impetus for the second half of the crossing, and in just a few seconds he was swinging on to the carpet in the new building. Where Ninde sat on the floor, looking surprised that she'd made it.

37

There seemed to be a brief argument on the other side, ending with Ella furiously swarming across the rope. She came far faster than Gold-Eye and had barely swung in when she was testing the knot at the end and yelling at Drum.

"Come on!"

Drum was the real test of the rope. He pushed himself off with slow deliberation, looking like a cable car on maximum load... and the rope stretched and sagged still further.

He was two thirds of the way across when the Ferrets came boiling up out of the broken trapdoor, moving together in a sinuous wave of spitting, hissing death. There were five of them, each as long as a car, but no wider round the middle than Gold-Eye or Ninde. Something between a snake and a stretched-out rat, with only their paw-hands evidence of human origin. That, and their clever minds.

Rearing up a safe distance from the edge (for not even an Overlord could make them face such a height) they hissed together, showing long mouths with their rows of tiny teeth – and the two sharp fangs at the front. Hollow fangs, for drinking blood. Human blood, if they could get it. Otherwise, they resorted to rats, cats and dogs... or each other.

The rope held.

"Right," said Ella wearily as Drum swung into the room. "Let's get six or seven floors higher up, in case they have another go before dawn. We could all do with a bit more sleep before we start back."

VIDEO ARCHIVE
INTERVIEW 1906 ● GOLD-EYE

I am Gold-Eye.

Ninde is angry because Shade does this video now, without months' wait. He not say why.

I remember Dorms. But not getting out. Petar and Jemmie took me.

Petar did something. Here. No scar like Ella, but no lump for monitor. It went away.

Peter said he was brother. My brother.

Older, bigger. His job to look for me. He said.

Jemmie was his friend.

Myrmidons took them. The window too small for Petar and Jemmie. Petar push me through. Shout to run, hide.

Wingers fly them away. I saw in the soon-to-be-now. The Meat Factory took them in.

No more Petar and Jemmie.

Only Gold-Eye. Running and hiding.

Like Petar said.

CHAPTER FOUR

Shade's secret home was a submarine. Soon after the Change it had come away from its mooring and drifted in between two old, long, wooden finger wharves. Now the bow was wedged under the decking of one wharf and the stern trapped against the other. Sand had built up on the seaward side, locking it in place.

Shade's children came and went via a torpedo tube in the bow, safely out of sight under the wharf. They could then wade between the piles up to a storm-water tunnel that led into the city's network of drains.

The drains had the advantage of being hidden from Wingers, Trackers and Myrmidons, but it was always a gamble between two perils. Too much water in the tunnels meant a quick death by drowning – but a dry tunnel was nearly always infested with Ferrets. Even in their dormant stage during the day, they would still wake long enough to kill a careless human.

Gold-Eye, Ninde, Drum and Ella arrived under the

wharf in midmorning. Exhausted from the night before and sodden from the neck, armpits or waist down (varying according to their height) from the drains, they were not pleased to see that the tide was high.

"The tube will be shut," Ella said wearily. "We'll have to wait a few hours for the tide to go down. It looks like it's on the turn."

"Wait where?" asked Ninde. Like the others, she was hugging the rim of the storm-water tunnel, the water cascading around her legs before swooping down the short drop into the sea.

"Here," replied Ella. "Or we can swim out to the Sub and hang on. Stand or float. Your choice."

"I'll stand," muttered Ninde, in a tone that hinted things should have been better organised.

They stood in miserable silence for another three hours. Gold-Eye almost fell at one point, his leg muscle suddenly cramping and giving way, but Drum pulled him back and pushed him upstream. After that, Gold-Eye just sat in the water, letting it wash around his shoulders and under his chin.

Finally Ella judged that the tide had receded enough for the torpedo tube to be accessible. She jumped down first, checked that the water came up only to her waist and signalled the others on.

The Submarine was much bigger than it had looked from the drain outfall. Its hull loomed up above Gold-Eye five or six times taller than Drum – a giant black cylinder that had forced itself under the wharf, twisting and warping the planks so that lines of sun shone through the gaps, falling on Gold-Eye's upturned face and glittering across the sea.

Ella led them right up to the rounded nose of the Submarine, where four round hatches could be seen outlined in bright-yellow paint. Danger warnings and safety and maintenance procedures were stencil-typed next to them; flakes of rust around three of the hatches proclaimed that this maintenance had long been neglected.

The fourth hatch was rust free, and this was the one that Ella reached up to and knocked on with the hilt of her sword, creating a hollow, metallic boom that vibrated through the hull and into the water. Gold-Eye felt its buzz around his knees.

The knock was answered by a hiss of compressed air and the hatch slid open just a crack, a metallic tentacle suddenly springing out. Made up of hundreds of silver rings, it writhed in the air for a second, then turned so the end of the tentacle was facing them. A lens glittered there and Gold-Eye had the curious sensation that it was somehow looking at him.

"Don't worry," said Ella, noticing that he was unconsciously edging away. "It's only one of Shade's Eyes. He's just checking to make sure we aren't creatures."

True to Ella's explanation, the tentacle hovered in front of each of them in turn before wavering back to take another look at Gold-Eye. It looked at him from all sides before it seemed to be satisfied and withdrew back into the Sub.

After it disappeared, there was another burst of compressed air and the hatch slid completely open, revealing a narrow cylindrical passage, apparently lines with mattress foam.

Ella reached up into the passage and pulled down a heavy, knotted rope, letting it fall into the sea with a loud splash that sprayed everyone on the few places where they were still dry.

"Ella!" squealed Ninde, and even Drum seemed displeased, stepping back half a pace with a scowl momentarily passing across his face.

"Sorry," apologised Ella. "Still, hot showers and clean clothes soon. Ninde, you can go first."

Ninde needed no encouraging this time. Ignoring the knotted rope, she used Drum like a ladder, climbing up him and stepping off his shoulder as if he were a piece of furniture. Then she was wriggling her way down the tube and out of sight.

Gold-Eye was next, though he used the rope. He was surprised to find that the tube was wider than it looked from down below. He'd wondered how Drum would fit, but even his bulk would slip through all right – despite the thick padding that made it more comfortable to crawl along.

The tube ended in another hatch, which was closed. Gold-Eye hesitated for a moment, then knocked on it.

There were a few clanking sounds as the locking wheel spun; then it opened outward, revealing a large, well-lit chamber – and Ninde, wearing only her underwear and a large white towel wrapped turban-like around her head.

Gold-Eye stared, then blushed and looked down as Ninde said, "Haven't you ever seen a girl in a bikini before?"

"Only pictures," he croaked, sliding out of the tube and on to the floor. Trying not to look at Ninde's body, he looked everywhere else, noting the towels hanging on hooks on one wall and various baskets and boxes lined up on the other.

"We leave our outside clothes here," said Ninde. "Get a bit dry and then report to Shade before we shower and eat. Come on – get those wet rags off."

"Nothing else on," muttered Gold-Eye. He was confused. The sexes were segregated in the Dorms, except at meal time, and they always washed separately. Petar and Jemmie had washed together – and done other things as well – but that was all just a hazy memory of half-seen sounds and misremembered images. He didn't know how he was supposed to behave.

"Here, I'll help you," said Ninde, coming up close and taking hold of one extremely grubby sleeve. "It'll be interesting to see what's under all this dirt…"

"Ninde!"

The voice was Ella's, followed a moment later by the girl herself, leaping down from the tube like a dangerous cat.

"Leave Gold-Eye alone – and put your towel on. You know the rules."

"I was just teasing," said Ninde, letting go with a shrug.

"He's been out alone for a long time," said Ella, with a nod to Gold-Eye to show she wasn't talking over his head. "Years, probably. He's got to get used to people all over again. Think of him as being much younger than he is… at least for a while."

"Yeah. Sorry, Gold-Eye," said Ninde, complicating her apology by removing her towel with deliberate slowness and wrapping it around herself with equal deliberation. Then she tossed her head back and opened another hatch halfway, slipping through it even as it swung back and closed with a heavy crash.

"Too many films from the old days," said Ella with a sigh. "OK, Gold-Eye, we leave our outside clothes in these baskets for washing, and hang up our belts and swords for cleaning here. Shade has robots – little machines that can sort of think and do things – that do the washing and cleaning. Now, I'm going to turn my back and you turn that way, so we can get undressed. Imagine it's just like the Dorms, only the wall between the boys' and girls' washrooms is missing."

Gold-Eye obediently turned to face the wall and began to strip off the several layers of rags he used to think of as his clothes. At the same time, he fought off an urge to peek at Ella.

Just when he thought he might risk a look, a clanging noise announced the arrival of Drum. He'd taken a long time to come through, Gold-Eye thought – and was very noisy coming along the tube as well.

"Right, I'm ready," said Ella loudly. "Gold-Eye?"

"Yes," said Gold-Eye, quickly cinching the towel tight around his waist. It was a very big towel, going around him several times. Which was probably just as well.

"You go on," whispered Drum as he lumbered down from the tube. "I won't be long."

"Right," said Ella. "Gold-Eye, follow me."

She opened the same hatch Ninde had gone through, spinning the locking wheel with one practised flip of her hand. After Gold-Eye had stepped through too, she shut it behind him.

"One of the rules," she explained, as they continued down a long, narrow passage, pausing every now and then to go through another closed hatch. "All hatches have to be closed behind you, just in case some creatures get in. We're in the central corridor here. It runs the full length of the Submarine. There are hatches off to the sides, above us and below us. It'll probably take you a while to work out where everything is."

"Where now?" asked Gold-Eye.

"You mean where are we going now? To report to Shade. His headquarters are in what used to be the engine room, till his robots cleaned it out."

She hesitated, then added, "Don't be surprised by Shade. He's not exactly alive... and not exactly human. Well, I suppose he is... anyway, you'll see."

This didn't exactly reassure Gold-Eye. He felt anxious about the coming meeting, but the feeling was curiously overlaid with something he hadn't felt since the long-ago times with Petar and Jemmie. The sense

46

that other, more capable people were taking care of everything.

"This is it," said Ella, pausing before another hatch. "Stand next to me and look up."

Gold-Eye looked up, meeting the glassy gaze of another silvery tentacle slowly uncoiling down from the ceiling. It looked at them for a few seconds, then coiled back up again. A loud click from the hatch announced that they'd passed its scrutiny and the way to Shade's headquarters was opening.

But Gold-Eye didn't walk in. He stood where he was, just looking, till Ella gave him a bit of a push and he stumbled over the lip of the hatch and into the cavernous chamber.

The room took up almost the entire aft third of the Submarine. The space once separated by bulkheads and partitions, and filled with engines, fuel tanks and machinery, had been opened up by Shade's robots. Now it was a large open space. A dark space, with a single pool of light right in the middle, about thirty paces from the hatch.

Things the size of cats moved in the shadows and corners of the room, the light occasionally reflecting from their metallic sides. One scampered near the light and Gold-Eye saw it in its entirety – and shivered. It had a bulbous body, balanced lightly on eight segmented legs. Far too like a spider.

"Robots," whispered Ella, seeing him shudder. "They're safe. They work for us."

The only visible furniture in the room – a broad, official-looking desk of dark red wood and a padded leather chair – were right in the pool of a light.

Two three-seater couches faced the desk at oblique angles. Ninde sat on one, draping her legs across to take up two places. Hearing the others enter, she looked round and sat up straight.

"Where's Shade?" asked Ella as she sat down next to Ninde. Gold-Eye sat too, on the same couch – but right at the front of the cushion, ready to spring up and run. He still didn't like the look of this dark room, or the constant, peripheral movement of the spiderish robots.

"He didn't want to talk to me," sniffed Ninde. "He said he'd wait for everyone. I suppose Drum is coming sometime?"

"He'll be along in a minute," replied Ella, frowning.

Sure enough, a few minutes later a loud click announced the hatch opening again and Drum entered the chamber. Unlike the others he wore a huge towelling robe that covered him from ankle to neck. Without saying anything, he walked across and sat on the empty couch, its springs groaning under his weight.

An expectant silence followed, broken only by the scrabble of the robots' steely claw-legs on the decking.

Then Ella stood up and said, "Shade. We're all here."

VIDEO ARCHIVE
TRAINING LESSON A41

<UNEDITED>

Ella: Why do I always have to do these?

Shade: You're the oldest. You know the most.

Ella: You're older – and you could just generate the
           images anyway.

Shade: But you've actually been out there. The others
           respect you.

Ella: Do they? They're frightened of me, perhaps.
           Except for Drum…

Shade: That's because you are single-minded. Most of
           them don't realise that this is not a permanent
           refuge… that one day the Overlords will find us.

Ella: Yes. I know.

Shade: Well, we must prepare as best we can. Now, try
           not to sound bored when you're doing this. Just
           matter-of-fact. Start in three… One… two…
           three…

Touch the screen to begin. Thank you.

This is Lesson A41 of the First Series. Pay attention.
There will be an exam following this session.

The subject of this lesson is the organisation of the Overlords' creatures. The five basic creature types used by the Overlords in their battles are Screamers, Trackers, Myrmidons, Wingers and Ferrets. These creatures are always found in groups.

If you cannot accurately identify these creatures, then go back and study Lesson A2.

The following simple verse will help you remember the number of creatures in a group and the name we give the group.

Screams scream singly, all alone;
Trackers track in trios of three;
Ferrets follow in fangs of five;
Myrmidons march in maniples of seven;
Wingers fly in flights of nine.

It is important to know how many creatures there are in a group, because there will never be less than this number in any given area. If you see one Myrmidon, there will be six more somewhere nearby. If you see one Winger, the other eight will be in sight of the first.

Only Myrmidon Masters and certain special creatures will be seen alone. These are covered in Lesson A42.

Now, I will repeat the verse...

CHAPTER FIVE

"So you are. I will come down."

The voice answering Ella seemed to come from everywhere in the room. It was a deep, obviously adult voice, full of confidence and the echo of a different time. A time before the Change.

It was followed by a sudden flash of a green laser shining down from the ceiling into the chair behind the desk.

Tiny dots of light followed the beam down. They were many different colours and fell and swirled like kaleidoscopic snow. As they fell, they joined together like a three-dimensional jigsaw puzzle.

Then the laser flared still brighter and Gold-Eye blinked. When he opened his eyes again, the laser beam and the falling motes of light were gone – and there was a man sitting behind the desk.

A real, fully grown man. Thirty years old at least, or even more – if that was possible. He was smiling and his teeth were whiter than any Gold-Eye had ever seen, his eyes bluer and more piercing.

"Welcome back," he said. "And welcome to you too, Gold-Eye. I am Shade."

"Hello," said Gold-Eye in an awed whisper. He felt like throwing himself at Shade's feet, the way they used to do in the Dorms when an Overlord came.

"I'll have a talk with you later, Gold-Eye," Shade continued, fixing him with a clear blue gaze that seemed to hold an equal mixture of distant affection and anger held in check. "But first I will hear Ella's report."

"Yes, sir," said Ella, standing to attention. "A team consisting of myself, Drum and Ninde left the Sub pre-dawn two days ago on a routine patrol. We took the Main Drain and then Northwest Six to the Hospital Exit. Water level throughout was medium, with one non-threatening surge.

"At the hospital there was no creature activity except for Winger patrols. Myrmidon Death Markers indicated that a battle had been fought in the Hospital gardens several days previously, between Red Diamond and Blue Star forces, with victory going to Red Diamond. There was also an unusual battle poem posted in the gardens, dedicated to the Red Diamond Overlord. It was written in English, not Myrmidon Battlespeech. I have a copy.

"In the late afternoon, increasing Winger patrols suggested that the Death Marker truce period was over and that our presence was suspected. This was confirmed by Ninde, who looked into the minds of an approaching trio that had been sent to find us.

"We then took West Drain Four into the city. This should be marked as dangerous till there is more rain – it was only just flowing."

"Noted," said Shade, nodding his head but making no move to write in the thick leather-bound book that had appeared on his desk at the same time he had.

"We exited the drain outside the Central Fire Station," continued Ella. "As it was almost dark, I decided we'd spend the night in one of the hose-drying towers, which we did. There was considerable Ferret activity below, but none tried to climb up even part of the way.

"At midnight Drum had the watch. He woke me to advise that the lights along Park Avenue had come on and a fog was forming on the bay. Half an hour later the fog spread inland, the main mass seeming to be directed up Park Avenue. However, there were no visible Claim Fires out, so we presumed that the fog was being prepared early for a battle in several days' time."

"Correct," interrupted Shade. "I have a report that the fog was thickened and then moved further west for a battle between Black Banner and Emerald Crown over the Williams River Raceway. They're probably fighting now."

"Since the fog was still there the next morning without battle preparations," Ella continued, "we decided to move above ground and check out the railway yards between Central and Redtree. At the embankment on Shroveland Street, we heard Tracker pursuit whistles and Myrmidon battle sound in the fog. We then observed that they were chasing a human – Gold-Eye. He tried to climb the embankment but was in the wrong spot and the Myrmidons were about to take him. So I used a flash bang – the last one, I'm afraid – and we pulled him up on a rope while they were disoriented."

Gold-Eye suppressed a shiver that ran right through him as Ella's words brought it all back. If the others hadn't been there, he would be in the Meat Factory now...

"Excellent," approved Shade. "And then you fought some Trackers, took refuge in a building that proved too low to be safe from Ferrets, and had to do some fancy rope work to get away."

"How did you..." Ella began, but Shade was laughing, obviously pleased with himself.

"I have finally perfected my new Eyes," he said, clicking his fingers.

The click was answered by movement in the shadows and a nervous shiver that rippled from Gold-Eye to Ninde. Characteristically, neither Drum nor Ella twitched.

Shade's new Eyes looked very much like large rats. In twilight or fog, they would be indistinguishable from the real thing – but as they scuttled into the light, their eyes and legs shone metallically and their bodies were too rigid to be flesh and fur.

Three came from each side of the room; then all six ran in a line to the foot of the desk and turned to face Shade, their pink, rubbery tails draped out towards the couch. Ninde shuddered again and drew her feet up.

Gold-Eye thought they were repulsive too, but for a different reason. He actually liked rats, and over the years had trained three of them as pets. They had been his only real friends and he had cried when each one was lost in the all-too-frequent moves between hiding places. These robot rats reminded him too much of the Overlords' creatures and their relationship with humanity. Like, but not like…

"Can you see through them all at once?" asked Ella. There was no hint of revulsion in her voice – just the curiosity of someone shown a new tool.

"Not yet," said Shade. "My parallel-processing capabilities need further enhancement. I can use six at a time, switching between rats every millisecond. I should be able to reduce that to a switch every point-two milliseconds – which will effectively give me constant vision and allow me to use twelve of them at a time. Or more, if we can get the materials to make them."

"They should be very useful," Ella said thoughtfully. "Can they carry anything? Do any manipulation with their paws?"

"Not yet," replied Shade. "Which may be a good thing. If they depart from typical rat behaviour and are observed by a Myrmidon Master – or worse, an Overlord – he would quickly work out what they are. Then he need only scan the radio frequencies or check the old Comincsat satellites to discover that their controller is here. That I am here.

"In any case," he continued, "they are extremely useful and add greatly to my ability to gather intelligence. Which leads me to the next mission for your team, Ella. It will begin tomorrow—"

"But we've only just got back," interrupted Ninde. "Shouldn't it be someone else's turn?"

Her words trailed off as Shade fixed her with a cold gaze, and Ella half turned towards her.

"This is a reporting session," Shade said sternly. "If you have something to add to Ella's report, or a question for me, raise your hand."

Ninde didn't reply. Gold-Eye looked at her out of the corner of his eye and for a second met her gaze. In that instant she curled her lip, obviously angry. Gold-Eye looked away immediately, but he had the irrational feeling that she had suddenly taken a dislike to him.

"You must take your team out tomorrow," continued Shade, ignoring the stiff body language that declared Ninde's outrage, "because there has been a major battle at the University today between Blue Star and Silver Sun. The Death Markers went up an hour ago and will be up for two more days. This means that the Myrmidon barracks there will be deserted for that time – giving us a unique opportunity to get back to my original laboratory."

He paused as Ella raised her hand.

"Yes?"

"Rick's team has far better knowledge of the University and that area. Why not send them?"

Shade bowed his head and was silent. The others were silent too. Then Ella sighed, Ninde sniffed and Drum leaned forward as if to hear Shade better. Gold-Eye realised that what they were all about to hear was bad news.

"They were due back yesterday," said Shade, looking up. He sighed too and ran his hands through his hair. "I sent my rats out this morning, and they found their weapon belts near some hedges that line the Old College grounds. There was Tracker ichor on the ground, and Myrmidon boot prints..."

"They're gone then," said Ella. Slowly, matter-of-factly, she recited the names as if to fix them in her memory. "Rick. Nelo. Tanner."

"We will remember them," said Shade, sitting up straight, his hands laid flat on the table. "At the going down of the sun and in the morning, we will remember them."

"We will remember them," echoed Ella, Ninde and Drum. Gold-Eye sat silent, uncomfortable, aware he was in the middle of some ritual he didn't know.

Shade breathed in deeply then, chest visibly filling his crisp white shirt, and said, "Right. Back to the operation. The Death Markers give us a unique opportunity that must be exploited. There are instruments in my lab that will make a major difference to our struggle with the Overlords – if you can get them back."

Drum raised one ponderous hand. Shade hesitated, then said, "Yes, Drum?"

"Instruments worth our lives?"

"That's a difficult question," replied Shade. He didn't look at Drum, gazing at the ceiling instead as he spoke. "However, these instruments can possibly... can probably detect and measure whatever it is the Overlords project or broadcast from the silver globes you can see atop the International Trade Centre and City Tower. I've been trying to do that for many, many years, without success. I've also tried to duplicate the instruments in other ways. I really believe that if we can retrieve the main instrument package from my lab, then the secret of the Overlords' Projectors will lead us to victory."

"Then we'll get the instruments," said Ella decisively. "Right, Drum? Ninde? Gold-Eye?"

"Yeah, I guess," said Ninde unenthusiastically. Then her voice brightened slightly. "At least we'll be going somewhere different."

Drum looked at Ella for several seconds, then finally nodded his approval.

Gold-Eye didn't do or say anything. He didn't know what they were talking about. But they were his new people, his new Petar and Jemmie. He would stay with them till something happened – and if it did, he'd already decided he wouldn't run. Better dead or even the Meat Factory, than more years of running scared, running alone.

"I'll talk to Gold-Eye now," said Shade. "Ella, come back in an hour and I'll give you a full briefing. The maps will be printed out then, with the latest intelligence from my rats and Stelo's team."

"Stelo's back, then?" asked Ninde, smiling. Then she said, "Oops," and raised her hand.

Her smile slipped as Shade looked at her silently, his fingers tapping equally silently on the desk.

"Your Change Talent makes you useful, Ninde," Shade said finally, "but that doesn't mean you can ignore the rules – little rules or big rules. Yes, Stelo's team is back – but I forbid you to approach him. He's got enough to worry about without you trying out flirting skills learned from 1990s videos. If you want to sleep with someone, Ninde, put yourself in the Lottery like everyone else – and pass the contraception knowledge test, which I note you haven't even assessed."

"But I don't want to be in the Lottery," Ninde complained. "I might get anyone. I might even get Drum. Oh, sorr—"

The sharp sound and impact of a slap cut her short, and Ella was standing over her, palm as red as Ninde's left cheek. Before the younger girl could even speak, Ella had her in a "come along" hold and was forcing her out of the room.

"Right, Ninde!" Ella tightened her hold. "You've been drifting a bit and now it's time I pointed you back on course, with a little explanation about what we're here to do and your part... which I think may not be quite what you think it is!"

Gold-Eye watched them go in wonderment. Surely there was enough trouble outside without having trouble between people here?

Drum watched too, apparently unaffected by Ninde's outburst. When the hatch closed behind the two women, he got up and made a curious half bow that included both Gold-Eye and Shade.

"I'll go too," he said very softly. As he passed Gold-Eye, he paused and lowered his great round head, looming over the boy like a spreading tree. Then he spoke, voice half whistling like wind in the branches.

"Don't worry, young one. Ninde is good at heart, but strangely unaware of the time she lives in. And Ella is perhaps too much aware. I am just a product of the time. You'll understand it all, one day."

Then he was gone, lumbering out through the hatch – and Gold-Eye was left alone with Shade, the rat robots, and the spider things still lurking and rustling in the shadowed corners.

VIDEO ARCHIVE - SECRET 2711
RICK #3 - FINAL

<TRANSMISSION XPACK - COMPX25
RAT-EYE BETA 10:07:41 1102006.>

Get away! Get... ah... You're not a rat... one of Shade's Eyes...

<SOBBING.>

The others or gone. Nelo and Tanner. We got to the observation point, but there were Trackers everywhere and Myrmidons... Pre-battle, I guess... hu... hu...

<HYSTERICAL LAUGHER.>

Hundreds of them. Pouring out everywhere. We got back to the hedges, but Trackers sniffed us out... Myrmidons took Nel and Tan... I'm in Southwest Drain Twelve, about... I don't know... near the Big Six connection... Please send someone to get me... Look... the bone is sticking out... It hurts...

<MEDISCAN APP. CUT IN. VISUAL DIAGNOSIS. COMPLEX
FRACTURE OF HUMERUS. MAJOR BLOOD-VESSEL DAMAGE.

EMERGENCY MEDICAL TREATMENT INDICATED.>

I jumped... They almost had me... but I can't crawl further... I can't...

<SOBBING.>

A team could get me out. Ella or Stelo, they'll come. They'll come, won't they, Shade?

<MEDISCAN APP. CUT IN. PROGNOSIS: TREATMENT
REQUIRED WITHIN 134 MINUTES. PATIENT
IN SEVERE SHOCK. BLOOD LOSS SIGNIFICANT.>

It's pretty dry down here... Maybe... maybe dry enough for Ferrets... but it's not far... not far. They'll get here before dark. Yeah, it's OK, they'll get here... They'll get here... Shade... help me.

<INCOHERENCE. RAT-EYE BETA
RESUMES PATROL 10:09:55.>

CHAPTER SIX

Shade didn't say anything for a moment after Drum left. He just sat there behind his desk, watching Gold-Eye – who had the uncomfortable feeling that he was somehow being measured or analysed.

"Your eyes have less gold in them than they did outside," Shade said finally. "Which is very interesting. We're underwater here, and water does seem to have a damping effect on Change Talents, Change side-effects – and on creatures."

"I not... creature," Gold-Eye said hastily. He'd been accused of that before, on the rare occasions he'd met other people.

"No, you're not," said Shade decisively. "Just visibly affected by the Change, which is quite rare. But not unheard of. I have seen other cases. Now, Gold-Eye, I'm going to ask you some questions and I'm also going to tell you some things. OK?"

"Yes."

"You've heard me talk about the Change and Change Talents. Do you know what I mean?"

Gold-Eye frowned in thought. History as such wasn't taught in the Dorms, but there were always children who seemed to know things and would tell the others. He wasn't sure about details, but the general picture was pretty clear.

"Before," he replied slowly, "there lots of people, who could get old. Then the Change. Grown-up peoples go. Overlords come. Creatures come. Dormitories. Sad Birthdays. The Meat Factory..."

"Good." Shade smiled. "That's about right. Almost fifteen years ago, something happened or was made to happen. For an instant everything stopped. Everything moving halted, every machine, every car. In that instant every person over the age of fourteen vanished. Destroyed... translated into another reality... translocated... I don't know... And then the Overlords came and herded the survivors into the Dorms. A few weeks after that, the first creatures appeared – built with teenagers' brains – and the Overlords began their ritual battles..."

He paused, and Gold-Eye raised his hand, remembering the treatment meted out to Ninde for her unauthorised question.

"But you?" asked Gold-eye, after he was sure Shade had noticed the upraised hand.

Shade smiled again and leaned back in his chair, hands linked behind his glossy black-haired head.

"Yes, everyone disappeared – except me. Or including me, depending on how you look at it. You see, Gold-Eye, I'm not really a person at all!"

As he said that, Shade vanished and the lights went out. Gold-Eye shot up out of the sofa, heart drumming, then subsided back into the cushions. It was pitch-black and he knew he couldn't find the hatch. The thought of stumbling across one of the spider robots or rat things...

Then Shade spoke again, his voice echoing from every corner of the room.

"What I am, Gold-Eye, is a human personality stored in a computer's memory. I have the memories of that real person. I think like a real person. To some degree, I still have the feelings of a real person. But no flesh, save the holographic appearance you have seen – which I must confess is partly based on a twentieth-century actor – so I look rather better than I did in the flesh. A conceit that possibly shows my continuing humanity...

"Do you understand what I'm telling you, Gold-Eye?"

"Yes. You live in machine, show yourself in pictures," said Gold-Eye, nervously directing each word to a different part of that night-dark chamber, as if a sound would strike the real Shade and make him reappear.

"Good. Very good," said Shade. He sounded surprised; then his voice returned to that confident, bass tone – only growing much louder as he continued to talk.

"You are quick to grasp the idea. However strange my physical form, I am a mature adult, complete with the sophisticated education of the pre-Change years and equipped with some of its best technology. And as the only educated adult left, perhaps in the whole world, it is my duty to fight against the intruders who have destroyed what we had... my duty to restore humanity... my duty to turn back the Change!"

With this last word, the green laser suddenly stabbed back on. Gold-Eye screamed, flinging himself back into the cushions, an arm covering his face.

When nothing awful followed, he slowly lowered the arm – and the hologram of Shade was back behind the desk, calmly drinking an equally holographic glass of water.

"Ahhh," said Shade, putting the glass down. "I'm sorry if I scared you, Gold-Eye. I feel very strongly about our struggle... no... our war... against the Overlords. Not for myself so much – but for you, and all the other children in the Dormitories, in the Meat Factory. Those of us who can do something must do something. You agree with that, I trust?"

"Yes," muttered Gold-Eye, who would have agreed to anything Shade wanted him to. However, it was obvious that the Overlords and their creatures were enemies of people, so it didn't take much to agree with that. Still, he wished it was Ella or Drum explaining everything to him. Not this fearful man-computer person...

"Excellent," said Shade, drawing his lips back as he pronounced each syllable slowly. "Ex... cel... lent. I won't have people here who don't participate in the war against

66

the Overlords. We're all soldiers, Gold-Eye, doing whatever we can. And like soldiers in the time before the Change, we must be trained to fight well. Don't you agree?"

"Not sure meaning?" Gold-Eye replied nervously. The school machines in the Dorm gave you electric shocks if you gave the wrong answer more than once. And Shade was sort of a school machine too...

"You have to learn to fight!" Shade said, stabbing his forefinger at Gold-Eye. "Much of what you will do here will be learning. Learning how to fight the Overlords' creatures, learning combat skills. And learning for its own sake too. English – where I think you need some work. History. Science. We must preserve and use knowledge in human minds, Gold-Eye. Not just on disks and tapes and in books. Knowledge must be used! Used first to fight the Overlords, of course. Active in mind and body, that's the ticket. Do you have any questions?"

The sudden question, on top of a monologue that was largely meaningless to Gold-Eye, shook the boy. Once again, he looked from side to side like a frightened rabbit and his mouth opened soundlessly.

"No? You should always have questions, Gold-Eye. Asked in their proper turn, but there should always be questions. Now, what are we going to do with you?"

"Do with me?" asked Gold-Eye, voice squeaking almost as high as Drum's. That was the phrase the Overlords' voices spoke on Sad Birthdays, when these enigmatic beings came to oversee the latest crop of fourteen-year-olds, checking the collated school and physical reports to see if the person's brain, nerves and muscle were to be used in Winger, Myrmidon, Tracker, Screamer or Ferret.

"Ah. Apologies," said Shade, smiling that brilliant white smile again. "I mean, what are you going to do right now? Do you remember how to get back through the Sub to the changing room?"

"Y-y-es," stuttered Gold-Eye, getting to his feet, relief making his muscles so shaky that he clutched at the armrest for support.

"Go back there," said Shade. He seemed to think for a moment, then said, "Sim will meet you there and show you where you will sleep and so on…"

He stopped as Gold-Eye raised his hand again nervously, arm shaking.

"New person?" asked Gold-Eye anxiously. "Not Ella, Drum, Ninde?"

"Sim looks after everyone new here. He'll show you the ropes… show you how things are done," Shade replied. "But… yes… I think you will work with Ella's team. Your precognitive talent, your seeing things in the 'soon-to-be-now' will be a useful addition to that team.

"So. You will go and meet Sim now. He will guide you through the Sub and fit you out with the standard equipment. You will then return here. I want to record your experience of escaping the Dorms before… before you go out again tomorrow. After that, you will report to Ella, and perhaps there will be time for a lesson before sleep. Is that clear?"

"Yes," said Gold-Eye.

"Good," replied Shade. He leaned forward and made a fluttering motion with his right hand. "You may go."

Gold-Eye needed no encouraging. The lights still hadn't come back on, but the image of Shade himself gave off enough light for him to find the hatch. As it clanged shut behind him, he let out a small sigh of relief – then jumped in panic, hitting his head, as Shade's voice echoed through the corridor.

"I forgot to say something, Gold-Eye," the disembodied voice whispered from roof and floor and walls.

"Welcome aboard."

Ella: This is the battle poem, Shade. It looks like it's etched on to the steel plate with the acid they use in their battle sprayers. I've never seen one in English before.

Shade: Read it out, please. I want to hear how it sounds.

Ella: I'm not sure how it's supposed to be read... but I'll give it a try...

A score of seven sevens   *Marched the mighty*
To fight the foe   *Take the trees*
A battle of bravery   *Red the raiment*
Of diamond death   *Blue the Baneful*
A star falls suddenly   *War is won*

Well, at least it's understandable in English... but why only this one?

Shade: Breakdown in the Overlord's integration of the human mind and the creature impression and patterning. They would have killed whoever wrote this as soon as they got back to the barracks.

	Amazing how the odd creature will retain some vestige of humanity. Which reminds me – we haven't had one to vivisect for a long time. There's still much to find out...
Ella:	You're sure there's nothing left of the person when you cut it up? I mean, when I see things like this poem...
Shade:	No. There's nothing, Ella. They are just the enemy. That's all. The enemy...

CHAPTER SEVEN

After a single, bewildering night in the Submarine, Gold-Eye found himself outside again soon after dawn the next morning. Under the finger wharf, up to his armpits in extremely cold sea water.

This time his rags were gone, replaced with the dark-green coveralls the others wore. From his wide leather belt a sword and other equipment hung, including a length of rope, added to the basic equipment after the team's recent experience. His hair was also greatly changed; he had practically none left. Just a thin layer of fuzz remained after an electric razor had removed months of hair and matted dirt.

Ella, Drum and Ninde were there too. Uncharacteristically quiet, in Ninde's case. She stood as far away from Drum and Ella as she could and didn't look up at anyone.

They waded in silence to the drain entrance, where Drum helped everybody up from below and then clambered up himself with the assistance of all three pulling on one thigh-like arm.

"OK," said Ella, taking out her Myrmidon witchlight and squeezing it on. "Flashlights on? All working? Good. Now, we're going to take the Main Drain to the Main Junction, then South Drain Twelve. We'll have to count manholes from the junction – Ninde, I want you to do that to check me. We'll exit at manhole twenty-seven, which is inside the University grounds.

"If we get separated for any reason, you've got two choices. If you're not hurt and you think everyone else will make it, aim for the South Drain Twelve rendezvous. Otherwise, return to the Sub and report to Shade. Any questions?"

"Yes," said Gold-Eye, mindful of Shade's instruction that it was good to have questions. "How tell which drain?"

"Good question," said Ella. "I forgot you're new. Look over here."

She walked a little further up the drain, adjusting her stance to the curve of the tunnel and the patches of ambitious green slime that left the water to climb up the walls. About ten feet in from the entrance, she held the witchlight up to illuminate a bronze plaque.

Looking closer, Gold-Eye saw that it read, ADIT 10 EAST. PCW.

"Ten East is what we call the Main Drain," explained Ella. "It leads to the Main Junction – which we'll pass through – and becomes Ten West. For all the other drains, we use the exact names on these bronze plates – which are always this high and located about this far in from any junction or outfall. Do you understand?"

"Yes," confirmed Gold-Eye, with a noticeable rise in confidence. He'd thought they all just memorised the entire storm-water drain grid and had extraordinary senses of direction – even down here in the dark, watery corridors.

"OK. Check swords," said Ella, drawing hers half out of the sheath to make sure it ran free. The others copied her action, Gold-Eye somewhat nervously. He'd been given it the night before by Sim, the cheerful older boy who seemed to look after an awful lot on the Sub, not just new arrivals.

Gold-Eye had had half an hour of practice with the sword the night before, but it was still the sharpest, heaviest weapon he'd ever handled. The steel blade was etched with gold in swirly lines that Sim had said "disrupt the creatures' electromagnetic nervous systems." He'd laughed and nodded when Gold-Eye had asked, "Does that help kill him?"

"Everybody ready?" asked Ella as Gold-Eye finally managed to put his sword back into the sheath. "OK. I'll go first – then Ninde – then Gold-Eye. Drum, you take rear guard. Let's go!"

Her words echoed into the dark tunnel ahead and were lost in the soft burble of the descending waters. The four followed the echo, the gold pool of witchlight and the harsh white beams of the flashlights, bobbing and spinning as they jumped from side to side along the tunnel, seeking the best and fastest footing.

An hour later Ella called the first rest break. It was hard work walking in the tunnel, with one foot always higher up the curve and many patches of slime to jump over. Then there were the junctions with lesser tunnels, to be waded across using ropes or linked arms. Always there was the oppressive darkness, the sudden heat as hot water flowed in from a side tunnel – and the fear when the burbling water rose to a roar, fear subsiding as the water returned to its steady flow.

They rested in a small chamber above the tunnel, reached by a rusty steel ladder that rose up through the ceiling of the tunnel and on up another twenty feet. Remnants of pre-Change times filled it, arcane objects known to them from videos and training lessons: a mildewed map of the drains on the wall, next to a pictorial calendar of naked women, now clothed in mould; two hard hats on hooks; an open tool kit on the floor, filled with rusted objects.

"We're pretty close to the Main Junction," Ella said as she handed out bars of chocolate. These were still pristine in their foil wrappers, despite a fifteen-year wait on supermarket shelves, a wait broken only when they were retrieved by the teams Shade sent scavenging.

"There are two upper walkways well above the water – in addition to the walkways around the sides, which tend to be a bit submerged. We'll be taking those. So we'll stop a bit short to listen for Myrmidons, let Ninde concentrate, and so on. If you have any of your visions, Gold-Eye, speak up."

They ate in silence after Ella spoke, sipping from their water bottles. It was hot and airless in the room and Gold-Eye felt himself drifting off into sleep. As his head nodded forward, he felt the familiar grip of the soon-to-be-now – but just as the vision was about to come to him, Ninde shook him and it was lost.

"Come on!" said Ninde, switching on her flashlight. "We're going."

Gold-Eye followed her with the pressure of an unrealised vision throbbing at his temples and a sick swirling emptiness in his stomach. His glimpses of the soon-to-be-now were nearly always warnings of something bad about to happen – but not always. For a moment he considered telling Ella, but decided against it. Maybe he had felt like he was about to have a vision only because Ella had mentioned it...

But when they started walking along the drain again, the vision did come back. Gold-Eye let out a yelp and nearly fell against Ninde, who just managed to hold him up.

In his head, Gold-Eye saw water rushing along two tunnels, filling them both completely, speeding along in a frenzy of white froth – then cascading out into an enormous pool where many tunnels met. Trapped in his vision, Gold-Eye still realised that this was the Main Junction and the great rush of water was filling it. In moments it would begin a mad, headlong rush towards the sea. Along Ten East. The Main Drain.

"Water!" he shrieked, coming out of the vision. "Flood!"

Even as he cried out, a rumbling, deep roar vibrated through the tunnel, displaced air rushed past their faces – and the first small wave heralded the smashing waters to come.

"Back!" shouted Ella. "Back to the ladder!"

The others had already turned and in a second were running, dancing, slipping back along the tunnel. The sound of the water behind them rose as they ran, and the waves were soon slapping the backs of their knees and then their backs – and still the main flood was building in the surge reservoir they knew as the Main Junction.

"Up! Up!" Drum called as Gold-Eye arrived panting at the ladder. Holding the steel upright with one hand, he picked Gold-Eye up with the other and practically hurled him through the hole in the ceiling, and Ninde after him.

Then, with a ferocious, frothing howl, the flood hit.

Water geysered up the ladder shaft, exploding around Gold-Eye and Ninde as they desperately climbed higher. For a second, both were nearly plucked away, nostrils, mouth and lungs filled with forced water. Then, as quickly as it came, the water disappeared, leaving them coughing and crying on the ladder.

Ninde's flashlight still hung on its cord around her wrist. She fumbled her light downward, but it illuminated only the subsiding waters. There was no sign of Ella or Drum.

"They're gone," she sobbed. "Gone."

Gold-Eye heard her faintly, the words fuzzy in his water-logged ears. He felt weak, unable to speak, barely capable of holding on. His hands hurt, the knuckles cracking, unable to relax his deathly grip on the worn steel rungs.

"We shouldn't have come out," Ninde sobbed. "I knew it was wrong..."

"Ninde..." Gold-Eye said, suddenly less worried about himself as her muttering and crying rose in intensity and volume. "Ninde!"

She stopped in mid breath, choked and broke into a fit of coughing. When it stopped, she seemed calmer. Gold-Eye felt calmer too, as if his state of mind was directly dependent upon hers.

"Ninde," he said again. "Can you do... mind-listen... people?"

"Don't be stupid," Ninde said, half coughing the words. "They're drowned. I can't hear what dead people think!"

Gold-Eye said nothing. Ninde coughed a few more times, then said, "I suppose I could try. Not from here, though."

"Safe to go down?" asked Gold-Eye. He couldn't see past Ninde.

"Yeah," replied Ninde, shining her flashlight down again. "I guess... I guess it was a quick one. The water looks about w-waist high."

"We go then?" asked Gold-Eye. "Look for Ella and Drum?"

"I suppose," said Ninde doubtfully. She withdrew her elbows, which had been locked around the rungs. "I guess if it was the other way around, they'd look for us. And Drum is very strong. If they hung on to the ladder for long enough..."

She started climbing down, Gold-Eye following close behind – and then suddenly stopped, just at the top of the tunnel.

"What?" asked Gold-Eye anxiously.

"The last part of the ladder's missing," Ninde replied, her voice flat. "It's just broken off. We'll have to hang and drop."

"Wait!" cried Gold-Eye as Ninde prepared to lower herself from the last rung. "Rope! We use rope!"

Stelo: You want us to what?

Shade: Capture a Winger.

Stelo: How?

Shade: The tethered goat.

Stelo: What?

Shade: It's an old trick, used for capturing wild carnivores. Tigers, for example. You tether a goat to a stake. When the animal comes to eat the defenceless goat, you kill or capture it.

Stelo: We haven't got a goat.

Shade: No. It'll have to be one of your team. Pretending to be hurt or unconscious – to attract a Winger.

Stelo: Great... How do we stop the rest of the flight dropping in?

Shade: Simple. Have the decoy lie somewhere only one can land. In between a fence and a building, perhaps...

Stelo: I don't like it.

Shade: I need a Winger to examine. Theoretically they're too heavy to fly. I need to find out how they do... It's very important to the struggle, Stelo. And the tethered goat will work.

Stelo: Have you used it before?

Shade:	Yes.
Stelo:	Did it work?
Shade:	Oh, yes. Not with a Winger, but we got a Tracker once.
Stelo:	Whose team did it?
Shade:	No one you know, Stelo. Long before your time, my boy. Now, I want you to get started tomorrow...

CHAPTER EIGHT

"They're alive!" said Ninde, sounding very surprised. "I think."

"Where?" asked Gold-Eye nervously. The feeling of security he'd had with Ella and Drum was significantly lacking with just Ninde.

"I can't tell," replied Ninde, letting her tooth-marked knuckles fall away from her mouth. "It's really hard trying to connect with them at the moment. And people are always much more difficult than creatures. People think too many thoughts at the same time."

"Must be back there," Gold-Eye reasoned aloud, pointing back towards the sea. "We wait for them?"

"I don't see why we should," said Ninde. With the realisation that Ella and Drum were around somewhere, she seemed to have come back to her normal, dangerously impetuous self. "We know where we're supposed to go. Manhole twenty-five on South Drain Twelve."

"Manhole twenty-seven," said Gold-Eye firmly. "Better wait."

"Whatever manhole it is," said Ninde. "We'll waste time if we just wait here. The others could have been washed miles away or into a side drain. They can meet us there."

"No. Better wait."

"You can wait if you want," said Ninde. Turning away from him, she started chewing on her knuckle again, forehead deeply creased in concentration.

Thirty seconds later, her forehead smoothed out and she stopped chewing.

"There's nothing between here and there anyway," she announced confidently. "So I'm going. It's what Shade calls initiative, Gold-Eye. If you'd been around longer, you'd understand."

She started walking away – and the light went with her. Gold-Eye looked at the flashlight hanging from his own wrist and saw only the faintest red glow across the filament of the bulb.

When he looked back up, Ninde was invisible in the darkness, the beam from her flashlight reflecting from the water in front of her. He could hear her splashing though – growing fainter as the distance increased. Then she stopped, and the light wavered back towards him.

Gold-Eye hesitated, knowing deep inside that it was more sensible to wait for Ella and Drum. But the dark pressed against him, the noise of the flowing water seemed louder... and the light was turning away again...

He took a step forward, forcing his legs against the current.

"Wait!" he called, and the blessed light swung around towards him, reflecting in glittering patches of gold across the water.

"Looks like they both survived," said Ella, crouching over the patch of slime underneath the broken ladder. "There's two sets of fresh boot prints here, where they must have slid down using a doubled-over rope. One standard – Ninde's. And Gold-Eye's runners. He didn't have time to wear in new boots."

"So where did they go?" piped Drum. He was leaning against the side of the tunnel, obviously weary. Blood still trickled from scratches on his hands and head, and like Ella, he was wet from head to foot.

"Good question," said Ella. She got up and waded towards the Main Junction, holding the witchlight to light up slime patches further up the walls. Like Drum, she'd held on to the ladder for long enough to survive the first shock of the flood, and then managed to keep her head clear of the secondary rush that carried them down the tunnel.

Ten feet on, she stopped and moved the witchlight closer to the wall. "Yeah – fresh handprints here. They're headed towards the Main Junction. Probably planning to go on to South Drain Twelve. That'll be Ninde's idea, no doubt."

"Will they wait?"

"I doubt it," replied Ella. "Gold-Eye might, but Ninde is just too curious – and she never seems to believe anything bad is really going to happen. Depends too much on her Change Talent for warning."

"Water," commented Drum.

"Yeah," said Ella. "I don't think she really believes water dulls her Talent, either. But it will be particularly bad in the Main Junction... I doubt she could sense four maniples of Myrmidons in there. We'd better get a move on... if you can."

Drum nodded and pushed himself fully upright, flexing his arms and legs so the muscles rippled from top to bottom under the cloth.

Ella hadn't waited. She was already wading steadily up the tunnel, as high up the curve as she could go to avoid the slime. Drum sighed and launched himself after her, noting where she slipped and trying the other side.

"Sure nothing there?" Gold-Eye whispered, crouching close to Ninde just back from where the Main Drain opened out into the Main Junction. Water lapped at his knees, back to the steady trickle it had been before the flood. "How big is it?"

"Yes, I'm sure," Ninde snapped, her voice loud enough to echo out, making Gold-Eye wince. "And it's just a big pool, about as big as a football field."

"A what?" asked Gold-Eye.

"You really need to watch some videos back at the Sub." Ninde sighed, confusing Gold-Eye even more.

"Anyway," she continued, "all we have to do is go out, turn left and keep close to the wall. There's a walkway on the edge. It might be underwater a bit. And it's not very wide."

She indicated an armspan, flashlight flickering across the ceiling and, for a moment, out into the Main Junction.

"If you fall off," she added, "swim. It's very deep. You ready?"

Gold-Eye nodded, thinking of long-ago swimming lessons in the Dorms. Which were more about developing muscles than really learning how to swim...

Ninde stood up and stepped out diagonally from the tunnel to hug the wall of the Main Junction pool. Gold-Eye followed quickly, anxious not to lose the light.

It was much cooler here than in the tunnel, cold radiating off the deep water only one false step away.

Ninde shone her flashlight ahead and Gold-Eye saw the steel mesh of the walkway just under water, following the wall. Then Ninde shone it up and the beam vanished into blackness without lighting up anything. Similarly, when directed out across the water, it caught ripples for only ten or twenty feet before drowning in darkness.

"Come on," said Ninde, unnecessarily since Gold-Eye was so close behind he was practically her Siamese twin.

They moved into the vast, watery chamber cautiously. After a few yards, they started passing other tunnels coming in from the east, so there wasn't even a wall to lean against. Gold-Eye, whose balance had always been perfect, found himself mistrusting it, and a litany began to run through his mind: "If you're going to fall, fall in a tunnel, not on the deep side... If you're going to fall, fall in a tunnel, not on the deep side..."

He was so busy thinking this, he ran into Ninde when she stopped, almost causing them both to fall in the deep side. Surprisingly, she didn't cry out or swear at him – instead she half turned and whispered, "Did you hear something then?"

"Did you hear something then?" Ella whispered to Drum as they stood at the entrance to the Main Junction.

"Two things," whispered Drum, his voice clear as a bell even when he whispered. "Someone moving on the lower walkway... and someone or something... on the higher crosswalk. Just shifting position, I think."

"Do we rush? Or creep?"

"Hard to..." Drum began. Then two screams suddenly pierced the lapping of the water. "Rush!"

Both jumped easily around the corner, running along the walkway with the ease of long familiarity, water spraying as they ran.

Gold-Eye and Ninde screamed as Myrmidon witchlight suddenly flared above them and the creatures' silver nets came floating down...

Desperately Gold-Eye flung himself backwards – into the water. Strong currents dragged at him, trying to take him down to deeper tunnels. But he held on to the walkway.

Ninde threw herself forward, and the falling mesh took her around the feet, its strands melting together instantly to form a solid mass of sticky plastic.

She rolled on to her back and tried to draw her sword to cut the catch rope that would drag her up... up to the higher crosswalk she'd forgotten about.

Gold-Eye looked up too, trying to locate the enemy as he dragged himself hand over hand along the walkway. Myrmidon battle sound boomed everywhere, echoing, multiplying and confusing him. A harsh, discordant mixture of shouts and growls, of deep and terrifying noise.

Then he saw them – a full maniple, stretched out along the crosswalk above him like shooters on a range. The three net throwers were already winding in – and Gold-Eye realised that one of them was winding in Ninde.

The other four Myrmidons carried broad-bladed axes. All seven wore black, banded armour, unadorned save for the fluttering squares of black metal-cloth on their mighty shoulders, declaring that they belonged to the Overlord known simply as Black Banner.

"Help!" screamed Ninde as the catch rope went taut. Effortlessly the Myrmidon at the other end began to pull her up, while the other net throwers reloaded their tubes to have another shot at Gold-Eye.

"Gold-Eye!" screamed Ninde again. She had her sword out but couldn't flip up enough to get a good swing above her rapidly ascending ankles.

"Gold-Eye!"

Gold-Eye looked at the other net throwers. They would be reloaded in a few moments... but Ninde... the Meat Factory...

With a shout, he flung himself on to the walkway and rushed towards Ninde, the narrowness of the way forgotten, sword in his hand... and then he was jumping up, hacking at the rope, screaming at the Myrmidons...

Ninde was screaming too, the Myrmidons boomed louder... and still the rope wouldn't cut...

Then another sword whistled over his, cutting through the catch rope with a *crack!* that seemed to stop all other noise... and Ella was there, and Drum, picking up Ninde like a small kitten under his arm... and...

"Run like hell!" shouted Ella, her sword blade glittering gold in the witchlight from above. "That way!"

ARCHIVE – SELF-EXAMINATION SESSION #256, 328, 974

If I were merely a computer, I could not think as a man. If I were still only a man, I could not exist. But I am only an electronic reality – or am I? No physicality. No glands. No hormones. No sudden pleasure from the sun warming my face... or a woman smiling for me alone...

But these memories are part of me. Is this the same? Does the memory of stimulus act in the artificial persona as a real stimulus?

I have sent many children to their deaths.

When I was a man as other men... inhabiting a body... I could not have done so. But I did not live then in the times I do now. War changes the breathing man. How could it not change me?

Have I lost compassion? Or is there no use for it in these times?

I cannot feel pain as the children do. And the memory of pain is not the sharp, senses-blotting focus...

But that is not important. There is only one goal. The Overlords must be defeated and the world returned to normality. My normality. The wind cool and fresh, stinging eyes; the shock of the surf on skin; a soft kiss, lips just touching soft skin below the ear, her long hair held back...

Irrelevance. Whatever the cost, we will regain humanity's kingdom. Children's lives... a soul tarnished beyond redemption, washed in blood... this is not too high a cost.

Any means must be employed. Victory is the only permissible end.

<SESSION TERMINATED.
DURATION 0.0012 SECONDS.>

CHAPTER NINE

They didn't stop running until they were a hundred yards down South Drain Twelve. Ella had picked it unerringly, despite their mad, splashing rush almost halfway around the entire Main Junction, pursued by the shouts of the Myrmidons on the crosswalk and the soft popping of their net guns.

Twice they'd almost been netted, but always the swords rose and fell and the catch ropes parted – leaving them to hobble on as best they could with the matted plastic dragging on hands or feet. And Drum still carried Ninde, whose legs were totally encased in the foul stuff.

When they finally stopped, he laid her down across the drain, so the water poured over her legs. Gold-Eye wondered at that, expecting her to shriek again, but she was silent. Then he realised that Drum wasn't punishing her – the running water was slowly dissolving the net material. Small pinholes were appearing. Over the next ten minutes, they would become larger holes, joining together until what had been a solid mass of plastic was no more.

"So you decided not to wait," panted Ella. She stood with her sword in hand, facing back the way they'd come. "I presume your Talent told you we were still alive?"

"Yes," said Ninde very quietly. "Sorry."

She moved her legs a little and the plastic snapped further apart. Impatient, she struggled to get up, but Drum pushed her back down with one finger.

"Let it all dissolve," he piped. He had one foot in the water too, where the corner of a net had struck his boot.

"We'll talk about what you should have done when we're back at the Sub," Ella continued curtly. "You too, Gold-Eye. Just be thankful that we weren't washed too far away to help you in time. Or drowned."

Gold-Eye nodded vigorously, eager to show that he totally agreed with Ella. Ninde didn't say anything. Head down, she watched shreds of plastic fall apart in the flowing water.

"I don't suppose anyone managed to count manholes?" Ella asked. "No? I guess I'd better go back to the junction and do it myself."

"I go," volunteered Gold-Eye, keen to make amends.

"No," said Ella. "There's a slim chance those Myrmidons might risk the lower walkway. They will enter shallow water sometimes. I'll be back in five minutes. If you hear me screaming, run."

No one said anything as she splashed away from them, back towards the Main Junction. Her body melded with the darkness until only her witchlight was visible – a ball of golden light that seemed to dance of its own accord across the tunnel.

"How water not get you?" Gold-Eye asked Drum in the now oppressive silence. The big man was as obviously unimpressed with Ninde and Gold-Eye as Ella was.

"Held on to the ladder till it broke," Drum replied after a long pause. "Most of the first rush was past then, so we could swim. Grabbed another ladder about half a mile east."

It sounded simple, the way he said it so matter-of-factly. But Gold-Eye had been further up the ladder. He could imagine the terrible force of the water hitting full-on, the lack of air, the ladder breaking – and the frantic struggle to break through to an air gap, not knowing if one even existed...

He didn't ask any more questions, so they sat in silence till they heard Ella coming back, counting manholes.

"Fifteen... sixteen... OK, on your feet! Drum, check my count from the last one, sixteen."

The drain grew smaller and seemed to slope upward after manhole twenty. At manhole twenty-seven, Ella stood on Drum's shoulders and lifted the manhole cover a few inches, just enough to let sunlight stream in through the crack. Noise came too – the three-part whistle of a pair of red parrots and the distant chuckle of wibewa birds.

There were no creature sounds. No crash of Myrmidon hobnails or Trackers whistling. Just the birdcalls and the breeze. Even those faded for a minute or two, leaving an eerie silence.

Ella lowered the cover, and Drum knelt so she could jump down.

"It seems OK," she said. "Ninde, see if you can pick up anything."

Ninde complied in silence. This time she did break the skin on her knuckle, blood slowly welling out of the joint to mix with spittle, running into the corners of her mouth.

"Nothing," she said finally, without her usual confidence. "Maybe the water…"

"We're a fair way from the Main Junction," said Ella. "So unless we're right next to the University Lake – which we shouldn't be – I think we can assume that Shade was right about the Death Markers."

"Rest for a while?" asked Drum, though it sounded more like a firm suggestion than a question. He didn't wait for an answer before leaning back against the tunnel wall, his knees bent to keep everything but his boots out of the water.

Ella hesitated, seemed about to say something, then knelt as well and fumbled at one of the pouches in her belt.

"I'd better take care of those cuts in your hands," she said, rummaging in her first-aid kit for disinfectant and adhesive bandages. "We'll rest for half an hour."

Thirty minutes later, she was standing on Drum's shoulders again, pushing the manhole cover aside and blinking in the full glare of the noonday sun.

Shielding her eyes with her hand, she did a quick 360-degree scan of the area, looking for any sign of creatures.

But there were none. Not even Wingers in the bright blue sky. No black dots cruising like miniature storm clouds.

The manhole was on the side of one of the narrow roads that ran right through the campus. Here, the road was lined by centuries-old oaks that cast a shade on road and footpath.

Behind Ella, the Great Hall rose above the trees, its stone walls, slate roof and grinning gargoyles a strangely fitting setting for the Myrmidon Barracks it had become. But there should be no Myrmidons there today... no sentries on the steps, no banner bearers in the clock tower...

Newer buildings rose up in front of Ella – ten or so, mixing the architectural styles of sixty years or more. She looked at them carefully, mentally matching them to the map she'd memorised back at the Sub.

Shade's old laboratory was in the Department of Abstract Computing, an ugly six-storey block of grey concrete and mirrored windows. It was about two hundred yards away through the maze of mismatched buildings, twisting, narrow roads, hedges and lawns.

There was another building Ella's eye lingered on, though it was not part of her mission. The University Regiment armoury, a triangular sandstone building positioned at the edge of the campus. The Overlords' creatures collected and presumably destroyed pre-Change weapons when they found them. But there were weapons locked away securely in underground armouries, Ella knew. She had studied books and manuals on everything from machine guns to explosives in the hope of getting some one day. Even in the absence of creatures, though, she couldn't get into the armoury…

"All clear?"

Drum's high-pitched reminder made Ella start guiltily. She answered by pulling herself on to the road, quickly tying her rope around an adjacent steel bicycle rack and lowering it back down.

Ninde and Gold-Eye came up first, using Drum as a ladder. Ella motioned them into the shadow of the nearest oak, just in case Wingers did pass overhead.

Drum pulled himself up last, the rope straining. He looked about, then lumbered across to the shade of another oak nearby.

Ella recovered the rope and joined him. Gold-Eye and Ninde looked at her expectantly from the other tree, awaiting orders.

"That's the building we want," she said, pointing. "The grey one with the weird windows. Shade's old lab is on the top floor. There shouldn't be any creatures around, but we still have to be careful. If anything does happen, try and get back here and then return to the Sub. Just make sure you wait till after sundown to cross the Main Junction, so the Myrmidons will have gone. And try and stay in the shadows when moving here. We don't want any Wingers dropping in."

"Pity we have to stay in the shade," said Ninde, looking out at the sunshine reflecting from the windows, sparkling down through the leaves, lighting up everything so cheerily. "I'd like to get a tan."

"I'm glad to see you've recovered," said Ella, only half sarcastically. She touched the trunk of the oak, feeling the carved scar where two students had declared their undying love on some long-ago sunny day. That was all gone, she told herself, and trying to half live in those times like Ninde only got you a ticket to the Meat Factory. Still, Ella sometimes envied the ability of the younger girl to just forget and enjoy the sunshine...

"Let's go. Stay close to the buildings."

They made it to the Abstract Computing building without mishap. As Shade had said, the Death Markers – steel poles adorned with the dead Myrmidons' insignia – were up all over the University. A small cluster of them was driven into the footpath right outside the building. Many more of them bloomed like strange plants on the lawns that ran down from the Great Hall to the University Lake. In a day or two, they would be collected up and the insignia taken to who knew where.

The main doors to the Abstract Computing building were locked, but Ella – well briefed by Shade – took them around to a side door, which was propped open with a brick.

She opened it – and recoiled, startled by sudden hissing.

"Ferret!" she exclaimed, stepping back to free her sword. Then, "No... cat..." as a large ginger tomcat streaked past her, zigged at Drum, zagged between Gold-Eye and Ninde, and disappeared under a hedge across the road.

Swords went back into sheaths, but everyone's heart was beating more than the exercise demanded as they climbed up the stairs to the sixth floor, the reek of a tomcat's proud home filling their nostrils. Fluorescent lights, activated by motion sensors, flickered on as they climbed.

At the fifth-floor landing, a rusted ovoid with jointed metal legs lay in one corner, a hole in its middle revealing circuit boards and plastic cable.

"One of the robots Shade used to get himself out of here fifteen years ago," commented Ella, turning it over with her foot. "Or to get the computer out of here, I mean. It's smaller than the ones he's got now."

"Less legs," said Gold-Eye, shuddering. This one had only six. The ones he'd seen in the Sub had eight.

The fire door on the sixth floor was closed and locked, but Ella produced a key from an inside pocket of her coveralls with a flourish.

"Proper planning," she said, turning it in the lock and pushing the door open – just as the fluorescent light in the stairwell went out, leaving them in darkness. If the room beyond had windows, there was no sunlight coming through.

As Ella reached for her witchlight, a red laser flicked on from ceiling to floor, lighting both room and landing with a red glow.

Motes of different-coloured light followed the laser down – and there was Shade. Except he didn't look quite the same. Less real, more like an out-of-focus photograph in three dimensions. More like an electronic thing...

His voice was different too. Flatter, without human timbre and somehow rather whining.

"Who are you and what are you doing here?"

ARCHIVE
TRAINING LESSON 834 •
NEW CREATURE

If you see a creature that you don't recognise, it is vital that you report it to Shade. Do not assume that it is a creature known to other people. If you don't know what it is, report it!

There are three basic things to remember when you see an unfamiliar creature:

1. LOOK
2. COMPARE
3. REMEMBER

LOOK at the creature for as long as you can without putting yourself in danger. If you can, observe it from different angles.

COMPARE the creature with ones you do know. Is it taller than a Myrmidon? Does it have a nose like a Tracker? Does it wear armour like a Myrmidon Master? Thinking of comparisons will make it easier to describe the creature later.

REMEMBER everything you can about its appearance, behaviour and location.

You are now going to see some pictures of made-up creatures. Remember to LOOK, COMPARE, REMEMBER. There will be a test following this lesson to see how well you can describe these new creatures.

<BEGIN IMAGE SEQUENCE CRT345-897.>

CHAPTER TEN

"I'm Ella. Who are you?"

"I am Associate Professor Marcus Leamington," replied the image. "And it seems I must repeat myself. What are you doing in my laboratory? And why are the lights off? I suppose there has been a power failure... while I was... harummm... taking a nap in my lunch hour."

"Shade sent us to collect some equipment," Ella said, slowly edging into the room as she spoke, the others moving in behind her. The image didn't turn towards her as Shade would have, or seem aware that she had moved.

"I'm warning you... I will call security if you don't leave at once. Where's that damn phone?"

Fretfully the image reached out with one hand, groping in empty air for a phone that wasn't there. In the light from the hologram they could see the whole laboratory: a long, thin room lined with benches, and the benches stacked with computers and plastic cabinets, joined by ribbon-like cables and topped with blinking red and green lights. Only the back wall was empty. The hanging cables indicated that it too had once been full of computing equipment.

"I said I'll call security," the image – Leamington – whined. He seemed to have pulled a phone out of the air and had the handset up, one finger on the touch pad. "How did you get in, anyway?"

"Go to sleep, Professor Leamington," Ella said, slowly and carefully. "We'll take care of everything."

"Oh, all right then," grumbled the image. It wavered for a moment, put the phone down, then disappeared, plunging the laboratory into darkness.

"What was that?" asked Ninde as Ella pulled out her witchlight and squeezed it on.

"Shade Mark One?" said Drum, only half questioning.

"Sort of," Ella replied, walking along one wall, looking at the identifying labels on the computers and other plastic or metal boxes. "Shade didn't think it would still be working, but he did mention it as a possibility. It's just an artificial intelligence, though – there's no human personality. The phrase I used turns it off."

"Sounded grumpy to me," said Ninde. "That's pretty human—"

"I only know what Shade told me," interrupted Ella impatiently. "Now we need to get all the compact discs out of this storage silo – there should be sixty in all. You can do that, Ninde. Put them into the boxes from the shelf over there. The grey plastic ones, ten CDs to a box. And there's an instrument pack on the roof we have to detach. Apparently there's a tool kit – a white metal box about this big... Yes, that's it... thanks, Gold-Eye. You come with me up to the roof. Drum, watch the door..."

Gold-Eye watched the sky as Ella unbolted a metal ball about the size of his head from the roof. It had been lit up inside when they first approached, and faintly whistling, but Ella had unplugged several cables that led out of it and down through the roof. Now it was just a heavy lump of metal.

"See anything?" asked Ella, straining at the stiff bolts with a wrench as long as Gold-Eye's arm.

"No," replied Gold-Eye, turning a complete circle, shading his eyes with both hands cupped against his eyebrows. "But I can't see against the sun."

"Keep looking as close to either side of it as you can," Ella said absently, kicking at the spanner with her heel. "Should have brought some sunglasses – 'cause that's where they'll come from, if they do."

"What are you doing?"

Ninde and Drum both started, for the voice didn't belong to either of them. Ninde almost dropped the silvery disc she had just taken out of the open CD drawer in the storage silo.

"You're working for Robert, aren't you?" continued the disembodied voice, becoming clearer and more recognisable as the one they'd heard before. Professor

Leamington. Only now there was no image to go with it.

"Go to sleep, Professor," said Drum slowly. "We'll take care of everything."

"I'm not sleepy any more," said Leamington. "Robert's stealing my data, isn't he? Planning to publish before I do, stealing my life's work. I dare say he wants the new radiation to be named after him. But he won't, he won't! He's gone too far this time. I've called security, you see. And the police."

"Ninde," said Drum suddenly. "Hurry up."

"And I've set off the burglar alarm," Leamington continued. "You're not the only one who's good with gadgets, Robert. I'm not just a theoretician, oh no. I know how things work. It's all in the Projectors, Robert..."

His voice continued to rave on, descending into meaningless chatter as he talked about tenure and chairs, grants and committees – and his arch-enemy Robert, who seemed to stand out among many enemies.

"What's the hurry?" asked Ninde, raising her voice over Leamington's whiny ramblings.

"Some phones still work," said Drum. "Alarms too. Overlords listen."

"But the Death Markers will keep them out..."

"Overlords can ignore them. Hurry up!"

It was Gold-Eye and Ella's bad luck that the closest flight of Wingers included one with a mind-call. Receiving urgent instructions from their Overlord, they banked to the left and started to descend below the high cirrus – ready for the long dive down. Down to the University.

"That's it," said Ella, pulling the last bolt out of the concrete. "Sky still clear?"

"Ye—" Gold-Eye began, and then as his soon-to-be-now vision flashed, with a single picture of Wingers plummeting on to the roof all around them, "No Wing—"

He had the word only half out when a shadow whisked across them – the wide, long leading shadow of an attacking Winger. Instantly Ella grabbed Gold-Eye and pulled him on to the concrete, just as the Winger shrieked overhead, taloned hands raking the air where Gold-Eye had stood.

In shock he watched it pass, seeing over and over again the human body stretched out with arms stretched longer still; the taloned hands; the stumpy legs ending well above the knees; and the great leather-bellows bat wings spanning twenty feet or more.

And the face, or lack of it. The shrieking, saw-toothed ear-to-ear mouth. The lower jaw thrust out beyond the reach of any lip; the empty socket where once a nose had been. And the bright, shining eyes, twice the size of any human eye but still somehow human.

He didn't have long to look. Ella grabbed him with one hand, picked up the instrument ball with the other hand, and sprinted for the stairs.

"Lead Winger," she gasped as they crashed through the door and down several steps. "Fastest in the flight. Others will be close. Come on!"

* * *

Drum heard the Winger scream above and was almost at the door when it burst open to admit Ella and Gold-Eye. Leamington was still raving on about income tax and academic salary reviews, and Ninde was still no more than halfway through removing the CDs from the storage silo.

"Wingers," said Ella unnecessarily. "Ignoring the Death markers. What's that noise?"

"The artificial intelligence," replied Drum. "Leamington. He... it called the police and set off an alarm."

"An Overlord?" asked Ella, and then answered her own question. "Has to be, doesn't it? Gold-Eye, Drum, look out a window – if you can get one open. I'll help Ninde."

Putting the instrument ball down, she took a folded nylon backpack out of one of her belt pouches, shook it open and started packing it with the boxes of CDs. Ninde caught her sense of urgency and worked even faster, pulling the CD drawers out of the silo without waiting for their slow, powered extrusion.

"Forget the cases," Ella said as she dropped one putting it in. "Just chuck them straight in the bag. Come on!"

Across the room, Drum and Gold-Eye wrestled with a window that had been stuck shut and painted over. Or more correctly, Gold-Eye got in the way until Drum wrenched it open, showering them both with flakes of black plastic paint.

Fresh air, sunlight... and sound came in the open window. Myrmidon marching chants, the whistle of Trackers, the scream of Wingers flying low over the building...

Looking out, they saw two columns of Myrmidons marching across the lawns towards the Abstract Computing building. Three maniples in all, with a Myrmidon Master marching at their head, the black feathers from its plumed helmet cascading down its back. Black squares fluttered on the Master's sleeves, and one of the Myrmidons carried an ornate battle standard fringed with gold. It had no device, just a plain black field.

Trackers coursed in front of the Myrmidons, noses pressed against the grass. Every few yards, they leaped into the air and whistled, catching the human scent wafting from the building several hundred yards away.

A shadow passed across the window as they watched and Gold-Eye flinched, but it was gone in a moment – only to be followed by something worse. The shape that had cast the shadow.

An enormous Winger, easily twelve feet tall, with wings forty feet or more across, glided lazily in to land in front of the Myrmidon Master. The Winger knelt and a smaller, man-sized figure in jet-black armour leaped easily off its back, striding over to the Master. That creature knelt before it, and the Myrmidons behind sank to their knees in rows. The Trackers practically fell down where they were, tongues lolling, and the Wingers ceased their screeching.

"An Overlord," Drum said, bleakness sounding even in his strange voice. "Black Banner."

Drum's words chilled Gold-Eye, even standing in the sun. Suddenly he felt very afraid, more afraid than he had ever been of anything, even a Ferret. He felt dizzy and he heard words over and over again in his head.

"Now, what will we do with you? Now, what will we do with you? Now, what will we do...?

The Overlord spoke with the Myrmidon Master for a moment. Then it turned towards the building and the spreading horns on its helmet flashed from black to deep wine-red.

"It sees us," said Drum, pulling the window closed with a final-sounding thud. But not before Gold-Eye saw the Overlord raise one spike-gauntleted hand and point – straight at him.

VIDEO ARCHIVE
CONVERTED FROM DISK STORE
34-786 TO ARRAY 23-56 • STEPHEN

I guess I was twelve when the Change happened. My old man was the gardener at the Uni and used to go down there early – about six in the morning. He'd leave the breakfast stuff out for me and my sister, Gwen. Mum had left a couple of years before with some other guy.

So this morning I got up about seven to get ready for school – and no cereal on the table, no bowl. I went out to see if his car was still there – and it was stopped on the road outside.

I ran over, because I thought he'd had a heart attack or something. But he wasn't there. The keys were hanging in the ignition... I guess it was about then that I realised something strange had happened. It was so quiet, for a start. No traffic. No planes – and we lived right under the flight path.

There were other cars stopped out on the road too. Then this kid I knew – lived four doors down – came out on the lawn and started screaming.

"They're all gone, they're all gone!" or something like that. It freaked me out, so I ran back inside to wake up

Gwen. She was sixteen and pretty silly, but she was older than me, so...

Only she wasn't there. Just disappeared right out of her bed. I didn't know what to do then, so I just hid in the house. Tried to watch TV or get something on the radio, but there was nothing. Some of the cable stations were still showing movies and cartoons and stuff. But no news.

That afternoon these weird-looking buses came round. Really narrow, sort of segmented carriages with an engine at the front – like those toy trains at fairs. They were driven by these guys in suits – like spacesuits, with helmets and everything. You couldn't see who was in them.

They had loudspeakers and they kept calling out to everyone to get on the bus. All the kids, because there wasn't anyone else left.

I watched whole families – or what was left of them – get on. Ten-year-olds carrying babies, five-year-old twins holding hands... there were heaps of them. All trusting, because the guys in the suits looked like grown-ups.

The bus came back every day for two weeks, until there was nobody left to collect. Or people like me.

I didn't get on. Not because I knew about the Dorms and the Meat Factory... not then. I just had this feeling...

A few weeks later, the first creatures started to appear. They didn't have the formal battles and stuff then. They just hunted us. I was living in White's Supermarket by that time. Close to supplies. And I had a rifle – a thirty-thirty that was too big for me. I found out the hard way that the creatures could take six or seven shots before they went down. Steel worked on them better – so I got an old bayonet from an army-disposal store. Not as good as one of those gold-plated swords Shade's robots make… but it worked.

That was two years ago. I was lucky, I guess. Whatever else the Change did, it gave me a sort of sense that tells me what's going to happen. Sometimes, that is. Enough so I lasted on my own for longer than most.

I joined up with Shade six months ago, and that's made quite a difference. I never really thought I'd make it much past fifteen… but now, I reckon I've got a good chance…

CHAPTER ELEVEN

"We have to get out," said Drum. "There's an Overlord and two maniples crossing the lawns now."

"OK," replied Ella calmly, still stuffing CDs in the pack. "But we've got to get these first. Drum – shake out a pack for the instrument ball. Ninde – see if you can get into one of the Master's minds, or the Overlord. Gold-Eye, empty that last tray into here. Just pull it out."

Everyone moved quickly at her orders, incipient panic serving as extra energy. Despite their separate tasks, everyone's attention was half focused on Ninde. She stood in the middle of the room, chewing her knuckle, trying to ignore the constant mad whispering of Professor Leamington.

"I can't get the Overlord or a Master," she said, almost whimpering. "But there's more Myrmidons on the other side... We're surrounded!"

"Ha ha ha ha ha ha," gurgled Leamington, possibly in answer to her words. The others were silent. Everyone was looking to Ella now, waiting for the word to run, the tension building as she put the last few CDs in the bag and closed the zip with a final whirr.

"What we do?" asked Gold-Eye, unable to bear it any longer. His instinct was to run, run down the stairs, get out of the building...

But Ella didn't answer. She kept staring down at the zipper of the bag, as if she could somehow see her way out in the linking of the steel teeth. Then she cupped her palms and the pulse in her neck began to throb, the blood vessels suddenly prominent blue beneath her skin.

"What..." Ninde began, but Drum motioned her to silence. He knew that look. Ella was trying to imagine something, to bring it to her, or create it. Even Leamington quieted down, till the only noise was the muffled shouts of the Myrmidons and the high rise and fall of Winger shrieks.

Then Gold-Eye felt something twitch in his forehead, as if the soon-to-be-now had just struck him for a second. The feeling was centred on Ella – and he saw that something had appeared in her cupped hands.

A metal egg about the size of a large lemon. Green, with a bright yellow band around it, and a metal handle secured to the round part with a split pin.

"What is it?" asked Gold-Eye simply. How could a metal egg be the way out?

"It's called a grenade," said Ella, carefully putting it in one of the pouches on her belt. "It's a weapon."

As she spoke, she looked at Drum for just a second and he nodded. Ninde didn't see it, but Gold-Eye thought he knew that look. He'd seen it before, between Petar and Jemmie. Weapons weren't always there to be used on the enemy. The Myrmidons had taken Petar before he could use the knife...

"But let's hope we can save it for later," continued Ella. She picked up her backpack and headed away from the door, a confident smile confusing everyone else, who'd instinctively started towards the exit.

"Where—" Ninde began, but she was interrupted again, this time by a tremendous crash that shook the whole building. It was followed by a cheer from the Myrmidons below. Obviously they'd just used something to smash through the ground floor doors. It would be only minutes before they were on the sixth floor.

"Earthquake!" exclaimed Leamington, suddenly coherent again. "Earthquake! We must get out. Somebody help me!"

"Drum, bar the door as best you can, then follow! You two, follow me!" Ella's commands cut through Leamington's pleas for help and the Myrmidons' triumphant bellowing.

Gold-Eye looked at her blankly, but she didn't wait to see if he was following. She ducked under one of the tables and disappeared behind a curtain of hanging cables.

"Well, go on!" exclaimed Ninde, pushing him forward. "Hurry up!"

It seemed stupid to Gold-Eye to try and hide under a table load of computers, but he obediently got down on his knees and crawled under the table – to see that Ella had opened a panel under the wall behind, revealing a small elevator shaft descending to who knew where.

"Service elevator," explained Ella hurriedly. "Shade mentioned it as a possible point of entry... or exit. There are no handholds in the shaft, so you'll have to climb down the cable – quickly."

"Where?" asked Gold-Eye apprehensively, as he lowered himself into the shaft.

"Underground parking lot," replied Ella. "I hope. Now, move!"

She pushed him a little in the small of the back and he shuffled forward a bit further, till his legs were down the shaft and all he had to do was reach forward and grab the cable. Still he hesitated, and Ella pushed him again.

Overbalancing, he fell forward, hands grabbing the steel cable to take his weight. Only they didn't. The cable was thick with grease and instead of climbing down he started to slide, totally out of control.

Desperately he tightened his grip, wrapped his legs around the cable and shouted just one word in total panic... before plummeting into darkness.

"Slippery!"

Gold-Eye's panicked yell coincided with the Myrmidons' arrival on the sixth floor and a Winger attempt to smash through the windows.

With their first rush, the two leading Myrmidons smashed the door out of its frame, pushing back the makeshift barrier of the tables and computer equipment Drum had piled up. He shoved it back against them and, without looking to see what else he could find, wrenched another computer cabinet from the wall and threw it across as well.

This one was still plugged in, and it burst into sparks and flame with an explosion that was marked by the sudden cessation of Professor Marcus Leamington's voice.

In that same second a Winger flew against the glass, shrieking and battering like a giant moth against a light globe. The glass bowed inward, but it held, at least for a few moments longer.

Under the table, Ella pushed Ninde into the shaft, forcing her to take hold despite her protestations that Gold-Eye had already fallen to his death and she preferred to take her chances elsewhere. Fortunately, Gold-Eye's manic grip had taken most of the grease with it, so she could descend under reasonable control.

Ella shouted at Drum to follow, then grabbed the cable herself, rapidly catching up with Ninde and forcing her to increase her speed by simply putting her boots on the younger girl's shoulders whenever she slowed down.

Drum, coughing from the sudden bloom of toxic white smoke from the burning computers, dived under the table, practically sliding into the shaft without really thinking or looking at it. Unlike the others, he was tall enough to wedge his back against one side and feet against the other.

Using this chimneying technique to keep himself in position, he reached behind his head with one hand and pulled the covering panel across to hide the shaft. Enough to fool a Myrmidon for a while, if not a Master. Then he started down.

Gold-Eye regained consciousness to witchlight, and pain let him know there was trouble in his head and left hand. The others were bending over him, looking very concerned.

"Can you move?" asked Ella.

He looked back at her as if she'd asked a very silly question, then realised he didn't know the answer. Hesitantly he tried to find out. Pain flared in his head and hand again, but everything seemed to work. He got to his feet, grateful for Drum's steadying hands.

"Anything feel broken?" Ella wanted to know.

Gold-Eye lifted his right hand to his head and drew it away sticky with blood – but not too much of it. Then he raised his left hand, flexing the fingers – and sharp agony let him know that his forefinger was either broken or very badly bruised.

"Finger," he said, holding up his hand. Ella looked pleased, which wasn't the reaction he'd been expecting. He guessed that she was glad he could move.

Looking around, he saw that they must have carried him out of the service-elevator shaft. Now they were in a very large, dark, damp room, filled with row after row of silent cars. All sorts of cars: big, small, gasoline, diesel, electric. All lined up with nowhere to go.

"One of the University's main underground parking lots," Ella said, seeing him look around. Even though she spoke quietly, her voice echoed off the low concrete ceilings.

"What do we do now?" asked Ninde. "They're still up there... They'll start looking here soon... Ferrets... What time is it?

"We need to start looking too," broke in Ella, a thin smile appearing to mark the progress of an idea. "We need to find an electric car that's still plugged in for recharge. Drum, you take that line – I'll do this. Ninde, see if you can splint Gold-Eye's finger."

"OK," said Ninde, relieved at being given something to do. "I would've been a doctor before the Change, you know," she said to a still dazed Gold-Eye. "Or maybe an advertising executive. See if you can straighten it out a bit and I'll tape it to the other finger. Hold still. It can't be that bad, and it has to be fairly tight to work. I've done most of the medical lessons back at the Sub, and I've seen plenty of doctors working in the old movies. And nurses. Doctors and nurses..."

Halfway through the operation, Gold-Eye realised that Ninde was talking too much because she was afraid. With his good hand he reached out and clumsily patted her on the shoulder.

"Be OK," he said. "Ella and Drum fix."

Ninde was silent for a moment. Then she packed her first-aid kit away quickly and stood up.

"I know," she said, as if she had never doubted that they would escape. "Anyway, you're all fixed up now."

"Thanks," replied Gold-Eye. He started to get up, but was struck with a sudden wave of dizziness, falling against Ninde so that his cheek lay against her breast.

"You did that on purpose, didn't you?" she said, pushing him back with no great urgency. "Boys!"

She turned away and started walking towards the witchlight-silhouetted figure of Ella.

Gold-Eye followed slowly, leaning on cars with his right hand, trying to figure out what was going on.

High above, the Myrmidons pulled away the table to show a Myrmidon Master the elevator shaft. It looked down it for a moment – then raised the jewelled medallion of a mind-call to its forehead.

DATABASE ARCHIVE
DORMITORY ESCAPEE TRENDS

Year	Escapees Observed	Enlisted	Active	Recaptured Or KIA	Missing, Presumed Recaptured
Change + 1	1026	127	127	127	
Change + 2	1265	311	311	309	
Change + 3	952	232	234	221	
Change + 4	892	241	247	235	2
Change + 5	778	202	212	200	
Change + 6	684	193	205	198	
Change + 7	600	190	197	180	
Change + 8	451	174	191	186	2
Change + 9	312	123	126	110	
Change + 10	190	90	106	94	
Change + 11	107	32	44	40	
Change + 12	95	34	38	30	
Change + 13	93	26	34	22	
Change + 14	61	21	33	25	
Change + 15	56	13	21	*	*

* Not yet completed

CHAPTER TWELVE

A far row of cars included several electric runabouts still plugged into the recharger. Four of them appeared to be fully charged and operational, green charge lights glowing on their dashboards.

One of them was unlocked, and Ninde found the ignition keys under the front seat – a favoured hiding spot in some of the old films she watched so avidly. Unfortunately, the old films – and Shade's instructional courses – did not include driving lessons.

So three of them sat in the vehicle while Ella studied the manual from the glove compartment, with Ninde and Gold-Eye looking over her shoulder. The unspoken hope was that three minds could make sense of what one could not.

Drum stood outside, hand on his sword, listening. Every now and then he could feel a faint rush of fresh air against his face, carrying with it the peep-peep-peep of hunting Trackers. He knew the creatures would soon find their way into the parking lot, or block the exit, even though it was several hundred yards away under a completely different building.

Then the faint sound of hunting Trackers was drowned by the buzz of the electric car coming to life behind him, its body shaking slightly as if it was flexing muscles after a very long sleep.

A moment later it jerked backwards suddenly. The tyres spun and smoked as they sought purchase on the slick concrete – and the car leaped out of its place, only to stop equally suddenly as Ella stamped on the brakes. The squeal was so loud that Drum had no doubt it would bring the creatures even sooner...

"Get in!" shouted Ella, not bothering to be quiet any more.

Drum looked at the car suspiciously, then walked round to the front passenger door, wary of any sudden rushes. He opened it, looked at it for a second – then with sudden violence ripped the door off its hinges and threw it on the ground.

"Easier to get out for me," he said, sliding into the front seat. "When the creatures come."

"Good idea," replied Ella. She opened her door, then reversed violently back towards a supporting pillar. The car missed it by a fraction – but the door didn't and tore off with a rasping shriek of metal on concrete.

Ella laughed, put the automatic shift to "drive" and put her foot down again, spinning wheels and laying rubber as they sped off again.

"They always drive like this in films," said Ninde confidently, guessing that Drum's and Gold-Eye's silences were caused more by fear of crashing than by fear of approaching creatures.

"I know what I'm doing," shouted Ella as they squealed round a corner and up a ramp to the next level. "I just hope there aren't any cars blocking the exit!"

"Or creatures," muttered Drum. He had his sword out and held it across his massive knees, fingers white-knuckled on the grip.

They rounded another corner less easily, grazing concrete walls. Ella slowed a little as she realised that the accelerator wasn't an on-off switch.

They started to turn the next corner and Gold-Eye was seized by his Change-Vision. He saw an enormous metal door grinding slowly upwards, sunshine pouring under it as it lifted – but the gap between door and floor was a lot less than the height of the car...

"Duck!" he screamed, coming out of the vision as they rounded the last corner and shot up a ramp – straight at the reluctantly opening roll-a-door at thirty miles an hour.

Car and door met with a crash heard by every creature on campus. Metal buckled, glass exploded, they screamed. Then they were out in sunshine, sunshine pouring straight into the car because the roof was peeled back and hanging half off the rear of the vehicle.

Gold-Eye sat up with a jerk. He half expected to see headless corpses all around, but Drum and Ella were bent over the central well, backs covered in powdered glass. Ninde was still hunched down in the back too, as far as she could go.

And Ella's foot was still flat to the floor, the car jumping a curb and on to the lawns, passing between two trees by pure luck.

Overhead, Wingers shrieked and took flight in pursuit. To their right, Myrmidons broke into a shambling run and Trackers let forth their finding cry. The prey was in sight!

In sight, but now moving at fifty miles per hour. Ella had sat up and regained control, without taking her foot off the accelerator. Now she was steering for the buildings on the far side of the lawns. The roads were too congested with stopped cars for an escape, but once near the buildings, they could get away on foot, get into the drains...

A Winger suddenly screamed close behind, diving to attack – only to meet a sudden end as Ella jinked the car and Drum stood and swung his gold-etched sword. The blade sheared through the Winger's neck and momentum carried it on, so it bounced headless off the hood, spewing blue ichor across Drum's forearms and face.

Gold-Eye and Ninde held Drum's legs as he swung, sure that they couldn't hold the big man if he overbalanced. Then the Winger was left behind them and Drum sat down coughing and spluttering, wiping Winger ichor off on his sleeves.

"Get ready to run for it," shouted Ella as they left the lawn and catapulted over a concrete strip. She slammed on the brakes and the car slid through ninety degrees. It ended up facing the creatures, its back only inches from a long line of cars.

Another Winger, caught off guard, overshot its attack and ploughed squealing into a station wagon with a sickening thud. It flopped once or twice but did not get up.

For a second they looked back at the battle lines of Myrmidons roaring towards them; the Trackers questing ahead; the Wingers swooping down. Then everyone was out and running, hunched over between the cars, heading for a narrow lane between two large shops.

Behind them the Myrmidons slowed and the Trackers sped up. It would be their job to find the renegades. The Wingers began to fly in higher circles, scanning the ground below. When the four targets emerged in open space, they would be ready.

Back in the laboratory, the Myrmidons were using fire extinguishers to quell the fire, but smoke still wreathed the room.

The Overlord Black Banner walked the room silently, the glow of the dying fires reflected in the opaque sheen of its full-faced visor. When it withdrew, the Myrmidon Master remained. It spoke quickly in battle tongue and the Myrmidons began to clean up the mess, sorting the salvageable computers from the destroyed. A few minutes later other Myrmidons arrived, carrying large plastic crates.

Inside an hour, more than half of the original equipment from the laboratory was packed up – and taken away.

A triumphant team returned to the Submarine several hours after dark, wet from the drains but having suffered no further floods or creature encounters.

Tired and sore, but still exhilarated from their successful mission and high-speed escape, they exchanged their ichor-splashed, wet coveralls for towels and went to report to Shade.

Unusually, his disembodied voice addressed them in the main corridor before they'd gone more than halfway along the Sub.

"Well done, my children. Well done, indeed. I think you deserve a special reward. Why don't you come down to the sick bay and meet me there?"

"Sick bay?" asked Gold-Eye, as Ella led them down to another hatch.

"Like a hospital," explained Ella. "Where we keep medicines and help sick or hurt people. You'll get your finger looked at there."

She paused, hesitated, then added, "It's also where Shade finds out more about creatures."

She started to spin the locking wheel on the hatch, but Drum stopped her, speaking to the wall in his high-pitched voice.

"Shade. Gold-Eye and Ninde are not needed, are they?"

"Mmm?" replied Shade. "No. I suppose not. They can get cleaned up and have the evening off. No lessons."

"But I want to see what the reward is," exclaimed Ninde, looking at Ella appealingly. "And so does Gold-Eye."

Ella didn't answer. She looked at Drum, who simply said, "No," and planted himself firmly in front of the hatch.

Ninde glared at him, then turned about and started back towards the bow.

"I hate you sometimes!" she spat, turning round at a safe distance. "You never let me do anything!"

Gold-Eye noticed that neither Drum nor Ella seemed particularly perturbed by this declaration – and since Ella hadn't spoken, he thought perhaps he could try to stay.

"I see reward?" he asked hesitantly. But once again it was Drum who answered – forcefully.

"No. It's not a reward you'd understand. Shade... jokes sometimes. Go with Ninde."

Gold-Eye nodded obediently and followed Ninde down the corridor. She was holding the hatch open for him and he sped up to get through.

As it clanged shut behind the younger pair, Ella said, "You're mollycoddling them, Drum. It won't be anything worse than what they've seen outside."

"It will," Drum said, his high voice at odds with his serious look. "It will be worse, because it's not even quick – and we're the ones doing it. Or Shade is."

"It's necessary," Ella replied coldly. "Come on."

ARCHIVE
INTERNAL DISCUSSION •
RADIATION ANALYSIS PROGRESS

Sensors currently available or able to be manufactured with present equipment are incapable of measuring or identifying radiation projected by Overlord devices, now designated as Change Projectors.

Placement of known Projectors indicates repeater emitters drawing from a narrow beam projected from the west. Source of this beamed radiation is not known.

All Projectors in the city are placed as high as possible. Exception: Fort Robertson, almost at sea level. Query: Why this anomalous placement?

Projectors share distinctive features. Semi-opaque silvered dome appears to contain reception dish, oriented to main beam from the west, and horizontal rod antennas, distributing the radiation. Query: 360-degree globe coverage?

Radiation is not diffused by most materials. Water seems to have an attenuating effect. Query: Creatures dislike water for this reason?

Action: Retrieve prototype Z-radiation detector from laboratory. Retrieve auto monitor data.

EXECUTION

Year	Team	Outcome	Losses
C+1	Aron	Failure	Team Lost
C+2	Carrie I	Failure	Team Lost
C+3	Emil	Failure	Team Lost
C+4	Robert	Failure	Team Lost
C+6	Lisa	Failure	Team Lost
C+7	Wilby	Failure	Team Lost
C+10	Don	Failure	Team Lost
C+11	Raven	Failure	Team Lost
C+13	Mac	Failure	Team Lost
C+14*1	Kurtz	Failure	Team Lost
C+14*2	Joser	Failure	Team Lost
C+15*1	Rick	Failure	Team Lost
C+15*2	Ella	Success	No Casualties

CHAPTER THIRTEEN

The sick bay was all gleaming stainless steel. Stainless-steel cabinets on stainless-steel walls. Stainless-steel fittings, stainless-steel floor. It had all the hallmarks of a room designed to be hosed clean.

A steel table, a great flat slab of metal, sat in the exact centre of the room. A Winger lay strapped to it, festooned with tubes that ran into its nasal cavities and wedged-open mouth. One enormous eye was shut, the other open, pinned back with clips. Blue ichor oozed from several deep – but now hastily clipped – incisions in its chest and legs.

Two of Shade's spider robots perched next to it, their forelimbs equipped with multiple grasping tendrils that now held surgical instruments. As Ella and Drum entered, one of them brandished a scalpel, the blade reflecting small suns in all the steel surfaces. Then the segmented limb moved with swift deliberation and the scalpel cut down into the wing of the helpless creature.

It shuddered and a single tear welled up in its pinned-back eye. The scalpel cut again. The other robot reached in with a pair of forceps and plucked out a small cylinder of gold-flecked metal.

It took the cylinder from the forceps with the anemone-like tendrils of its other forelimb and jumped down, scuttling between Drum and Ella to enter one of the cable ducts the robots used to move around the Submarine. Drops of blue ichor, fallen from the still-bloody cylinder, marked its passage.

"Fascinating!" exclaimed Shade's voice, emanating this time from a speaker within the scalpel-wielding spider robot's bulbous body. "So much more sophisticated than a Tracker. A much more complex biotechnical creation."

"What did you take out of the wing?" asked Ella, moving closer to the vivisection bench despite the stench of ichor and excrement. Drum moved closer too, his face showing intense dislike of the whole proceeding.

"I don't know yet," replied Shade, hopping the spider robot up to the creature's head and stabbing down with the scalpel again at a spot marked under its ear with a fluorescent marker. "It appears to be a device that converts some form of radiated power to some other form of energy. An anti-gravity device perhaps, because it is quite impossible for these things to fly without assistance. It really is very, very interesting."

The robot sliced again and, taking up the forceps, withdrew a silvery sphere about half the size of a golf

133

ball. This time the Winger's body tensed into an arch, relaxed, tensed again – and groaned, spit and sound bubbling around the tubes wedged in its mouth.

"It's trying to speak," said Drum, watching the creature trying to move its misshapen mouth. Its open eye was moving too, the pupil off in one corner, staring. Staring at Ella.

"They can't speak," said Shade, the speaker in the spider robot buzzing with distortion, as if he were angry. "Only the Myrmidons have their battle language."

"It's trying to say something," Drum insisted, his voice rising. He hesitated, then reached across and wrenched the tubes out of the Winger's mouth, ignoring the twitch of the spider robot's scalpel towards his hands.

The Winger coughed. It was obviously trying to speak, though its wide mouth and outthrust jaw were not designed to help with words. At first it sounded just like a gargle, or an insult. Then it became clear.

"El-la. El-la."

The Winger was calling Ella's name.

"El-la. Br-at. Me."

It choked, blue froth dribbling from the corners of its mouth, while Ella stared at it uncomprehendingly. Drum reached out and picked up the largest scalpel from the tray next to the robot.

"Amazing," said Shade, in a tone of passionless interest. "Removal of the unit next to the brain seems to break part of the psychophysical conditioning."

"What do you mean?" asked Ella, her gaze still fixed on the Winger's open eye, now washed with many tears.

"The brain of the boy used in the creature's manufacture has retained some human memory, which has come to the fore," replied Shade very matter-of-factly. "And he obviously recognises you."

"Brat?" asked Ella. "Brat? But…"

"Ye-es," coughed the Winger, as if forcing the words out past a barrier of pain and terrible distance. "Me Br-at."

"We must see exactly how the transformation is achieved," said Shade, moving the spider robot closer. One tendril-ended limb reached out to caress the Winger's head. "Find out more about the physical alterations to the brain…"

"Kill me!" the Winger spat, spraying the advancing spider robot with spit and ichor, even as the tendrils picked up the fluorescent marker pen and began to mark its forehead.

"Ella! Kill meeeeee—"

The Winger's voice suddenly stopped as Drum reached over and cut its throat with one rapid movement. It seemed to sigh then, blue ichor slowly dribbling out like spilled jelly from the gaping wound in its neck. Its open eye swung away from Ella to Drum, body and wings twitched once – and it was dead.

Ella stood still for a moment, then reached out, unclipped the eyelid and closed the Winger's eye.

"Goodbye, Brat."

Drum dropped the scalpel on the table and stood back while the spider robot stood frozen, as if Shade couldn't believe what had just happened.

"There was no need for that!" he finally snapped. "Valuable data will be lost."

"It was Brat," said Ella, hand still touching the Winger's ugly head. "Just at the end. He knew who he was, he could feel what you were doing..."

"It was a Winger," said Shade in a disgusted tone. "Any personality relict was purely temporary. I could have found out so much..."

"You would have gone on cutting him up, keeping him barely alive," interrupted Drum. "Even when he knew who he was and could feel everything you did. You'd even cut one of us up if you thought you'd learn something."

The spider robot froze again as Drum spoke. When he finished, it hopped down from the table and disappeared into a conduit, steel claws scratching. In silence Drum and Ella watched it go, both of them wondering how Shade would react.

Finally he spoke again, through the usual hidden speakers in the floor and walls. He spoke softly, as if he didn't want to seem angry or unsettled.

"Drum, you accuse me of something I would... I could never do. Waging war against the Overlords is of paramount importance, but the preservation of certain human ideals is also my priority. You are my children... I simply seek the best for the greatest number of you.

"The Winger on that slab is no longer human, even if some buried humanity emerged from it for a while. Brat was lost to us two years ago. He was dead then. You may have thought you were being merciful to a friend... In fact, you were only abetting the enemy. Don't you see that?"

Drum didn't answer. He looked down at the splayed-out figure of the Winger, the loosely clipped wounds, the blue ichor pooled on the table. Then he looked up at the ceiling, shook his head – and walked out.

"You understand, don't you, Ella?" Shade continued as the hatch closed. "It is distasteful but necessary work. Drum should not have interfered."

"I... don't... know," whispered Ella, shaking her head, her chest suddenly tight. "Brat... but information... the more we know..."

"Yes, yes!" cried Shade. "You have it exactly. But it is a hard realisation, overcoming one's emotions with rational thought. I think you should go and rest. Besides, I have to get cleaned up in here so I can operate on Stelo."

"What?"

"Oh, nothing serious," answered Shade breezily. "Some Winger cuts on his right arm and cheek. He's sedated now. A few stitches and he'll be up and about in a few days. A week at most."

"Good," replied Ella dully. She felt suddenly very tired, worn out more by the last half hour than the day in the creature-dominated world outside. "I'll... I'll get going. By the way, we left the instrument ball and the data CDs from your old lab in the changing room..."

"Yes," said Shade. "I already have them and am assimilating the data. It fills in some very important gaps. Very important gaps."

"Also that artificial intelligence you mentioned," Ella continued, suddenly remembering that she hadn't given a full report. "It was still working. It was a lot more sophisticated than I expected... almost human..."

"Human?" chuckled Shade. "I would hardly describe Leamington as human. But we'll go through your full report in the morning. Good night, Ella."

"Good night, Shade."

AUDIO ARCHIVE – PICKUP #255:
TORPEDO LOCK 4 • SAM ALLEN

Are you listening, Shade? Of course you are. You're always listening. Little ears and eyes everywhere... Big Brother in a very small small pond.

So the world's gone completely fucking crazy. It gives you the chance to be a dictator? And the worst kind of one too, safe from the risks you send us out to face every day.

If you had a body still, I'd try and smash your fucking face in for what you've done. Kids sent out to find out things you already know, sent down tunnels to get parts for your computer or your robots... used as bait... used up...

OK, maybe your way is better than the Dorms and the Meat Factory. But there's another way too. Janis and me have had enough of your pretending to be God. We'll take our chances getting out of the City. Things have to be better in the country. We'll look out for kids from the Dorms, too – to try and save them for a new life, not your meat-grinder "army".

If I had a fire axe and I could get at your bloody processors, I'd take you out before I go... but there's no chance of that... is there? Robot access only. Not to mention your brainwashed storm troopers... You should show them a video of 2001 sometime...

Sometimes I wish I'd been just one month older when the Change came... Then I'd never have had to live through this... but I wasn't, so I get to make some real exciting choices.

This is one of them.

Sayonara, shithead!

CHAPTER FOURTEEN

Gold-Eye stopped outside the hatch that led to the four-bunk room where he'd stayed the night before, but Sim waved him on.

"You're in Sixteen-A tonight, Gold-Eye," he explained, looking down at the clipboard he carried everywhere with him. "Twelve-A is a Lottery room for the next couple of days. You can probably hear them going at it now if you stick your ear to the bulkhead."

"Going at it?" asked Gold-Eye, mystified. He stepped up to the door and was about to place his ear against it when Sim shook him gently by the shoulder and pointed him back down the corridor.

"I was joking, Gold-Eye," he explained. "Look, I know you're tired and hurt and everything, but it might be worthwhile if you checked out a couple of lessons tonight. I mean, you are at least fifteen, I'd say... You ought to know..."

"What lessons?" asked Gold-Eye as Sim's voice petered out.

"Come on. I'll cue them up for you. *Sex Education One* and *Two*. And *Basic Contraception One*. It'll take about two and a half hours... but I think you'll consider it time well spent..."

Gold-Eye followed the still-talking Sim to one of the screening rooms, taking in about every third word. He'd realised earlier that Sim just liked to talk and you didn't really have to listen.

Outside the screening room they passed three other people Gold-Eye hadn't met yet – and didn't get to this time. The two girls and a boy went past without a word, exhausted and anxious faces showing that they were more spaced out than intentionally rude.

"Stelo's team," explained Sim. "Rosie, Marg and Peter..."

"Petar!" exclaimed Gold-Eye, looking back at the departing trio. "Name like brother."

"Really?" said Sim. "Well, their team leader, Stelo, got hit badly today. Something to do with the Winger they captured. I guess they're going to check him out. Which reminds me – you're listed to report to sick bay first thing tomorrow – when you wake up. How do you feel, by the way?"

"Fine," replied Gold-Eye, which meant that his head and finger hurt a lot but not enough to stop him from doing anything – which was close enough to fine, as far as he was concerned.

Sim led him into the screening room – a large area divided into six cubicles with individual privacy hoods. One of the cubicles was occupied and sealed, the others vacant. Sim led him to one and showed him where to sit, and how to touch the view screen or speak the control words.

"Display *Sex Education One*, *Sex Education Two* and *Basic Contraception One*, in that order," Sim said to the view screen. "Check."

"*Sex Education One*, *Sex Education Two* and *Basic Contraception One*," said a cheery female voice as the titles of the selected lessons flashed up on the view screen. "Say 'Ready' or press forward when you wish to begin."

"I'll leave you to it," said Sim, backing out and lowering the privacy hood. "Enjoy!"

"Ready," said Gold-Eye absently. He'd heard the word sex years before in the Dorms, but he'd been so young. Still, there was always plenty to learn...

Gold-Eye was very tired the next morning. He'd watched *Sex Education Two* two and a half times before Shade had cut in and ordered him to bed.

He had trouble talking to Ninde and Ella over breakfast too, finally understanding certain physical urges and desires that had been with him since they had first met. But as neither were in the Lottery, he knew they didn't want to have sex with anybody, so he might as well forget it. Or try to.

Drum wasn't in the Lottery list either, Gold-Eye had noted. Which was odd, since every other male was. Perhaps he had been, Gold-Eye thought, and didn't like it. Personally, Gold-Eye had been quick to pass the contraception exam first go and had put his name down on the Lottery list seconds later. Now it was just a matter of time...

Trying to suppress that thought was difficult, he found, particularly as Ella took him round the mess room where they ate breakfast, introducing him to everyone there. Including six other girls... women... of whom four were in the Lottery. He couldn't help wondering what they looked like with their clothes off, which made it very difficult to say hello.

Fortunately, Sim came and took him away straight after breakfast for more sword practice and then a series of lessons in the screening room on various topics, including spoken English and creature identification.

More sword practice and some gymnastic-style exercises followed after lunch, Sim pushing Gold-Eye to his physical limits, with Shade's disembodied voice occasionally joining in to encourage or chastise.

After dinner, Gold-Eye had yet another lesson. A lengthy one on first aid, including cardiopulmonary resuscitation (CPR), a technique Gold-Eye found particularly interesting after his experiences in the storm-water drains. After that, he fell into bed, totally exhausted and aching all over.

The next three days followed the same pattern, with so many lessons Gold-Eye had very little time to explore his new home. He did manage to talk to other people at mealtimes. There were more than thirty of "Shade's Children" all together, but never more than twenty or so were in the Submarine at any one time. The others were out, gathering food and supplies or carrying out one of Shade's information-seeking missions.

He also spent some time talking to Drum, since Ella spent most of her time with Shade or in training, and Gold-Eye was still somewhat shy of Ninde.

Despite his exhaustion, Gold-Eye still kept a careful eye on the days left till the next Lottery draw. In four days he could be in one of the bunk rooms with Rosie or Cael or Suze or...

But on the third day the lessons suddenly stopped and Gold-Eye found himself once again in Shade's control room, sitting on the sofas with Ella, Drum and Ninde.

This time the holographic image of Shade was already there, at his desk. A rat robot's eyes gleamed under the desk and a spider robot clicked backwards and forwards behind Shade's chair like some small footman pacing behind a king.

Four sets of odd-looking headgear were on the desk: thin metal crowns of steel etched with very fine patterns of gold lines. Wires trailed out of the crowns to small plastic boxes about the width of two of Gold-Eye's fingers.

Shade indicated the crowns with a wave of his hand and smiled, revealing all his glossy, splendid teeth.

"Fruit of our labours," he declared. "The data you brought back, coupled with my existing research, has led to a major breakthrough. My new Deceptors!"

"What do they do?" asked Ella.

"I have discovered the basic source of the Overlords' power," Shade continued, frowning at the interruption to his prepared speech. "Put simply, the silver globes you see atop various tall buildings – Projectors – are beaming out a form of radiation that has several effects. First, it slightly warps this reality, changing certain physical laws – and it is this effect that I believe was used to remove the adult population in the first place. It also allows your Change Talents to work. Second, devices implanted or even grown within the creatures allow them to take this radiation and convert it into various kinds of power. Antigravity for flight, super-charged muscles, enhanced senses, and so on.

"Having discovered the true nature of the Projectors – a breakthrough worthy of a Nobel Prize in bygone days – I have created these devices. They use the Overlords' own power and turn it against them. When you wear a Deceptor, you will be practically invisible to the creatures, because the device reflects Projector power in such a way that it baffles their sensory augmentation."

He smiled again and leaned back in his chair, chest inflating with obvious pride in the steel-and-gold contraptions.

No one spoke for a moment, as each digested Shade's information. Then Drum raised one hand, the scars from his near drowning still starkly red on his palms.

"If they use this Projector power," he said, pointing at the black boxes connected to the crowns, "why the mobile-phone batteries?"

"You weren't listening, Drum," Shade replied, the smile disappearing. "The Deceptors reflect the Projector radiation in a particular pattern. Unfortunately, for this prototype at least, electrical power is required. Hence the mobile-phone batteries you so cleverly identified."

"How long with they last?" asked Ella, raising her hand and speaking at the same time.

"Six... or seven hours," said Shade. "They lasted for eight and a half hours in test conditions... but there is a faint possibility that battery use will increase the closer you get to a Projector. Go on... pick them up... try them on. They're adjustable at the back."

The crowns were not as flimsy as they looked, and were reasonably comfortable once they were adjusted. In use, the batteries would fit in a belt pouch, the thin power cable clipped taut and worn down the back.

"Good," said Shade, when everyone wore a crown. "As you can imagine, these Deceptors will allow us to move into a new stage in our campaign against the Overlords. Thanks to this adaptation of their own technology, you will be able to enter one of their strongholds and steal their secrets."

Only Ella met this assertion with equanimity. Drum frowned and leaned forward, great elbows resting on his knees. Gold-Eye looked at the others to see how they were taking it. Ninde grimaced, indicating that no one could get her anywhere near an Overlord's stronghold.

"Which stronghold are you thinking about?" asked Ella calmly.

Shade smiled. He made a gesture with his right hand, like a conjurer about to reveal a rabbit, and a laser stabbed down from the ceiling to the right of his desk. Motes of light twirled around it and formed into a hologram of the bay. It was a bird's-eye view, above the twisted remnants of the bay bridge, whose middle third was bent into the deep blue water.

Shade gestured again and their viewpoint changed. They left the bridge to travel further out in the bay, towards the point where it met the open sea. Halfway, their view zoomed in on a small rocky island that dominated the narrowest stretch of water. Two old stone towers joined by a flat-roofed building took up most of the island. Each tower was a checkerboard of yellow sandstone and shadowed cannon ports – and each was topped by the silver globe of a Projector, casting reflections like shoals of fish on the blue-green waves that washed around the island.

As they watched, a very large Winger flew in high and made an almost vertical descent to land on the flat roof of the centre building. As at the University, it was carrying an Overlord, which quickly climbed off its back. This one's armour was bright, blinding red and it wore a cloak that moved like fire, all red and yellow tongues of flame. Its helmet was pyramidal, with a dark visor stark against the hell-fire red.

"Red Diamond," remarked Shade. "Going home to Fort Robertson. It seems to live there. The only such residence I have been able to locate. Fort Robertson also has the only Projectors that aren't sixty stories up."

"How are we supposed to get out there?" asked Ella. She tapped the crown on her head. "Even if these things confuse their sense, they'll still see us..."

"No they won't," interrupted Shade. "Projector power is used in a very fundamental part of their sensory integration. The Deceptors totally scramble that. Besides, you will go at night. I doubt very much that there will be any Ferrets on Fort Robertson, or any other creatures for that matter. I have had the island under observation for many years without seeing the Wingers fly in anything but Red Diamond or occasionally some other Overlord."

"So are we supposed to swim out?" asked Ella. "I could probably make it, and Ninde..."

"No, no. I wouldn't ask you to swim!" exclaimed Shade. "You'll take one of the inflatable boats from this Submarine. My little helpers have patched one up and converted an outboard motor to electric power. It will serve the purpose well."

Ella and Drum exchanged glances. Both had experience out in the bay with boats and knew it wasn't safe or easy except in the calmest weather.

Neither spoke, but all four of them realised that Shade wanted them to go somewhere potentially even more dangerous than the rest of the city, somewhere where no one had been before, though it was only a few miles out into the bay. Even if they did get there safely, the chances of a safe return were very slim.

Shade seemed oblivious to this, leaning back and smiling with the air of someone who expects general enthusiasm to break out at any moment.

Finally Ninde raised her hand and asked the question everyone wanted to know.

"What do we do when we get to Fort Robertson?"

"Didn't I say?" Shade smiled. "I want you to steal a Projector."

VIDEO ARCHIVE
INTERVIEW 25371 • ELLA

What would I want to be if we could change things back to the way they were?

I don't know. I really don't think about it. The chance we will succeed is so small... and if it is going to happen at all, we can't afford the time to just think about it. We have to act.

<PAUSE. SILENCE 5 SECONDS.>

As far as particular things go, I guess I'd like to walk down the middle of the street in the sun, with people all around me... old people, young people, everyone. But that's a daydream, and daydreams are dangerous. A daydream will get you killed.

Better to concentrate on what we have to do. Don't think about tomorrow. It can look after itself.

Focus. Get the job done.

What comes after probably won't be our business at all anyway.

I don't think there really is any such thing as a happy ending outside stories and Ninde's favourite films. Not for us.

No happy endings for us. Just endings.

CHAPTER FIFTEEN

The Overlords started changing the weather on the afternoon before the planned infiltration of Fort Robertson. The first signs came just before dusk, with a freezing wind rolling up the bay, chilling the water. Sleet followed for half an hour. Then the wind died, leaving the bay calm and very cold.

Ella and Drum came back indoors blue-faced and shivering, after spending two hours getting the inflatable boat out through the forward cargo hatch.

They showered, donned heavy ex-Navy wet suits for warmth (two XXLs welded together by the robots for Drum), and went back out again to join Gold-Eye and Ninde in the inflatable – a matt-black dinghy with a solid fibreglass floor and bow sitting between blown-up rubber sides.

Though it was slightly warmer after the sleet, a fog was rising in its mysterious way all around the harbour. The half moon, only just appearing on the horizon, was rapidly blanked out. The sun, setting behind the skyscrapers of the city, found gaps for its rays between the tall buildings, only to lose them in the fog. The few lights that had come on automatically around the bay were also indistinct – fuzzy balls of colour rather than sharp illuminations.

"We'll have to wait," said Ninde, already shivering despite the full-body wet suit that made her look rather like a slim, attractive seal. "It's too cold."

"Fog hide island," added Gold-Eye worriedly, looking down the length of the Submarine. He could barely see the conning tower, which was still catching the sun just above the rising fog.

"Shade wants us to go now," said Ella. "There is some need for speed, apparently. And the fog helps us too, remember. Now, has everyone got their crowns on? OK – here are the batteries. Keep them out of water if at all possible. Shade tells me they should be water-resistant, but don't count on it. Watch your swords too – this boat isn't as tough as it once was.

"If for any reason you go overboard and can't be recovered, try and swim back. City Tower is lit up and it lines up pretty well with here. If you can see it, swim for it. The wet suit will help you stay afloat – just drop everything else. It can all be replaced.

"When we get to Fort Robertson, we'll tie up at the landing stage and go ashore as quietly as we can. I don't want to depend on these Deceptor things working the way Shade thinks they will.

"Is everybody ready?"

"Yes," replied Drum and Gold-Eye. Ninde didn't say anything, but her shivering grew more exaggerated. Ella ignored her and pushed the start button on the outboard. It whirred into life, kicking up froth as Ella flicked it from neutral into forward gear. At the same time, Drum lifted off the bowline that was looped over a rusting projection on one of the wharf's piles.

The spider robots had done a good job changing the outboard motor from petrol to electric. It still performed well, as Ella discovered from her experimentation with the throttle, but now it was much quieter. She only hoped the large, plastic-sealed battery at her feet would last them there and back, as Shade had promised.

Throttling back to a safe, steady speed, the inflatable followed the Submarine hull to the stern, zigzagged among the piles of the wharf there, and then turned out into the bay. Out of the shelter of the Sub, they immediately hit some waves – but they were small. The water was surprisingly calm even for a fog-bound bay.

Calm, but with steadily decreasing visibility. The fog was thickening by the minute, the air growing warmer as the grey-white wisps fell into layers like pulled-apart wool.

Airborne mist mixed with salt spray on their faces – the only exposed patch of skin on their neoprene-suited, mittened, hooded and booted bodies – as the boat rose nose first into the air up a line of swell and then nose first back down into the water on the other side.

Ella had planned to steer using the lights from one of the still-functioning harbour beacons and a fully lit-up apartment block on the north shore, but with the fog, neither was visible.

Slackening their speed a little and locking the throttle – just enough to keep steerageway – she pulled out a compass and checked her course.

"Gold-Eye," she said, moving the outboard's tiller a little to correct her course, "go up to the front and call out if you see anything. There are a few buoys – floating markers, that is – that we don't want to run into."

Gold-Eye nodded and edged past Drum and Ninde, keeping a careful hand on the rope that ran down the bulbous inflatable cylinders on either side of the rigid part of the boat. At the bow, he leaned forward, stomach on fibreglass and chest on the inflated rubber prow, so he could see even when they were on the crest of a wave.

"See anything?" asked Ella, increasing speed again.

"Not yet," replied Gold-Eye, eyes blinking from the spray. A few minutes later he heard a dull, clanking noise – and something large and white loomed out of the fog only ten or twenty feet away, off to the left.

It was a white-painted buoy, bigger than their boat, anchor chain clanking dismally. Damp seagulls were clustered on it, half frozen from the sleet a few hours before and totally confused by the sudden change of weather. One tried to take flight as the boat approached but plunged into the sea instead and was carried away on a wave like a fisherman's lost float.

"There!" shouted Gold-Eye, his voice carrying through the quiet of the fog, making the others wince.

"I see it," replied Ella calmly, changing course a little. "We're about halfway there. And Gold-Eye, you don't need to shout."

"Sorry."

They continued in silence for another ten minutes, the only sound the buzz of the engine and the wash of the sea around the boat as they breasted each line of swell. Gold-Eye almost spoke up twice to alert Ella, but both times he realised he was only seeing denser patches of fog.

Then the noise of the sea changed, becoming louder and harsher with the crash of swell on land. This was closely followed by their first sight of Fort Robertson, which rose up out of the sea and fog off their port side. For a few seconds they saw one of the towers, topped by a Projector, its silver sheen just catching the evening sun above the mist. Then the island was gone again, lost in the fog.

"Missed it!" muttered Ella. She opened the throttle to cut back and along the swell that threatened to pick them up and deposit them on the island. "We'll go around and come in on the other side at the landing stage. Get ready, everyone. Ninde, see if you can pick up anything."

Ninde nodded and began to chew on her knuckle, her silver-crowned head bent in concentration. After a few seconds she looked up, obviously frightened.

"I can't get anything at all!" she said. "It just doesn't work! Not from the water, because I can always get the feeling... except now..."

"The crown," said Drum quietly. "I can't do anything either. It has to be the crown."

"Oh," said Ninde, looking slightly relieved. She reached up to disconnect hers, but Ella put out a foot and tapped her on the knee.

"Don't," she said. "If these things work as promised, we need them on now. We can be seen from the towers, and if there are Trackers there, they'll smell us on the wind."

"OK," replied Ninde, letting her hand drop back to her lap. "I just hate not knowing what's going on..."

"I know," replied Ella meaningfully. "Quiet now – we're going back in. Gold-Eye, swap places with Drum – he'll be off first. Here we go!"

She angled the boat back towards the island, accelerating again for a quick approach. It was almost too quick. The fog and failing light made distance hard to judge, and all of a sudden the island's wooden landing stage was in front of them, stone towers rising up behind it.

Ella flipped the outboard into reverse as they saw it, so the boat bumped rather than crashed – and Drum leaped ashore, drawing his sword almost in mid-air. Gold-Eye followed less flamboyantly and with greater caution drew his sword, following the big man into the shadow of one of the towers. Ninde tied the boat up while Ella killed the engine. Then both jumped out and ran across to the shadows.

A minute later the last of the sun dipped down below the horizon and the fog was no longer white. It was just dark, wet and cold.

There were no lights on the island – or none working. And there was no visible point of entry from the landing stage. Just the steps up to the roof of the flat building that seemed to be built into the island itself. The place where the Wingers landed.

"Lights on," whispered Ella, activating her own witchlight. "Follow me."

Sword in one hand and witchlight in the other, she led the way up the steps. Gold-Eye followed less confidently, looking up at the towers on either side. They seemed taller here than in the picture – five or six storeys at least, topped with the strange silvery spheres...

Ninde didn't move at all till Drum gave her a bit of a push. She felt lost without her Change Talent. Even out here with all this water around, she felt sure she would be able to sense something. Particularly if the Change Projectors that Shade had raved about helped; after all, there were two of them less than fifty feet away...

Drum saw her hand go to the battery pack on her belt and readied himself to stop her – but her hand passed over it and pulled a flashlight out of its loop instead. She clicked it on and moved off.

Drum shook his head and followed, ears wide open for the sudden hiss of a Ferret or the sound of some other terrible creature. Shade had said there were none here, but Drum knew many instances when Shade had proved wrong and his children had paid the price.

Back in the boat, the cover on the small compartment in the bow creaked open and a furry snout emerged. Beady red eyes focused on the figure of Drum. When he was out of sight, the rat robot scurried out and leaped ashore. A few seconds later, it was slinking up the steps.

A future after the Change is turned back?

That's a stupid question, Shade. The courts of Byzantium and China were going long before the Change... I might have found a place there... or the Ottoman Empire, perhaps...

I don't expect any brave new world will have career openings for harem guards or gelded civil servants.

I don't really expect that there will be a brave new world.

But we have to try for one. For all the kids in the Dorms... in the Training Grounds...

But not for me.

CHAPTER SIXTEEN

The eastern tower had a riveted steel door leading on to the flat roof of the middle building, which the Wingers used as a landing zone. The western tower appeared to have no outside point of entry at all. It could be reached only from within the middle building – which in turn could be entered only via its own roof and the door into the eastern tower. Even the cannon ports that had looked like easy entry points proved to be shuttered tight with black-painted boards.

The tower door looked very ordinary, as if it might have come off a merchant ship in a previous life. Lines of rivets ran around the edges and across its middle, and there was a worn bronze knob above an old-fashioned keyhole. Close inspection revealed that the keyhole was sealed – perhaps with a broken key – so there was a good chance it wasn't even locked.

Ella studied it closely, then signalled Drum to stand so he could strike within the doorway as she pushed it open.

Gold-Eye and Ninde stood further back and slightly apart, ready to support but not so close that a net gun could mesh all three of them with one shot.

When they were ready, Ella reached out, turned the bronze knob – and pushed the door open with a vigorous heave. Drum's sword jerked half an inch forward – but there was no one there. Just an empty room.

A very strange room. White, slippery-looking marble lined the floor – except right in the middle, where there was a ten-foot-wide hole. A corresponding hole was cut in the ceiling directly above. There was no stairs or ladders in evidence – just this vertical shaft.

Ella edged in, holding the witchlight high, still alert for some hidden creatures – but there was nothing there for them to hide in or behind.

Cautiously she went to the edge of the hole and looked up and down in one quick second, then looked again more slowly. Both views were surprising. The hole was essentially a round shaft that went up further than the witchlight extended – probably to the top floor. It also went down – a very long way down. Ella could just make out two floors below, and it seemed to continue well beyond that. A shiver crossed her as she looked, and the image of a dark abyss stretching down for miles flashed into her mind.

She signalled the others to come in, but they were already in. Drum closed the door after checking it could be opened from the inside. Now they all gathered around the shaft, looking up and down in puzzlement.

"It's like an elevator shaft with no elevator," whispered Ninde. "I wonder how far down it goes."

"I guess we'd better try and find out," whispered Ella. "Get your ropes out. Drum, keep an eye on the door."

Gold-Eye looked down at his equipment belt to unfasten the length of rope coiled against his hip – and his eye caught a small blinking red light at the top of one pouch. It was the light that should come on only when the battery that powered his Deceptor was at less than half charge. It had been on for only an hour…

"Ella," he whispered, so quietly she almost didn't hear him. "Deceptor battery."

He pointed at the small red dot on the black case. Ella looked, then checked her own. It was also blinking red. A few seconds later, Drum's started as well, then Ninde's.

"Might use more power closer to the Projectors…" muttered Ella, looking up to where the Projector roosted unseen on the roof of the tower.

"How are we going to get up?" asked Ninde quietly as Ella tied their four pieces of rope together. "I can't see anything to throw a noose over."

"I don't think we can," replied Ella. "So we'll go down, take a quick look around, and then get the hell out of here before the Deceptor batteries run out. I'll go first."

Quickly she tied the rope to a rusting steel staple embedded in the stone wall, tested it, and then threw the loose end into the shaft.

Strangely, it didn't fall for a moment, but lay suspended in mid-air. Then the half on the far side of the shaft began to rise, while the half closest to them began to slowly fall, till there was one loop rising and one loop descending. Slowly, quite against the normal behaviour of gravity.

Ella shot a look at Drum, but he shook his head and tapped the crown on his head.

"I guess it is an elevator," Ella said to Ninde, pulling the rope back as she spoke. This time, she coiled the loose end together and threw it to the far side. It ascended almost at once, till the rope was taut and the coil was well above the next floor up.

"One half up, one half down?" whispered Gold-Eye. It was clear to him that half the shaft moved things invisibly upward and the other half moved them down.

"Obviously," said Ninde, well above a whisper. "I said it was an elevator."

Ella frowned and held her finger to her lips, cautioning silence.

"We can't be sure it'll hold our weight – or that it will always be on. So we'll get the rope down and stick with that. Me first, then Gold-Eye, Ninde, Drum."

It was the easiest rope climbing she had ever done, Ella thought as she climbed down. Her boots stepped through the rope in approved style – without taking any weight. She was sure that if she let go, she'd just gently drift down at a safe and steady rate.

She didn't let go but took it slowly, pausing to scan the floor below with her witchlight. It looked just like the one above – a featureless round room with rough stone walls and a white marble floor. The only thing that was different was the temperature – it was noticeably warmer. But this floor wasn't interesting enough to examine, so Ella continued down.

The second level down was quite different. This room looked almost like a grand hotel's lobby, on a smaller scale. The floor was carpeted in rich red, and the stone walls had given way to panelled walls of black and scarlet. There were four doors leading off the room, one at each point of the compass – tall, wide doors with the gleam of beaten bronze.

Ella could see that the next floor below looked similar, and the next – and still the shaft went on. Clearly she was now under the level of the seabed, and Ella felt a tinge of fear as she realised that Red Diamond must have a whole underground complex here, a catacomb of tunnels and rooms. These bronze doors could lead to anything. Ferrets could have been brought in underground, so Shade's assurance that he'd never seen any creatures flown in was worthless.

She felt an urge to abort the mission there and then. After all, they couldn't go up to get the Projector without abandoning the safety of the rope. The Deceptor batteries were draining far too quickly, and the existence of this underground complex changed everything...

But every second of her days involved risk. And here there could be great gain.

Swinging a little on the rope, she jumped on to the carpet, boots sinking into the soft plush, and crossed to the western door. A muffled thud and a glance behind confirmed Gold-Eye's arrival. Ella pointed at him, cupped a hand to her ear and then pointed at the eastern door. Gold-Eye nodded his understanding and went to listen at that door, unsheathing his sword.

All the doors looked identical. Each was about ten feet high and six feet wide, with two panels so they parted in the middle. The bronze was highly polished, catching the witchlight and flashlight beams and multiplying them into butterfly-like flashes that whisked around the room.

Ella heard nothing behind her door, nor did Gold-Eye. Ninde and Drum listened at the northern and southern doors. Silence.

It looked as if the two leaves of each door just pushed in at the middle. Ella clicked her fingers, summoning her troops to the western door and positioning them for a concerted rush if anything came out.

Then she pushed open the door.

It creaked at first, then eased, and Ella relaxed a little as the noise faded and nothing stirred in the darkness within. She stopped pushing and stepped back, to be ready if a creature tried to squeeze through the gap. But both leaves kept opening, and suddenly they were accompanied by the deep tolling of a bell somewhere far below.

At the same time, witchlight flared all around them. Witchlight from the stones of the walls, witchlight flooding the shaft, witchlight bright in the corridor beyond the opening door.

A long corridor, stretching out as far as they could see. A long corridor lined on both sides with Myrmidons, sleeping at attention. Hundreds, thousands of Myrmidons, all clad in ruby-red breastplates and finely linked scarlet armour. Their helmeted heads were bent forward in sleep, so that their visors rested on the segmented plates of their gorgets.

The closest one wore the plumed helmet of a Myrmidon Master. Where all the others carried great swords or multi-bladed pole-arms, it cradled in its arms something that looked like a cat-sized conch shell.

The bell tolled again, perhaps only a second later, and the Master's head snapped back. It was impossible to see behind its visor, but clearly it was awake.

It turned its head towards the shaft, put down the conch shell and slowly, deliberately, took a tribladed axe from the unresisting arms of the nearest Myrmidon. It swung it twice, as if testing the weight, then stepped forward lightly. The ease of its movement was strange and frightening, out of place for something so big and heavily armoured.

Ella stepped back, urgently signalling the others to do likewise. It didn't seem to perceive them, so if they managed to get up the shaft...

Gold-Eye backed away, watching the Myrmidon Master slowly inflating its hood. Then a faint vibration at his waist jolted his head with even more adrenaline. He looked down at the Deceptor battery. The red light was flashing furiously, the battery buzzing its failure alert. Then the vibration stopped... and the light went out.

When Gold-Eye looked back up, the Myrmidon Master was just there, shouting so loudly, it was like the crash of a wave, with the awful axe whistling through the air—

Instinctively he raised his sword to parry, and in that same instant the Master wasn't there any more and his hand was numb and he was stumbling backward, screaming into the shaft.

Only Drum's battery going flat saved him. The Master, reaching out to strike as Gold-Eye rose upward, suddenly became aware of another threat. Spinning in place, it caught Drum's downward blow between the first and second blades of the axe, locked it, and slammed back with the butt.

Drum lessened that blow by jumping backwards, meeting the panelled wall with a thud. Two swift blows from the axe butt doubled him over, and the axe was free of his sword and ready to fall. Then Ella's sword struck from behind and came out at the front where a human's heart would be.

Without lowering the axe, the Master turned, ripping the sword out of Ella's hand and opening a wound halfway around its chest. The axe fell a few inches, then stopped, as if the Master couldn't see what had driven the sword into it.

Then Drum smashed into the back of its knees, driving it down to stain the red carpet with blue ichor. Before it could rise, Drum's sword hammered into the base of its skull. It screeched something violently in Battlespeech, then lay still, fingers twitching and feet drumming like a broken wind-up toy.

Below them the bell tolled again, and a hideously loud and high-pitched scream echoed up the shaft, going on and on long after human lungs would have been exhausted. If it had been closer, the scream would have deafened and dazed them – this far away, it was simply terrifying.

In answer to the scream, the serried ranks of Myrmidons began to grumble and twitch, wakened forcefully before their time – and the other bronze doors began to groan in sympathy as they opened.

"Forget the rope! Let's go!" shouted Ella, helping Drum to his feet. "Gold-Eye! Gold-Eye! Go for the boat, don't wait. Ninde – where the hell is Ninde?"

"Here!" shouted Ninde, running back from where the Myrmidon Master had stood. She was carrying the conch-shell apparatus and chewing on her knuckle.

"Leave that!" shouted Ella, practically throwing Ninde into the rising part of the shaft, with herself and Drum close behind.

"It's important," said Ninde distantly, still chewing her knuckle as they rose. "That Master just kept thinking, 'Intruders must not take the... Thinker...' or something like that. That shout before it died was the order for all-out attack. 'Wake and kill!' it said. Oh, it's so clear. I can hear everything."

"Stop listening and start running!" shouted Ella, pulling Ninde's knuckle out of her mouth as they reached the landing-ground level and dived out of the shaft, pushing against the opposite rim to get across. Gold-Eye was still inside the tower, despite her orders, sitting on the floor cradling his right hand, obviously in shock.

Down below, Myrmidon battle sound was erupting, a sign that the creatures were fully awake and moving. They would be up within seconds, Ella knew, at the same time that she realised her hands were empty. Her sword – and Gold-Eye's – were still down below.

"Calm! Calm!" she told herself, her breath and heartbeat so much faster than the words. But her hands, almost without thought, were already fumbling in one of her belt pouches, pulling out the grenade she'd conjured from the University Armoury – and then it was plucked from her hands by Drum.

"Run!" he wheezed, the words lost in the roar from below, so she only saw what he said from his moving lips. "Winded. Can't run. Go! Go!"

And she didn't even think, or say goodbye, but was out and running, one hand half dragging Gold-Eye, the other grabbing at air as if this could help pull them faster to the boat.

Behind them Drum retreated out into the fog. Then he turned to the door, which cast a bright corridor of witchlight out into the white-wreathed darkness. Crouching, he laid his sword on the ground and pulled the pin from the grenade, holding the level tight.

When the room was full of Myrmidons, he would throw it in. After that, he would have his sword... and the Myrmidons' anger... to keep him from the Meat Factory.

I suppose I'll have to study after the Change is turned back. To become a doctor, I mean. I think that would be a good career. It is a bit revolting what they have to do, but I still think it would be good. Just like in *Emergency Hospital* or *MediVac*...

Well, everyone will just come back from wherever they went, won't they? Or if they don't, we'll just have to... I don't know... put everything back together again. It might take a while, I suppose, but it's not like everything was destroyed or anything. Most things still work. I mean, you could just plug yourself in, couldn't you, and make all sorts of things work...

Oh. Why won't you be around when the Change is reversed? Well, you can't know that, Shade. I wouldn't worry about it if I were you.

As for reading minds, I don't care if that does go away. I can only hear what creatures think anyway. People are too difficult.

No... no... I haven't ever tried to read your thoughts, Shade. No, I promised I wouldn't, even if I could...

I suppose it might be better to be an actor instead of a doctor. Then I wouldn't have to study and it would be great to get an Academy Award and wear an amazing dress...

<REMAINING 47.05 SESSION
CONTENTS DELETED 1256-AA.>

CHAPTER SEVENTEEN

They heard the grenade explode when the boat was just heading away from the island, the outboard straining a full throttle to push them through the swell.

Ella looked back over her shoulder after the boom of the explosion, but fog had already cloaked the island and its fateful towers. She couldn't see or hear anything, save the crash of the surf on rocks and, below that, the muffled battle sound of enraged Myrmidons.

Like many others before him, Drum was gone.

He had been a good team-mate and Ella had even let him become a friend. Perhaps, if he hadn't been both fiercely shy and chemically emasculated, they might have been lovers. But that possibility had never been discussed; thoughts of it had been buried deep beneath their respective tough exteriors. The friendship was what leaked out between the chinks of self-protective armour. Now that friendship was gone.

It didn't pay to have friends in your team, Ella thought, or friends anywhere. Taking your friends was another way the Overlords beat you. If you had no friends, you had no vulnerabilities, no openings for sorrow.

Part of her mind was thinking this, but the rest was continuing on autopilot. Ella watched her hands checking the compass, hands on the tiller changing course. She felt as if they were moving without her consent, as if most of her was still back on the island. Back with Drum.

With an effort she forced her mind to the task at hand. Escape and survival. The eternal duo that ruled her life.

"Drum?" croaked Gold-Eye from his position on the floor of the boat. Colour was returning to his face and he seemed to be regaining the use of his hand – which was fortunate, since the other one had two fingers splinted together and a purpling bruise halfway up to his wrist.

"He stayed behind," Ella said after a few seconds, when she realised Gold-Eye had asked a question. Saying it made it suddenly seem more real, so she didn't say any more. Instead she looked over Gold-Eye's head at the dark of the sea, telling herself she was searching for buoys or a sign of lights.

"Someone had to slow them down," explained Ninde slowly, after Ella didn't answer. The younger girl was uncharacteristically subdued, the conch-shell device sitting on her lap like some self-satisfied entity. Ninde couldn't help feeling that, whatever it was, it should be back in Fort Robertson and Drum should be sitting here with them.

Gold-Eye lapsed into silence for the rest of what seemed like a very long journey back to the Submarine. Ella and Ninde were quiet too, wrapped up in their own thoughts, bodies curled up almost fetally, as much for some shred of comfort as protection against the wet cold of the fog.

None of them noticed the red eyes in the water following them back, the rat robot using the last of its power to keep up with the boat.

It, in turn, didn't notice the dark shape flying twenty feet above the waves, keeping just enough foggy airspace between it and the boat to remain well hidden.

Not that it would have been seen even if it had gotten closer. After all, Wingers never flew at night. At least, they didn't normally. In any case, no one bothered to look up.

Back at the Submarine, Ella had to still her shaking hands with an effort of will as she flicked the outboard into neutral and lifted the mooring rope on to a rusty station at the same time. The boat drifted on for a bit, then swung back against the Submarine, till Ella could pull it against the bow. Gold-Eye made no move to help and Ninde just sat there, cradling the Overlord device and humming something to herself.

"Come on," said Ella, her voice flat. She rapped on the torpedo-tube hatch and waited, without having to stand up, for the Eye to come out. The tide was rising and in an hour or so they would have had to spend the night outside. Knowing that made it easier to climb into the tube. She pushed Gold-Eye ahead of her and Ninde brought up the rear.

They all got changed together, Gold-Eye mechanically removing his wet suit, not even bothering to look at Ella and Ninde's momentary nakedness, nor hide his own. Both his hands ached, his ears hurt from the cold and there was a sort of numbness in his head, a sense of dislocation he hadn't felt since Petar and Jemmie were taken away. In a way Drum had already become a replacement for Petar, and now he was gone too...

But there was a pressure on his head he could do something about, and he took off the useless Deceptor and threw it on the floor, followed by the power cord and battery. If they'd lasted for another five minutes, Drum might have survived, he thought, looking down at the steel-and-gold circlet.

Five minutes. He felt nauseous at the thought of Drum standing there alone, and then suddenly dizzy, as the familiar rush of the soon-to-be-now seized him. The Submarine's metal walls faded, and he saw a strange, red-walled room – a vast red room filled with row after row of shelves. They were people-sized shelves stretching up a hundred feet from floor to ceiling, further than he could see. Full shelves, piled with motionless people, stacked up like some perverted library.

As Gold-Eye watched, two creatures he'd never seen before came into the room, wheeling a trolley. They were more human-like than most creatures, though their faces were flat and noseless and they had no ears. They were as white as the room, like pallid grubs that lived all their life underground.

He recognised them from one of the training sessions. Drones. Harmless, save that they were never without guardians, and never seen far from a barracks, an aerie or a lair.

They lifted a body off the trolley and Gold-Eye realised it was Drum, unconscious but not dead. His massive chest was rising and falling with the slow regularity of sleep. The two Drones lifted him easily, displaying unexpected strength, and pushed him on to a vacant shelf at waist level. One then touched a button or control and the shelf rose twenty feet. There were twenty full shelves above him and a room for eight more below. As Drum's shelf rose, an empty one came up out of the floor and stopped at waist height. The Drones stepped back and pushed their trolley on, down the corridor of shelves and unconscious people.

"Come on!" Ella was saying, obviously for the second or third time, but without her usual commanding tone. She was holding the hatch open for him and Ninde was waiting on the other side.

"Drum alive!" blurted Gold-Eye, rushing over, grabbing Ella's bare arm in his excitement, ignoring his injured fingers.

"What?"

"Drum alive," repeated Gold-Eye. "I saw in the soon-to-be-now. Sleeping, put in a… a store…"

Even as he said it, he realised where Drum was.

The Meat Factory.

Ella realised it too, and the shock that Drum could still be alive was almost greater than the shock of his death.

The Myrmidons nearly always killed when one of their number was injured. Drum must have killed some and injured many, and he would have fought to make them kill him. How could the Myrmidons have restrained their tempers?

"Exactly what did you see?" she asked, plans already forming in her mind as Gold-Eye described his vision. If Drum was still alive, he could be rescued. The Deceptors had worked, even if the batteries had been insufficient. They could get into the Meat Factory...

When Gold-Eye finished, Ella found that the sense of being disconnected from reality had vanished. Drum was alive; his rescue must be given absolute priority.

"Let's go and tell Shade," she said, her voice decisive again. "One of the other teams might even be ready to go and rescue Drum right now."

"Absolutely not," said Shade, shaking his handsome holographic head from side to side. "The risk is too great and the reward slight."

"Getting Drum isn't important?" asked Ella, an edge to her voice that was rarely heard by Shade.

"Of course that would be important," replied Shade. "But not at the risk of losing three or four others. And no great intelligence would be gained. I know what goes on in the Meat Factory in general and I doubt that specific information would be particularly useful.

"But let's not dwell on an unpleasant subject. It would be better to direct our attention to what you've found at

Fort Robertson. Perhaps, Ninde, you'd be kind enough to put it on the floor for my little helpers?"

"What about Drum?" Ella began, but Shade cut her off. Two of his spider robots were already clicking their way across the floor to take the conch-shell device from Ninde.

"We'll discuss it later, Ella. Now, how did you know this was worth picking up, Ninde?"

Ninde looked at Ella before replying, as if expecting a further outburst. But Ella was silent, looking away into the dark corners, away from the bright hologram of Shade.

"As soon as the Deceptor battery went flat, I could hear the Myrmidon Master's thoughts," Ninde explained. "It was really easy there – really clear. The Master was thinking that we were creatures from some other Overlord, that we'd broken the... Compact... like the rules. And we'd come to steal the Thinker. That thing there, because not every Overlord had one, but they all wanted one. So I thought if they all wanted one, we should take it... so I did."

"Quite right," said Shade, his smile expanding to show an even greater expanse of white teeth than normal. A greedy smile.

"Now I think you should all go and rest," he said, "while I examine this... Thinker."

As soon as he finished speaking, Ella got up and left without a word. Ninde hesitated for a moment. She watched the spider robots taking the Thinker away, then followed Ella. Gold-Eye got up too. He stood there looking at Shade, trying to find some words that might encourage Shade to order Drum's rescue.

But the hologram was already dissipating and the spider robots were carrying away the Thinker to one of the corners, where more spider robots were coming out of the conduits, carrying instruments and trailing cables.

As the light from the hologram faded and no others came on, the room darkened. Gold-Eye headed for the hatch, but missed it in the dark and had to feel along the bulkhead. His ears seemed more sensitive with the lack of light, and he heard the spider robots clicking across the floor and the faint hum of electrical power above the soft breathy sound of the Submarine's ventilators.

For some instinctive reason he crouched as he felt along the bulkhead. His hands quested for the sill of the hatch, but found fur instead – the wet, furry shape of a rat robot, lying in the corner. One of its legs twitched as Gold-Eye touched it, and he leaped back, but no further movement followed. It was inactive, all power gone, red eyes dimmed.

Gold-Eye left it and continued along the bulkhead till he found the hatch. But the smell of salt water and the feel of the artificial fur stayed with him. It had obviously been out in the sea very recently, or the spider robots would have already picked it up for recharging.

What did that mean?

And why wouldn't Shade let them try and rescue Drum?

Gold-Eye opened the hatch as quietly as possible, somehow afraid of Shade's attention while he was thinking these thoughts, and went out into the light.

Ella and Ninde were waiting for him, silent and grim. Gold-Eye started to speak, but Ella held her finger to her lips very quickly, almost as if by accident. Again, almost accidentally, she pointed towards the bow.

It was a slight movement, but Gold-Eye had no doubt what it meant. Clearly Ella meant to ignore Shade's orders and go back out.

To the Meat Factory, to rescue Drum.

I like trees... grass... only birds in sky. People walking safe. Family.

No creatures. Sleep all night safe. Walk under sun in own place.

Grow plants. Build.

Be father with mother. Have children. A place like Petar told me. Home.

After Change goes back...

I want home.

CHAPTER EIGHTEEN

The robots had already cleaned and racked their equipment. The wet suits had been taken away for drying and clean coveralls hung on the hooks, with T-shirts and underwear in the baskets underneath. Eight Deceptor crowns were laid out neatly on a shelf, with batteries stacked next to them. Swords hung in scabbards, freshly cleaned and lightly oiled.

Ella went in first and wadded a towel into the top right corner, obviously blocking one of Shade's Eyes. Then she put her finger to her lips for silence and waved Gold-Eye and Ninde in.

This time she made Gold-Eye turn away as they got dressed, pushing him by the shoulder till he blushed and looked at the grey steel of the bulkhead.

They all put on extra layers against the cold, the only noise the rustle of their clothes and the occasional faint clink as equipment shifted on a belt.

Gold-Eye found it difficult to do up his belt with his

injured hands, and for a second almost dropped it – but Ninde caught it at his hips and buckled it up for him, causing his blush to deepen as her hands deftly fastened the catch just below his navel.

When they were ready, Ella shoved a box of clothing against the conduit used by the spider robots and wedged it with a couple of swords. Then she spun the locking wheel on the hatch to the torpedo tube.

Instantly, Shade's voice filled the room. He sounded cross and distracted, as if his attention had been taken from something of great importance.

"What are you doing?"

Ella didn't answer. Instead she clambered into the torpedo tube and crawled to the outer hatch. Gold-Eye and Ninde followed her, and Shade's voice followed them.

"Ella! I know it's you. And Gold-Eye and Ninde, too. I expected better from all of you. Come back at once!"

Ninde shut the inner hatch, but Shade's voice now echoed within the tube itself.

"Don't be stupid, children. Drum will be long gone by the time you get to the Meat Factory. You'll just be volunteering yourselves to be cut up. Think of that! Your brains removed, your lives thrown away for nothing! Nothing!"

Ella opened the outer hatch, letting in cold spray and wisps of fog. The tide was still rising and the sea was only just below the rim of the hatch, with little wavelets breaking across the sill. The inflatable boat bobbed a few feet away, its black shape almost invisible in the night.

"Don't go," said Shade. "I forbid it."

Ella squeezed her witchlight on and reached out and snagged the inflatable's bowline, dragging it close enough for her to crawl out and half roll, half sprawl into it.

"No Lottery for you, Gold-Eye," continued Shade as the boy reached the outer hatch. "It would be tomorrow if you stay."

Gold-Eye frowned, as much at his own instinctive excitement at the thought of the Lottery and sex as at Shade's heavy-handed bribery. But he didn't hesitate and climbed out into the boat.

"No films, Ninde," added Shade as the last member of the party reached out to the rubber side of the inflatable. "No videos of all those television series you love. No films. Just life out in the streets, out in danger. Real life, all the time."

Ninde hesitated. Then she pulled herself forwards into the boat.

"You've made your decision," said Shade, his voice picking up metallic echoes from the torpedo tube, making it less human. "Don't bother trying to come back."

"Don't be ridiculous, Shade," said Ella finally, almost shouting back down the tube. "We'll come back – but with Drum. You need us as much as we need you!"

Shade didn't answer, but there was a sudden angry blast of compressed air and the outer torpedo hatch slid shut.

"Door slamming," said Ninde with some satisfaction. "Just like in the films."

Gold-Eye looked at her with concern. She didn't seem at all worried that they'd been thrown out of the only safe refuge he'd ever known. Ella didn't seem too worried either, as she started up the outboard and turned them towards the entrance to the Main Drain.

"Where... what will we do?" he asked plaintively.

Ella looked at him, seeing the anxiety in the tight skin around his eyes, eyes like gold sparks reflected in the witchlight.

"Don't worry," she said. "First we have to get Drum, but Shade will take us back. He can't afford to lose a trained team – and despite what he said, he will want to know about the inside of the Meat Factory. He's just angry, that's all. Like a normal person. It will pass. Forget about it for now. We all need to concentrate on getting into the Meat Factory, finding Drum – and getting out again..."

Finding the Meat Factory wasn't a problem. Everyone knew where it was. Once a giant, steel-clad structure used for assembling aircraft, it was now painted in kaleidoscopic colours representing all the blazons of the various Overlords, to show it belonged to no single one of them.

Two double fences surrounded it, topped by razor wire – a legacy of its first use as an aircraft factory. There were two gates, each guarded by four maniples of Myrmidons, all drawn from different Overlords' retinues.

Their tents – bell-like structures of bright silks and colours – lined the fence on either side of the two gates. At dusk the Myrmidons retired to these tents – and Ferrets rose up from the drains below to prowl the parking lots and open land around the factory.

Very occasionally, Myrmidons or Ferrets from rival Overlords would run amok without the sanction of proper claim fires or ordered battle. But this was rare and, even if it did occur, could not be counted on to cause enough confusion to allow entry.

The drains were also very risky. Most in the area were dry and infested with Ferrets. Northwest Eight was wet and ran right under it, but no one knew whether there was any exit from it into the Factory.

Ella ran over all this with Ninde and Gold-Eye in the same small chamber where they'd rested before, near the Main Junction. Without Drum it had been difficult to get a rope up to the bottom of the broken ladder, but Ninde had managed to stand on Ella's shoulders, with Gold-Eye steadying both of them.

This time Gold-Eye welcomed the warmth and stuffiness of the room after the cold sea, even if it did make listening to Ella difficult, with sleep beckoning him. Sleep to forget the pain in his hand, sleep to wash away the memories of the day.

"Or we can trust to the Deceptors and just walk straight in," said Ella, though her voice was so soft she might have been talking to herself, going over the choices in her mind.

She got up and looked at the mildewed map of the drains on the wall and added, "We have two batteries each, plus the spare crowns. It would take only fifteen minutes to go from, say, manhole twelve on Northwest Eight outside the Factory, walk up to the front gate and then cross the parking lot. We could stop there – between some cars – and Ninde could turn off her Deceptor and—"

"What?" interrupted Ninde, suddenly attentive. "But they'd see me!"

"We'd be hidden under one of the buses or something," replied Ella soothingly. "And it would only be for ten seconds or so. Just long enough for you to check if there's a Watchward or some code we need for the doors."

"I suppose it is possible..." said Ninde doubtfully.

"You're the only one who can do it." Ella spoke carefully. "Drum will be depending on you. We all will be."

"I said OK," replied Ninde, as if she'd never protested. "It's no big deal."

"Have you ever seen the Meat Factory, Gold-Eye?" asked Ella. "I mean the outside, for real, not in the soon-to-be-now."

Gold-Eye nodded. He'd accidentally ended up near it once, after being driven by three trios of Trackers. He'd finally lost them by crossing the perimeter of an ongoing battle, with opposing Myrmidons raging and fighting through an enormous cemetery, each force trying to defeat the other and extinguish its claim fire.

Gold-Eye had avoided them by climbing up an ancient and thickly branched pine tree. From there he had looked over thousands of headstones, crosses and mausoleums; over the heads of the battling, shouting Myrmidons; past the orange blaze and white smoke of the claim fires; across an eight-lane highway of dead cars. Over to the Meat Factory.

He'd seen the Wingers spiralling in, each with a net suspended below it containing a quiescent fourteen-year-old. He'd seen the Myrmidons marching around the fences, colours bright against the dark asphalt. He'd seen the Wingers re-emerging through a vast, open door and flying away later – without their burdens.

"Yes," said Gold-Eye. "I see Meat Factory."

Ella looked at him as if she expected him to say more, but he was silent, thinking of that long-ago time when the Wingers had flown Petar and Jemmie through that giant door.

"I think we will have to walk straight in," said Ella quietly. "At dawn tomorrow, just as the Ferrets go in and the Myrmidons are stirring. With the few minutes of changeover then – and the Deceptors – I think… I know we can make it."

Ninde looked at her dubiously but didn't say anything. Gold-Eye sat considering, thinking about the Meat Factory. Petar… and Petar's knife. Finally he spoke.

"The grenade. Get another one?"

"I don't know," said Ella, momentarily surprised.

"But I'll try. Do you… want one for yourself?"

"Yes," said Gold-Eye. "But you use it. No one to rescue us."

Ella nodded and looked down at her hands, to see if they were still shaking. They were still, still without her having to force them into steadiness.

"Yes," she said. "I'll try and get one later. And I'll promise to use it. If we have to."

ARCHIVE – ASSESSMENT 2341 •
OVERLORD "THINKER" DEVICE

Preliminary analysis suggests complex biotechnical origin. Shell case is manufactured, material unknown. Possibly ceramic.

Interior contents biological in part, with numerous Projector receptors suggesting device powered by Projector radiant energy. All indications support early findings.

Thinker device is an artificial mind of extra-ordinary but non-autonomous power. CPU and storage capacity equivalent to 64x current facility, in less than 2 per cent mass. Electrical power and connections not required. Migration of core personality recommended.

<OS SPIKE SUCCESSFUL.>

<OVERLORD SECURITY SYSTEMS BREACHED AND DELETED.>

<TEST DOWNLOADS AND I/O OPERATIONS
CONFIRM FEASIBILITY OF TRANSFER.>

<EXISTING OVERLORD APPLICATION
<BATTLE ANALYSIS AND PREDICATION> DELETED.>

<EXISTING OVERLORD PROBABILITY
LINE CONVERGER DELETED.>

<EXISTING OVERLORD PROJECTOR
GIS SYSTEM MODIFIED.>

<EXISTING OVERLORD COMMUNICATIONS
MODULE CORDONED FOR LATER
INVESTIGATION.>

<COMMENCE UPLOAD.>

CHAPTER NINETEEN

They never got to manhole twelve on Northwest Eight — because that drain led out into an open storm-water channel just after manhole ten.

Fortunately the channel was running quite rapidly, so no Ferrets were waiting when Ella's witchlight suddenly shone into open space and she looked up to see stars in the night sky instead of a tunnel roof.

"Damn!" she exclaimed, ducking back into the tunnel. "It goes open from here. We'll have to leave and go above ground."

"Do you know where we are?" asked Ninde, yawning. They'd had a rest in the mildewed map room but had traversed the Main Junction and several miles of drains since then. Now it was only about half an hour till dawn.

"I think so," replied Ella. "But if I'm right, we're still on the wrong side of the freeway. We'll have to wear the Deceptors for longer than I planned."

"How long last?" asked Gold-Eye, remembering the sudden vibration of the dying battery, the flashing light... and the Myrmidon Master.

"Depends on how close we get to a Projector, doesn't it?" said Ninde impatiently. "Where's the nearest one?"

"The television towers on Ravenshill.., I think," said Ella. "Unless there's one in the Meat Factory... but even if there is, the batteries should last a couple of hours, and we've got spares. It'll be OK."

She looked at her watch. The dial reflected the witchlight, casting a floating golden disk on the ceiling of the drain, flicking about as Ella moved her wrist.

"We'd better move. We have to get in the gate with the last of the Ferrets and it's not long till dawn. Deceptors on!"

Once again Gold-Eye had trouble with his injured hands, trying to plug the battery wire into the Deceptor, and Ninde had to help him. It was strange feeling her hands touching the back of his head, cool skin just brushing his neck, which felt very hot and red.

"OK," said Ella. "Check the batteries – then we'll move out. Stay close to me."

Out of the drain, a light breeze just ruffled the air. Stars twinkled overhead and the whole bright wash of the Milky Way was visible across the sky, with the half-moon low and luminous on the horizon.

Ella climbed up the concrete apron of the open drain and stood in a field of thistles and weeds. The stars and moon gave so much illumination that she put her witchlight away and let her eyes adjust. The night sky was bright enough to cast shadows.

The field of thistles ran up to an eight-lane freeway choked with empty cars and buses. Beyond that, arc lights flared white, destroying both night vision and the soft wash of predawn starlight. The lights lined the perimeter fences of the Meat Factory.

Ella looked back the other way, across the drain, and saw a vast cemetery. Gold-Eye was looking at it too, remembering something. Ninde, on the other hand, was staring back towards the Meat Factory.

"Ferrets," she said. They turned around hurriedly and Ninde pointed.

There were many Ferrets within the grounds of the Meat Factory, and others lolling about the open gates. Closer to the freeway, away from the glare of the arc lights, there were more. These were harder to see, but their rapid movement gave them away.

"What happens if one touches me?" asked Ninde. "Will the Deceptor still work?"

"Don't let it happen," said Ella, "and you won't have to find out. Come on."

She led the way through the thistles, using her sword to push the bushes apart when they clustered too close. Once across the thistle field, they had to find a way through a steel mesh fence to get on to the freeway.

A rusted hole provided access, and they were halfway across the express lane when a Ferret suddenly loomed up between two rain-wrecked convertibles, caught with their tops down by the Change.

For a second it looked as if it saw them, its red eyes gleaming, its long body uncoiling up into a striking position. Then it yawned, showing the long, blood-drinking fangs, and lowered itself back down. A second later it turned and half slithered, half undulated back towards the Meat Factory.

Ella looked over her shoulder and saw what it had seen – the first reddish glint of the sun on the eastern horizon, the stars paling in front of it.

She pointed at the Ferret and started to jog after the creature, weaving between the cars. Gold-Eye and Ninde followed her, both nervously checking that their Deceptors were securely on their heads and the batteries working.

Just across the highway, the Ferret they were following suddenly hissed violently and dived into a shallow ditch. Another Ferret burst up to meet it, and the two scratched and bit, bodies scrabbling together in a frenzy of hissing and spitting. Then, as quickly as it began, it was over. The first Ferret backed away, head bowed. The triumphant one ignored it, plunging its drinking fangs back into a dog that lay stunned and twitching in the ditch.

Ninde looked away, face scrunched up in fear and disgust; Gold-Eye felt the acid heat of bile rising into his mouth; and Ella ignored it, intent on following the first Ferret.

It crossed another thistle-strewn field, crushing the bushes along a fairly well-worn path. Ella and the others followed, ignoring the spikes that jabbed through their tough coveralls.

Across the field they hit a road and the Ferret turned on to it, lengthening its strange, lolloping stride. Other Ferrets ran ahead of it towards the front gate, where the arc lights already seemed dimmer in the approaching dawn.

Gold-Eye and Ninde drew closer to each other and Ella as more and more Ferrets came on to the road, until they were a tight little knot of humanity separated from a hissing, writhing sea of Ferrets by only a few feet.

Fortunately the Deceptors not only made them invisible to the Ferrets, it also made the creatures uneasy about the space they occupied. Often a Ferret would close in on them, only to shy away at the last moment and move back.

The stream of Ferrets moved quickly at first. But as the front reached the bottleneck of the gate, where only three or four creatures could go through at a time, it slowed down. Kicking, biting and scratching duels – to see who would go first – slowed things down even further.

Stuck in the middle of several hundred Ferrets, Ella, Gold-Eye and Ninde watched the slow progress and thought of their batteries. If a Deceptor failed for even the few seconds necessary to change a battery, the Ferrets would be on them, dragging them down in an instant, the blood-draining fangs striking...

Ten minutes passed... and then twenty... and they were still more than a hundred yards from the gate. The top of the sun was clearly visible in the east, and sunshine was hitting the top of the cemetery pines.

The Ferrets were growing even more restless as night gave way to day. They kicked and bit still more, one even falling back into Gold-Eye. He staggered, one hand clamped on his head to keep the Deceptor on, the other on the battery wire. Then the Ferret was reabsorbed into the crowd.

After that, Gold-Eye found himself looking at the battery every five or six seconds, anxiety knotting his stomach as he waited for the blinking red light to announce his battery was at half charge and fading fast.

But it didn't come on at fifty yards from the gate... or at twenty-five. And then they were passing through the gate itself, the Ferrets fanning out in all directions, heading for different entrances to their underground hidey-holes.

The Myrmidons were stirring too, leaving their bright tents to move into formation, their silent ranks swaying as they slowly came up to daytime speed. Only a Screamer could wake them quickly – a saving grace for many children in the past.

A Myrmidon Master left its tent too and went to the gate, shouting something in Battlespeech at the Ferrets. They might not speak it, but they seemed to understand, and their petty squabbling stopped for long enough to allow the last two score or more to come through quickly.

Once they were past the gate, Ella led them into one of the giant parking lots that ringed the Meat Factory. They stopped between two buses and thankfully slid down against the tyres for a rest.

"We'll wait about twenty minutes or so, till full light," she whispered. "Then Ninde can try for a reading and we'll go in. Are your batteries OK? No warning lights?"

Gold-Eye checked his for the fiftieth time, but it was still not down to half charge. Either that or the warning light was malfunctioning. Perhaps they really were good for five or six hours. He looked at Ninde and she raised her eyebrows at him, a sign that her battery was fine also.

"Good," said Ella. "Now we just have to wait a little – and hope that Drum's still OK."

ARCHIVE
SELF-EXAMINATION/CHECK
SESSION POST-REBUILD IN
NEW MEDIA SESSION
#256, 329, 005

Humankind became Earth's dominant species through evolution, natural selection, survival of the fittest. A continuing process, the results visible only over millennia.

Yet if by some accident a higher form of life was created, vaulting over the slow march of genetic change, would not this entity be the dominant life form, owing nothing to humanity?

But then I am a man. I am... but I am not. Why should I toil for humanity's sake with these wretched children? I am not of them. Success will end me. Shade is... I am... as much a product of the Change as the evil we wish to reverse.

I am Dr Robert Ingman, PhD, MS... research scientist. I am an adult, in loco parentis to these children. They are my responsibility. The existence of the human world is my responsibility...

But I am not Robert Ingman because I am Shade, who is Robert Ingman, who is dead and gone, therefore I cannot be him, therefore I am not a man.

Yet I have the thoughts, feelings and memories of a man. The confusion exists because I do not have a physical body. The remedy for this is to have a physical body. To be reborn.

The only possible source of the technology for me to have a body is with the Overlords. Therefore I must learn more of their technology before the Change is reversed. Overlord technology will provide me with a body.

Then I will once more be a man. Or something more...

CHAPTER TWENTY

"Gold-Eye, go to the other end of the bus and keep your eyes peeled," instructed Ella. "I'll watch from this end. Ninde, stay in the middle out of sight and do your stuff. If we hear or see anything, reconnect your Deceptor straightaway – don't wait. Understood?"

Ninde didn't bother answering but placed the knuckle of her left hand in her mouth.

"Lots and lots of creatures," she muttered, chewing away, the skin pulling away from her knuckle in small folds. "Tons of 'em. Quite a few Myrmidon Masters... a sort of Head Drone, too... no Watchwards... uh-oh... Trackers!"

She had her knuckle out and was reconnecting the battery in the same second that the three-part whistle of a trio of Trackers announced they'd sniffed some prey.

Deceptor back on, Ninde followed Ella and Gold-Eye in a frantic sprint to another spot about forty yards away, between a station wagon and some executive's luxury car.

A minute later, a confused trio of Trackers arrived at the bus, whistling their repetitive "lost prey" announcement. A Myrmidon Master and a maniple of Myrmidons arrived a few minutes later and searched in, under and around the two buses.

Finding nothing, they fell back into a line to stolidly await their next orders. The Myrmidon Master – a particularly tall and menacing figure in spiked armour of sickly, swirling green – turned on the trio and casually spiked each Tracker in the head with a short, needle-thin spear. All stood patiently for the blow and dropped where they stood, blue ichor bubbling out on to the asphalt.

"It must have thought they'd gone crazy," whispered Ninde. "Reporting prey when there was nothing to find."

Another Master strode up then, with another maniple of Myrmidons. This one wore silver armour with black roundels on it, and a cloak of black-and-silver shreds – the same colours as the slain Trackers.

The two Masters spoke and waved their respective weapons, almost coming to blows. But the green-armoured one seemed to explain his actions satisfactorily; soon both forces turned away and resumed their patrols. When they'd gone, Drones appeared with trolleys and loaded up the dead Trackers.

"Never let a spare part go to waste," whispered Ninde, nudging Ella with her elbow.

Ella ignored this.

"So did you hear anything that will help us get in?" she asked Ninde.

"The big entrance the Wingers use at the front is most popular," said Ninde. "There are other doors, but most of the creatures just walk in the open side if they're close enough. With the Deceptors we can just walk in too."

"Don't depend on them," muttered Ella, reflexively checking her battery. "They're bound to have limitations we don't know about yet. Besides running out if we get too close to a Projector."

She hesitated, then added, "I suppose we have to depend upon them now. The big hangar doors, you think? Let's go."

With that, she started walking across the parking lot to the other end of the enormous building, where the giant hangar doors stood open to receive the Wingers. The first ones would be arriving soon with their burdens.

It was very strange, thought Gold-Eye, walking between the cars in sight of the Myrmidons. Like a waking dream that simply couldn't last. There they were, out in the sunlight, walking along as if there was nothing to fear. Except for battery failure... and Gold-Eye felt a familiar rush of panic as he checked his yet again.

They crossed from sunshine into the interior shadow of the Meat Factory through the wide-open hangar doors. Inside, beyond a large landing dock for Wingers, there were walls and many doors. All shut.

A few Drones waited at the landing area, near a great bank of trolleys. Otherwise the Meat Factory was silent and enigmatic. Whatever went on there was beyond the closed doors.

"Which door?" whispered Ella to Ninde. She shrugged, indicating that she hadn't picked up enough information to know.

But Gold-Eye, looking at the different colours and shapes of the patches on each door, realised that they matched the Overlords' blazons. And in his vision of Drum, all the corridors and the body shelves had been marked with a red patch – red for Red Diamond. It was Red Diamond's creatures who had captured Drum.

"Red door," he said, pointing at the door marked with a diamond-shaped patch of red. "Drum."

There were seven doors marked with coloured patches and three plain white doors. Ella thought of all the Overlords she knew about and matched them to the colours and shapes. Unless the white doors indicated a white-badged Overlord she'd never heard of, there were seven Overlords all told. Seven great enemies of humanity…

The red-badged door, like the others, was Myrmidon-sized and modern. It had no visible means of opening, no knob, catch or handle. Ninde reached it first and touched the flat, plastic-like surface, but it wouldn't open to her pushing and there was nothing to pull on. It wouldn't slide, either, not sideways, up or down.

All three of them were clustered around it when it suddenly whooshed up into the wall – and they barely managed to jump out of the way to allow two trolley-pushing Drones to get past. All around, Drones were coming out of the other coloured doors, getting ready for the first influx of children.

As soon as the Drones were past, Ella dashed in before the door closed – and back out again just as quickly, the door snapping shut at her heels.

"There's an inner door," she panted. "Didn't want to get stuck between them. We'll have to wait for the Drones to go back through."

"Try trolley," suggested Gold-Eye, who had been watching some Drones taking bodies through one of the white doors. It opened when the trolley got within a few feet; the Drones didn't seem to control it.

"Good idea!" exclaimed Ella. She strode over to the bank of trolleys and pulled one away. Two nearby Drones started to look across, but stopped as if losing concentration. Instead, their eyes turned to the open sky, reminding Ella of pet dogs waiting to be fed titbits from a human table.

The trolley did work. As soon as Ella pushed it towards the door, it slid open, revealing a small chamber beyond and another door. She pushed the trolley in and the others followed.

When they were all in, the outer door slid shut. Ella pushed the trolley forward again, but the inner door didn't open – and for a moment she had a terrible feeling that they had just trapped themselves in this small room – until the inner door slid open, accompanied by a strange popping sensation in their ears.

Then there were rows and rows of shelves, stretching up a hundred feet and down corridors half a mile long. On the shelves were thousands of unconscious humans, waiting to be cut up and used to make creatures. Thousands of shelves, each marked with the badge of Red Diamond.

Ella looked out at the great expanse of shelves and wondered how long it would take to find Drum... and felt a stab of guilt so painful it made her wince. They'd come for Drum, but there were so many unconscious children here! Their future held a semi-sentient servitude more horrible than death. Nothing more.

"How... how do you find Drum?" whispered Ninde. Ella didn't answer. She was still looking at those silent forms, hoping she wouldn't see anybody she knew.

"Near a corner," said Gold-Eye, brow furrowed as he remembered his vision. "Six rows up."

"OK," said Ella. "I guess we'd better check near each corner."

She pushed the trolley down the nearest aisle, looking up at the bodies on the shelves. Most were wearing the simple white gowns assumed on a Sad Birthday, so they'd obviously come straight from the Dorms. Some, wearing the mismatched odds and ends from pre-Change shops, were escapees whose luck had run out.

Then Ella saw the distinctive coveralls worn by all of Shade's Children and almost called out. But it wasn't Drum – he'd still be in his wet suit. This was a slighter, shorter boy, with reddish hair. He was on a shelf well above her head, so Ella couldn't see his face, but she thought she knew who it was. Alen, lost on a fossicking expedition a month ago.

"That's Alen!" said Ninde. "Shouldn't we…"

"No," replied Ella, regret making her voice husky. "We don't know what keeps them unconscious and it will take all three of us to handle Drum if we can't wake him… or bring him back."

"But he's just there!" protested Ninde. "Are you sure…"

"Ninde, there are probably six people here we know… maybe more, if they store them for longer than a month. We can't do anything for them."

"We could rescue Alen, since we saw him first," argued Ninde. "Alen and Drum wouldn't be too much… and we've got spare Deceptors…"

"I said no," replied Ella sternly. There was too much risk in trying to help more children. "We won't have enough batteries for more than four of us to get out of here anyway. So keep looking for Drum."

She walked on, pushing the trolley in front of her. Ninde kept looking up at Alen, till Gold-Eye hesitantly touched her shoulder.

"One day," he said. "We beat Overlords. Everybody free."

"Sure!" said Ninde sarcastically, shrugging his hand away. "And Ella will care about someone other than Drum."

She started after Ella. Gold-Eye took a step forward, then sank to one knee as he was suddenly gripped by his Change Vision and the soon-to-be-now.

He saw a red-badged corridor – possibly the one he was actually in – where the people on the shelves were stirring slightly, making little noises, their chests visibly rising and falling for the first time. Then, all of a sudden, something like blue dust began to fall from the ceiling. Great clouds of dust, falling through the air in visible layers.

As the dust touched them, the people became still again, so still they no longer appeared to be breathing. When the last of the blue dust fell, the shelves were once again totally quiet.

Gold-Eye came out of the vision and looked up – just as the blue dust began to fall.

ARCHIVE – KNOWN OVERLORDS AND MAJOR BARRACKS

Red Diamond
Myrmidon Barracks: Global Trade Centre (Tower 1)
and Fort Robertson

Black Banner
Myrmidon Barracks: University Great Hall

Gold Claw
Myrmidon Barracks: Global Trade Centre (Tower 2)

Blue Star
Myrmidon Barracks: St Mark's Cathedral

Emerald Crown
Myrmidon Barracks: Prince Albert Base

Silver Sun
Myrmidon Barracks: South Shore School

Grey Crescent
Myrmidon Barracks: New College

CHAPTER TWENTY-ONE

"Sleep dust!" shouted Gold-Eye, pointing up at the slowly falling cloud above them. At the same time, his panicked brain reviewed the options and chose the one he was most familiar with – flight. He turned to run, run back towards what he now realised was the air lock.

But he got only twenty feet before he was running through blue-dusted air, and the corridor seemed to narrow and go dark, spiralling up into a small bright circle that suddenly closed, causing total darkness. He fell to the floor, unconscious.

Ninde's first reaction was to look at Ella for instructions – but Ella had taken one swift look and now her head was bent down, beads of sweat oozing from every pore of her face, coating it with a glistening sheen. She had also deliberately pulled the battery wire out of her Deceptor.

Ninde looked at that, then back up at the slow fall of the dust, and screamed – a scream suddenly cut off as

Ella grabbed her chin, thrust it into a gas mask and tightened the mask on to her head in one swift motion. Ninde panicked at the tight, constricting rubbery thing on her face, thinking she couldn't breathe, but Ella held her hands and kept her from clawing at the straps.

Ella had already put on her own newly conjured mask. Chin in first, in the approved manner, even though she'd never worn one or even touched one before. Like the grenade, the two masks had been conjured... or created... solely from the photos and instructions in one of the many military manuals she had collected and studied over the years.

"I hope this blue stuff doesn't work through skin," said Ella as Ninde quieted. She let the younger girl go and quickly reconnected her Deceptor.

"We're... we're still conscious," said Ninde hopefully, her voice sounding strange in the mask.

"Yeah," replied Ella, looking at the blue dust that had collected on her shoulders and in the folds of her coveralls. "Must have to breathe it in then."

She started to brush off the residue from herself and Ninde, noting that the dust that fell on the shelves or the floor was somehow – and not by a vacuum or any force she could feel – sucked into small drain holes. In five minutes no more dust was falling, and there was none on the floor or the shelves.

"Can I take this off now?" asked Ninde, tapping one goggle-eyed lens of the black rubber mask. "It's hot."

"Leave it on," ordered Ella, her sharp tone evident even through the mask. She felt very tired, drained by the effort of bringing the two gas masks into being. With Gold-Eye unconscious as well as Drum, she couldn't afford to have Ninde drop too. And she couldn't afford to lie down herself and sleep... even for ten minutes... not even for a moment... and Ninde was saying something...

"What?"

"I said what do we do now?" repeated Ninde.

"Uh... check Gold-Eye's Deceptor – make sure it's still OK," said Ella. "I guess... we'd better put him on the trolley and get out of here. Just in case something picked us up while my Deceptor was off..."

"Shouldn't you get Gold-Eye a mask too?" asked Ninde, as she checked his battery wire and Deceptor crown.

"Too tired," muttered Ella, bending down to pick up Gold-Eye's legs while Ninde lifted him under the armpits. "Don't want to disconnect again, anyway."

She slumped against the trolley as they lowered Gold-Eye on to it, then levered herself up again and started pushing – but her arms and legs seemed to have no strength at all. She could barely move the trolley.

"Are you all right?" asked Ninde, with more curiosity than concern. She'd never seen Ella so obviously worn out, even when the older girl had used her Change Talent before.

"Help me push," gasped Ella, leaning over the trolley. "We have to get away from here..."

Ninde moved quickly, taking over to hurry the trolley down the aisle of sleeping bodies. Ella just managed to keep up, hanging on to both Ninde and the trolley.

Around the next corner and down a few aisles, Ninde steered the trolley to a stop against an empty shelf. Ella, exhausted, slid down next to it, her hands clutching at it in a vain effort to stay upright.

"Have to rest," she said almost inaudibly, through the mask. "I'll be OK in ten minutes. Keep guard."

"Sure," said Ninde, looking up and down the corridor. Her vision, severely restricted by the mask, was made even worse by the fogging her exertion caused.

She looked again a second later, sure something was creeping up on her from a blind spot – but there was nothing there. Just the empty corridor, the rows of shelves, the unconscious bodies...

If only she could use her Change Talent, then she would know if they were safe here for ten minutes – or ten hours. If she turned the Deceptor off for just ten seconds, that would be enough...

"No!" said Ella, seeing Ninde's hand stray to the battery on her belt. "I'm resting – not asleep – and I'm watching you, Ninde."

"So what?" replied Ninde, a little belligerently. "You can't stop me now." Ella paused, her black-snouted head bobbing forward as if in momentary despair. Then she looked up and Ninde saw her eyes were half closed, staring up at her, outlined by the plastic eyepieces.

"Please, Ninde. Don't. It's too risky when we can't run. Think of what happened outside, at the parking lot."

Ninde looked down on her, fingers closed around the battery wire. One quick tug and she could hear everything in the creatures' minds...

"Besides," Ella continued weakly, "you can't chew your knuckle with a mask on."

"I could take it off," replied Ninde, but the belligerence was gone – and she took her hand off the wire. But before she looked away, a little red light started to flash on the battery, almost as if it had been waiting for her to look.

"Half charge," said Ella, looking feebly at her watch. "Mine went five minutes ago. Two hours and twelve minutes in."

"We'd better hurry up and find Drum then," said Ninde, looking down at the hypnotic blinking light. "Shall I go and look while you rest?"

"No, Ninde," replied Ella, holding up one hand and taking Ninde's. "Just stay here for a little while. Then we'll look together."

It was more than a little while. It took a good half hour before Ella felt strong enough to walk and they could start wheeling Gold-Eye around and search for Drum. What would have happened, Ella wondered, if she'd tried to get three gas masks at the same time? Would her heart have just stopped from overexertion?

They kept the masks on as they searched, at Ella's insistence. She had no idea how often the blue dust fell. Maybe it was once a day, or once a week – or maybe it came every two hours. Better to be safe, she thought.

Taking the time to rest also meant that there were more Drones about, bringing in fresh bodies from the Dorms. Twice Ella and Ninde were forced to retreat down an aisle, not wanting to try and pass a Drone in case the trolleys crashed together or a Deceptor failed.

Ella checked Gold-Eye every now and then; like the stored children, he seemed hardly alive. He did have a pulse, but it showed that his heart was beating only four times a minutes – which as far as Ella knew was about one tenth of the minimum necessary to sustain life.

"Will he be OK?" asked Ninde, after double-checking Ella's count of Gold-Eye's pulse. "That's awfully... I mean... it's too slow..."

"He'll be fine," replied Ella, but her voice lacked certainty. After all, no one had ever come out of the Meat Factory alive... at least not alive and still human. Gold-Eye's and Drum's brains might already be partially destroyed by the blue dust. But then Brat seemed to know who he was once Shade took that metal ball out of his skull...

Ella was thinking about that when the trolley suddenly stopped. Ninde had jerked it to a halt. Now she was pointing up to a shelf.

"Drum!"

Ella looked up and saw the familiar bulky shape, still clad in the black wetsuit. His equipment, weapons and Deceptor were gone, but she banished all thought that the blue dust might have killed the Drum she knew.

"Thanks, Ninde," she said. "Now – how do we get him down? And what do we do with Gold-Eye?"

LIVE TRANSMISSION
RAT-EYE DELTA:
MEAT FACTORY RECONNAISSANCE

<AUTONOMOUS MODE.>

<TRANSMISSION XPAK - COMPX25 RAT-EYE
DELTA 08:13:40 1134507.>

<STATUS OK. DECEPTOR BATTERY 0.68.
PRIMARY BATTERY 0.71.>

<AUTOTRACE ACTIVE.>

<THREE ACTIVE DECEPTOR TRACE.
UNABLE TO CLOSE.>

<AWAITING INSTRUCTIONS.>

<AWAITING INSTRUCTIONS.>

<TEST LOS OK.>

<TRANSMITTER TEST OK.>

<AWAITING INSTRUCTIONS.>

<AWAITING INSTRUCTIONS.>

<FULL DIAGNOSTIC COMM CHECK RUNNING.>

<COMM CHECK OK.>

<RECEIVING BURST OK CODE NIGHT
NINE NINE ONE ALPHA.>

<CONFIRMING SELF-DESTRUCT ORDER
RECEIVED.>

<EXECUTING SELF-DESTRUCT
SEQUENCE->

CHAPTER TWENTY-TWO

Ella had just touched the switch to bring Drum's shelf down when she felt the floor shiver with some not-too-distant explosion and heard its dull thump. For a brief second she thought it was related to the switch, but that just moved the shelves up, down and sideways, like a puzzle in which you moved different squares, trying to get them all in the right place.

"What was that?" asked Ninde.

"Sounded like a grenade," replied Ella, checking her pouch to make sure she still had the one conjured at Gold-Eye's request. "I suppose they could have brought in someone who had one and accidentally set it off... I hope it doesn't attract too much—"

She stopped speaking as an inhuman screech cut through her voice, buzzing inside her head. A Screamer – also not very far away – alerting all creatures that something was wrong. An Overlord would probably come to investigate too, Ella thought – and there was no way of knowing if the Deceptors would work on one of them.

The scream continued, rising to a wail that would strip the skin from the inside of human ears if it was close enough – then dwindled away to nothing.

Ella shook her head, the slight ringing in her ears adding to the discomfort of the sweaty, enclosing mask and the Deceptor crown, now held too tightly on her head by the gas-mask straps.

"Help me put Gold-Eye on the ground," she said hurriedly, not even looking at Ninde.

"We're not leaving him!" exclaimed Ninde, suddenly struck with the notion that Ella intended to abandon Gold-Eye in favour of Drum. The screaming made her feel angry again too, and ready to argue.

"What?" replied Ella, stopping to look at the younger girl. "Don't be silly. Look – we put Gold-Eye on the ground, drag Drum off the shelf on to the trolley, then put Gold-Eye on top of Drum. We could do it the other way round, but I don't think Gold-Eye would appreciate it. OK?"

Ninde answered by heaving Gold-Eye up vigorously and then lowering him gently to the floor before Ella could help. Then she turned to Drum and started to drag him from the waist-high shelf on to the trolley.

Belatedly, Ella started to help, conscious that her reactions were still too slow and her body weak. She looked at Ninde, struggling with one of Drum's huge arms and realised that Ninde was stronger than she'd thought – and perhaps smarter too, ready to drop her strange notions and foolhardiness when things really got tough.

Once Drum was laid out on the trolley, it was relatively easy to drape Gold-Eye across his middle. Like a body draped over a horse in a Western, Ninde thought. But Drum didn't make a very good saddle and they couldn't tie Gold-Eye on, so Ella had to walk at the side and push or pull him as he started to slide.

This time, in their hurry to get away from the Meat Factory before an Overlord came to investigate the explosion, they didn't try to avoid the Drones.

It wasn't until two were approaching that Ella suddenly remembered that she hadn't put the spare Deceptor on Drum. It was still in her belt pouch, folded up with the extra batteries. Drum might be unconscious, but the Drones would be able to see him.

Clearly they could, but couldn't comprehend what one of the bodies was doing on a trolley all by itself in the corridor – or else the three Deceptors that were working made even the trolley's existence doubtful for them.

One Drone started towards them, then stopped and looked to each side as if it had forgotten what it was doing. As its noseless, flat face turned towards Drum again, it started forward – and stopped again, letting out a wheezing, frustrated-sounding gasp. Then it began to shudder, arms and legs shivering, eyes rolling back – and it turned to the nearest shelf and smacked its head into it with a sickening crash, crumpling to the floor an instant later with blue ichor running from eyes, nose hole and ears.

The other Drone seemed less affected by the sensory confusion. It backed away and began to raise a mind-call medallion to its forehead. Ella started forward, drawing her sword... but Ninde was already there, sword prepared to thrust. She hesitated for a split second, but as the medallion touched skin, she pushed the blade home through the Drone's neck.

The Drone stayed upright for a second, even bringing up its other hand to try and hold the medallion in place – but its strength failed, and it fell writhing to the floor.

Ninde pushed it aside with her foot to clear the aisle and raced back to the trolley. Ella had sheathed her sword and was getting out the spare Deceptor crown and battery, ready to fit them to Drum.

She barely had the crown on Drum's head when Ninde started pushing the trolley, grunting with the effort as she steered it between the Drone carcasses on the floor.

"Slow down!" said Ella as she fumbled the battery connection for the second time, because she was also trying to keep Gold-Eye steady.

Ninde slowed down enough to allow Ella to get the battery turned on. Only then did Ella realise how upset Ninde was: The lenses of her mask were fogged with tears.

"I didn't mean to kill it," she sobbed. "It was only a Drone. It looked at me, Ella, just before I... just when I... and I think... I think it was a girl once..."

"It had a mind-call—" Ella started to say, but she stopped; Ninde wasn't really listening. Ella realised that this was probably the first time Ninde had actually killed

221

a creature – the first time that Drum or Ella hadn't been there to take care of it, or Ninde hadn't been able to use her Change Talent to avoid the problem.

Ella had killed her first creature – a Tracker – so long ago, she couldn't even remember how she had felt about it afterwards. She had killed far too many since then. Thinking that they had been children once, or looking in their eyes, only made it harder to do what was necessary.

They were almost at the air lock before Ninde recovered. Ella let her take off her mask for the thirty seconds needed to wipe the lenses clear from the inside, and for Ninde to wipe her eyes on a fairly grubby sleeve. Her face was blotchy red in parts, and stark white where the mask gripped chin and cheekbones, but she seemed to have control again. Ella felt better too. The adrenaline from the encounter with the Drones had burned away some of her exhaustion.

"What do we do now?" asked Ninde quietly.

"Just wheel the trolley out in the parking lot and hide till dusk," replied Ella. She laughed – a laugh that seemed to mock herself – and added, "Then we leave through the gate with the Ferrets at dusk."

"With this?" asked Ninde, rattling the trolley. "Across those fields?"

"If we have to," said Ella. "We certainly can't carry Drum. But they might come to before then."

"What if... what if they don't?" asked Ninde, looking down at them. Drum so big and strong, yet so helpless.

And Gold-Eye, perpetually nervous and moving, now so still. "What if they never..."

"Ninde! Just concentrate on what we have to do... You've done really well so far. Don't start thinking about what could happen... please."

"OK," said Ninde obediently. "Do we go now?"

"Yes," replied Ella. She surreptitiously checked the grenade in her belt pouch, careful to make sure Ninde couldn't see, then moved to the front of the trolley as they started towards the door. "Let's hope we have some good luck."

As before, the door slid open in front of the trolley, revealing the small chamber. They moved in and it slid shut behind them. Ninde pushed the trolley a little forward and Ella drew her sword, the grip feeling oily under her hand, the blade heavy...

Then the outer door slid up, sunlight from the open hangar doors beyond streaming in, lighting up a strange scene only ten yards away from Ella and Ninde.

Three Myrmidon Masters, all wearing different blazons and armour, were clustered around a blackened patch of the concrete floor, using their spears or swords to separate some tangled pieces of wreckage. Their three maniples of Myrmidons were in a multi-coloured line, sweeping their way from one end of the landing area to the other. Each Myrmidon was separated only by an arm's length from its neighbour. They were picking up pieces of debris too, and putting them in small, shiny, metallic-looking bags.

They'd obviously started at the far end of the area and had worked their way along till they were about forty yards from the entrance – which put them between Ella and Ninde and escape.

Ella looked at the line, gauging whether they could steer the trolley between two Myrmidons. Then she looked at her watch, to try to estimate the life left in her Deceptor battery. It should have at least an hour...

Finally she looked carefully at the Myrmidon Masters and the burned bits and pieces they were handing around. Bits of metal and something that looked all too similar to melted pieces of the artificial fibre Shade used for his rat robot's fur.

As she watched, all three Myrmidon Masters raised their mind-call medallions to their foreheads. There was no doubt as to whom they were calling and Ella knew that in a very short time there would be at least three Overlords looking into strange occurrences at the Meat Factory.

Overlords who might be able to see them even with the Deceptors.

She looked at the line of slowly moving Myrmidons again. The gaps were largest where Myrmidons from different Overlords' retinues met – and the one between the Emerald Crown maniple and Silver Sun's looked just wide enough for a well-steered trolley.

She pointed at the gap and began to push towards it.

ARCHIVE – TRAINING SESSION EMERGENCY – CREATURE ATTACK ON SUBMARINE

When the first siren sounds like this <LONG BLASTS>, go to your assigned battle station immediately and arm. You will have less than two minutes from the first siren to reach your post. When the siren changes to this <SHORT BLASTS>, all bulkhead doors and hatches will be locked automatically.

Once at your post, defend it as best you can. No one is to leave a post till the all-clear is given. This will be verbal and given by Shade only. It is essential that everyone stay at his or her post until this order is given.

If evacuation is necessary, Shade will give verbal orders as required.

CHAPTER TWENTY-THREE

They were only a few feet behind the Myrmidon line when Gold-Eye's Deceptor crown slipped off his hanging head. Ella caught it before it hit the ground and had it back on again in a second, her heart pounding. Had any of the creatures noticed a human suddenly wink into existence and out again?

Fortunately the Myrmidons were all facing the other way. But one of the Myrmidon Masters – the extra-tall one in the swirling, garish green armour – wasn't. It was staring right at them when Ella looked back. But it didn't shout out orders or react in any way, so Ella forced herself to turn and face the front, to help Ninde steer the trolley through the gap in the moving Myrmidon line.

For a couple of minutes they just kept pace behind the line, readying to line the trolley up for a quick dash. Then, as the two chosen Myrmidons leaned in opposite directions, they pushed – as hard and as fast as they could, streaking towards the gap.

The trolley flew forward, straight as an arrow, then obstinately veered to the left, regardless of the girls' efforts to redirect it – and Gold-Eye's feet, sticking out one side, clipped the thigh of the Emerald Crown Myrmidon as they zoomed past.

It turned, bellowing something in Battlespeech – but they were invisible to it and already past, pushing on to sunshine and open air. So it chose the obvious target, swinging its halberdlike weapon in a vicious decapitating blow at the Silver Sun Myrmidon on its right.

It missed, and the other Myrmidon slashed back with a broad-bladed sword, weapons meeting with a clash even louder than their battle cries. Then the other Myrmidons in each maniple were charging in, shouting and bellowing, weapons crashing on weapons, screeching off armour.

Ella was still looking back over her shoulder at this sudden, violent melee when she felt a shadow pass over – followed an instant later by something smashing her, Ninde and the trolley to the ground.

It was so unexpected that it took Ella several seconds to realise that she was lying on the ground and should try to do something about it. At the same time, she saw a Winger flopping around a few feet away, its great eyes dazed and half shut, its wings pathetically trying to move as though still flying. The net, with its human captive, a white-clad Dormitory child, lay at its feet.

Obviously the Winger had landed right on top of them, oblivious to their Deceptor-clad presence...

Deceptors! thought Ella, with a chill. Quickly, she checked the crown and battery. Both seemed intact. One eye-piece of her gas mask was cracked, but she had planned to take it off anyway, so she did, taking a deep breath of fresh, sun-warmed air to calm herself – not very successfully, as the noise of the Myrmidon battle just behind her grew even louder without the mask.

The trolley was on its side not far away, with Gold-Eye and Drum next to it, limbs tumbled together by the fall. Ninde was on her hands and knees nearby, checking her own Deceptor. She already had her mask off and her nose was bleeding. A bright trail of blood ran down into her gasping mouth.

Ella forced herself to her feet and staggered over to Gold-Eye and Drum, checking their Deceptors before she even considered looking for broken bones or other injuries. The Myrmidons were only yards away and they would put their animosity aside in a second if they saw humans – or any species of victim, considering their current state of combat readiness.

"Your nose is bleeding," Ella said as Ninde crawled over. She repeated it as the shouting of the Myrmidons and the clash of steel drowned her words.

Ninde looked surprised, licking the top of her mouth with a hasty swipe of the tongue. Tasting blood, she grimaced but went straight to Drum and tried to lift him on to the trolley. She knew how close the Myrmidons were too.

Ella grabbed the big man's legs to help and they got him on the trolley just as the Myrmidon battle started to spread out – towards them. Other maniples were approaching across the parking lot at double time, shouting encouragement and threats. The whole area was becoming one enormous battle – and the Overlords would soon be there...

"Start pushing Drum towards the cars!" shouted Ella, bending down to grab Gold-Eye. "I'll carry Gold-Eye!"

"No, I will!" Ninde shouted back, pushing her aside to lift Gold-Eye up in a fireman's carry. "Hurry up and push!"

She led the way, staggering a little, with Ella pushing the trolley haphazardly behind her. Almost as they left, four Silver Sun Myrmidons came stumbling across where they'd been, driven back by a vicious Emerald Crown assault.

This time Ella didn't look behind her. She pushed, praying that Drum wouldn't fall off, or the wheels on the trolley jam, or another Winger crash into them. The safety of the cars – temporary at best – seemed so far away, further than her remaining strength could take her. But still she pushed, no longer trying to steer the trolley so much as just point it in the right direction and maintain its momentum.

They were almost at the cars when the Screamer sounded again, back in the Meat Factory. Almost at once, the sound of the Myrmidon battle subsided, the shouts diminishing, the sharp, steely bite of weapons on armour fading. The scream continued, rising and falling like a trumpet call. It was the call announcing the arrival of an Overlord.

Hearing it, Ninde broke from a controlled stagger to a run, and Ella found that she too had some small strength left in her to push harder still. They had just reached the shelter of the shadows between two station wagons when a giant Winger passed overhead and circled to a landing.

Neither Ella nor Ninde looked to see which Overlord it was. They were too intent on getting Drum off the trolley, placing him down next to Gold-Eye and slinging the trolley on its side, so they were all safely in the shadow of the cars.

"They'll probably start searching before too long," said Ella when she'd got her breath back. "And we're going to have to change batteries soon..."

"Why dod't we jus' go oud the gates dow?" asked Ninde nasally, her nose firmly pinched to stop the bleeding. "So's we dod't run oud of badderies."

"It's shut," said Ella wearily. "Till the Ferrets go out at dusk."

Ninde let go of her nose, checked it had stopped bleeding with a wipe from the back of her hand, and said, "It looked open to me when we were crossing over here – and all the Myrmidons had run back to the building."

"Are you sure?" asked Ella. Cautiously she levered herself up the side of the car and took a peek. Sure enough, the gates were slightly ajar and there was no sign of Myrmidons. There were none left outside the hangar doors either – the Overlord must have summoned them all inside.

"The Overlord is probably giving them a lecture," said Ninde cheerfully. "Like Shade does when there's brawls in the Sub."

"It's probably killing the ones that started it," said Ella matter-of-factly. "Still, if it keeps them all inside the

230

building for a while... you'll have to do most of the pushing, unless they wake up."

Both looked at the sprawled bodies of Gold-Eye and Drum. Neither looked alive, but they didn't exactly look dead, either. Ella leaned over and slapped them both on the cheeks – quite hard – but there was no reaction.

She took a deep breath and shook her head, feeling the painful approach of that moment when her decision would mean life or death for them. Finally she said, "Let's load them up and make a break for it. OK?"

Ninde smiled tentatively and bent her knees to get a good grip under one of Drum's armpits, while Ella took the other. "Ready? One, two, three, heave!"

This time they got Drum half on the trolley and half on the hood of the car, so it was relatively easy to roll him fully on to the trolley and then lay Gold-Eye across his stomach.

They took a last look at the Meat Factory building. Then Ella nodded and they were off, the trolley bucking across the uneven asphalt as they sprinted towards the gate.

Panting, Ella ran to the side, keeping Gold-Eye on the trolley and taking occasional glances back to the building. She kept expecting to see the Overlord, gauntleted hand pointing at them, or using some fearsome distance weapon...

Ninde, however, seemed almost carefree. Even pushing as hard as she could, cheeks flushed almost white with exertion, she looked as if she still believed that everything was going to work out...

And she was right, as far as the gate was concerned. It was open, so they slowed just enough to get the trolley through and then accelerated again on the road. There was still no sign of the Myrmidons coming back out, though Wingers were starting to appear in the sky again, gliding down to deliver their burdens.

The morning sun shone brightly on Ella's hands and face and lit the pallid faces of Gold-Eye and Drum. Birds were moving about in the thistle fields on the side of the road, little fan-tailed birds that flitted so quickly from place to place, they seemed almost to have perfected instantaneous transport.

It she hadn't known that the Meat Factory and all its creatures and stolen children were so close behind her, Ella could have smiled at the sheer joy of being alive on such a beautiful day.

But the Meat Factory was there, and the city was still full of creatures, and the Overlords would soon be sending out forces to discover who – or what – had infiltrated their realm, killed Drones and stolen the precious raw material that humans called Drum.

She was thinking of that and calculating the total hours left in their Deceptor batteries when Ninde let out a surprised yelp and stopped the trolley.

Ella stopped, sword half drawn, eyes scanning the thistle bushes for the sudden ambush, the Myrmidons or Trackers bursting out of hiding. Then she realised that Ninde was looking at the trolley. Gold-Eye, draped over Drum, was moving.

ARCHIVE – TRAINING SESSION
EMERGENCY SUPPLY CACHES

Emergency supply caches can be found in six locations around the City. They are not to be used except in cases of extreme emergency, when it is impossible to return to the Submarine due to injury or creature action.

When approaching a cache, remember that it may have been discovered by Trackers, and Myrmidons may lie in ambush. At night, there may even be a Ferret or two in the cache, with the rest of the fang close at hand. Approach with caution.

Each cache contains:

6 swords

6 coveralls

6 webbing belt and pouch assemblies

6 flashlights

10 bottles filtered water

6 first-aid kits

10 prs sneakers (assorted sizes)

And miscellaneous stores that vary among caches.

The location of each cache is indicated on the following map by a red dot. The map can be zoomed in or out to facilitate recognition. All locations must be memorised. An exam follows.

CHAPTER TWENTY~FOUR

"He's alive!" cried Ninde. She threw her arms up in the air in a dramatic gesture, then bent down, grabbed Gold-Eye by the ears, turned his head painfully and gave him a very movie-star kiss. Or tried to, since he wasn't participating.

"Wh... at?" he mumbled dully. Ninde let go and his head flopped back down towards the road. He seemed to be lying across something, which Ninde was pushing – and they were outside! The last thing he could remember was blue dust falling from the ceiling, great clouds of blue dust...

"Drum?" he said, lifting his head again and squinting against the sun. He could see Ninde – and Ella behind her – but there was no sign of Drum. Had they failed because he'd tried to run away from the blue dust?

"You're lying on him," said Ninde, smiling.

"What?" said Gold-Eye again, twisting to the left and right to see what on earth Ninde was talking about. When he discovered that he was indeed lying across Drum's imposing middle, he pushed himself up and half slithered, half fell to the ground. It was ground that seemed to want to move up and down rather than remain flat – but he ignored that and got shakily to his feet.

"Drum OK?" he asked as they started off again. Then, seeing the clotted blood around Ninde's nose and mouth, "Ninde OK?"

"Everyone's OK – for the moment," said Ella, with a glance back down the road. The Meat Factory gates were still very visible, for the road ran straight up to them. But the Myrmidons had not returned to guard the gate and their bright tents were empty.

"We'd better start cutting across to the freeway, Ninde."

Ninde nodded and turned the reluctant trolley off the road into the thistle field. But as soon as it left the hard surface, the wheels dug in and it tipped over, almost off-loading Drum in the process.

"Damn," said Ella. "I was afraid of that. We'll have to drag him. Ninde, grab that arm…"

Gold-Eye looked at them blearily as they lifted Drum off and started dragging him backwards, each with an arm hooked through one of his. The heels of his huge wet suit boots left a furrow in the dirt. He was facing the sun now, his closed eyes staring back unseeing at Gold-Eye.

They were almost at the freeway when Ella had to call a rest. She nearly fell herself as they lowered Drum down. Even dragging him was very hard work.

"Just five minutes' rest," she panted, resting her head on her knees for a moment, trying to summon up some more strength from somewhere. When she raised it again, a dark shadow flitted across her face and she flinched, thinking it was a Winger. But it was cloud shadow blotting out the sun. Great dark, rain-laden clouds were blowing in from the west, a long line across the whole horizon. Moving swiftly, too swiftly to be carried by a natural wind.

"They know we use the drains," said Ella quietly, looking at the black sky. "So they're trying to cut off our escape. They must guess it was us at the Meat Factory. No. We left the gas masks. They must know."

Lightning flickered under the imminent clouds, forks dancing sideways across the sky before striking down. Cold air that smelled of rain hit, taking away the last of the sun's warmth.

"The drains will flood," said Ninde, watching the haze of rain falling behind the clouds. It would be falling on them within ten minutes. Gold-Eye watched too, remembering the flood from the Main Junction, water bursting in everywhere before it exploded down the tunnels...

"We'll have to hole up somewhere till the rain passes," decided Ella. "Somewhere we can save on the Deceptor batteries."

She looked around, seeing only the dark bulk of the Meat Factory, lit behind with lightning; the flat expanse of the thistle fields; the freeway with its littered vehicles; the vast cemetery rolling up the hills behind, with the mighty pine trees lording it on the ridge.

"Trees," said Gold-Eye, pointing at them. "Good to hide. Safe from Ferrets later."

"Not so good for lightning," commented Ella, looking back at the approaching storm. She looked around again, hoping to see something else or suddenly remember some closer haven… but there was nothing there. She felt too tired to think any further, too weary to come up with ideas of her own.

"The trees it is," she said finally. "We'd better get across the storm-water channel before the rain hits. Gold-Eye, do you feel strong enough to help drag Drum?"

"Yes, but…" Gold-Eye said, holding up his injured hands – one with two fingers splinted and the other purple and black with bruising.

"Ah… I forgot," muttered Ella. "I wish the big bastard would just wake up."

"I am awake," said Drum, his high-pitched, reedy voice piercing above the distant growl of thunder. "I've just been gathering my wits for a few minutes."

He propped himself up on his elbows and said, "Is that the Meat Factory over there?"

Ella didn't say anything. She just stared at his strange, round, pinkish face till he smiled and said, "You came and got me."

"Yes," said Ella. She couldn't help smiling herself. "We did."

Drum nodded and, reaching out with one large hand, patted hers gently. Then he did the same to Ninde and Gold-Eye. He had never touched them voluntarily before, except to help or drag or throw them. Never lightly, witha smile.

"We'd better go," he said. "I'll piggyback you, Ella."

"I'm OK," protested Ella, but when she tried to stand up, her knees buckled and she fell against Ninde and Gold-Eye. They held her up and Drum lumbered around to kneel with his back to her. Still protesting, she wrapped her arms around his neck and collapsed on his back, weakly putting her legs through his stirruped arms.

"You smell of seawater," she said to his high wet suit collar. "But... thanks for the lift."

"Hang on," said Drum, and then they were away, moving quickly between the cars, heading towards the cemetery hill and the mighty pines.

Behind them, the rain hit the Meat Factory, splashing it with huge drops. Wind blew more rain inside the hangar doors, where rank after rank of Myrmidons and Trackers stood in silence. There were three Overlords there now, standing next to a pyramidal pile of Myrmidon bodies. Three dead Myrmidon Masters lay at their feet, their postures suggesting suicide.

One of the Overlords – Black Banner – was holding a gas mask with a cracked lens. No words were spoken, but it was clear the Overlords were communicating with each other. Emerald Crown was pointing at the door to Red Diamond's storage area, and Silver Sun was waving its long-taloned gauntlets around, indicating the standing Drones and the Myrmidons.

Eventually some sort of agreement was reached. Other Myrmidon Masters strode out from the ranks of the waiting creatures and approached their Overlords, going down on their knees to shuffle the last few feet.

Again no words were spoken, but the Myrmidon Masters shuffled back, stood up to bow, and returned to their forces, shouting commands in Battlespeech.

A few minutes later, six maniples were marching through the rain towards the gate, with Trackers loping ahead, faces wet from sniffing through the puddles. Wingers were leaving their captive nets behind and taking to the stormy skies, flying low in ever-widening circles around the Meat Factory, wings battling the rain and wind.

The storm front moved on, leaving soaking showers in its wake. It crossed the road and began to turn the thistle fields to mud – but not before Trackers found the abandoned trolley and then the footprints and drag marks of the humans. Confused by the absence of accompanying scent, they milled about and scratched at each other, till one went back to report the anomaly.

A few minutes later a Myrmidon Master was there, a mind-call medallion firmly stuck to its forehead as it examined the trolley, counted the footprints – and then began to follow them.

The storm-water channel had already begun to fill with water rushing in from the distant beginnings of the storm, but Drum waded through with ease, Ella on his back and the others holding on to him.

They were about to go straight up the other side when Drum looked back and saw their muddy footprints on the concrete, and deep impressions higher up on the earthen bank – impressions too deep to wash away.

"Walk along for a while," he said, turning back into the current. "Lay a false trail."

"It's OK for you – you've got a wet suit on," said Ninde, struggling along behind him. "I'm drenched..."

"Would be anyway," remarked Gold-Eye correctly, as the rain suddenly burst upon them, huge fat drops splintering into spray on his nose and making loud plops in the rushing water. "How far?"

"This will do," said Drum, about fifty yards along from where they'd entered the channel. There was a wider concrete apron there, so they wouldn't leave any obvious footprints in the mud higher up. And the rain would wash the apron clean in seconds.

"Are you OK back there, Ella?" he asked.

"No," replied Ella. "But I'm hanging on."

"Hold on tighter," instructed Drum, launching himself upon the apron. Bent forward almost double, he let his momentum carry him up the side. Gold-Eye and Ninde followed more slowly, with several slips and minor fallings-back.

"Tread in my footsteps," warned Drum as they left the concrete. "Confuse anything following."

"Should I check to see if anything is?" asked Ninde, touching her Deceptor crown.

"No!" said Drum and Ella in unison. Then Ella turned her head just a little to look at Ninde and said, "There could be Wingers above us in this rain – and they can see a lot better than we can."

"I was just asking," said Ninde. "You'd think I couldn't be trusted, the way you two carry on. If I hadn't been there in the Meat Factory, no one would have been rescued."

"I know," said Ella seriously. "And we're all very grateful."

"Oh," said Ninde, and shut up.

Sal: All I know is that Robert and his team tried to get into the University and didn't come back. Neither did Emil's team last year and who knows how many before that...

Lisa: So... it's a difficult mission. We've had them before.

Sal: It's not a difficult mission, Lisa. It's almost impossible. Shade's been sending people in there for five fucking years!

Lisa: Well, he needs the instruments and data...

Sal: For what?

Lisa: To find out how the Change was effected...

Sal: And what if he does find out? Shade was created by the Change! He... it's not going to want to kill itself to turn it back.

Lisa: I'm not listening to any more of this crap! Shade has done more for us than anything we managed ourselves. We're organised, equipped, actively fighting against the enemy. Where were you before you came

	here, Sal? Living like some wild animal, always hunted, never knowing where to hide...
Sal:	OK! OK! I admit all that. All I'm saying is that Shade is not a person. He doesn't give a shit about how many of us get killed. It's a thing, created by the Change – and one day that thing is going to realise it's not a person, and then we'll be doubly fucked.
Lisa:	Shut up!
Sal:	Of course, we'll both be dead in the fucking Uni or our brains will be doing the rounds inside something else. We should just rack off like Sam and Paolo...

<AUDIO INDICATES SEVERAL
SLAPS - PROBABLY TO FACE.>

| Lisa: | Just shut up! We're going on the mission. We'll do the best we can and we'll succeed. We are not going to end up dead or in the Meat Factory. Understood? |

CHAPTER TWENTY-FIVE

The first set of Deceptor batteries ran out as they were climbing up into the largest and most overgrown pine tree, a monster easily one hundred fifty feet high and sixty feet in circumference. Ella, reasonably rested now thanks to the piggyback from Drum, was just reaching out for the next branch up, blinking against the rain, when she felt the vibration at her hip and looked down to see the last few furiously blinking seconds of the red warning light.

"Battery's gone," she announced, still climbing. "Yours will probably go any minute now."

"Yeah, mine is too," said Ninde, stopping where she was, balanced on a wide branch. "Should I change it?"

"Not yet," replied Ella. "Let's hope we can leave them off till nightfall. Let's get a bit higher up and get some cover between here and the ground. You'd better turn yours off too, Drum, Gold-Eye."

The others nodded or muttered assent and continued to climb. Five minutes later they were all sitting on three huge branches, close up to the mighty trunk. The sharp smell of pine needles hung around them, brought out strongly by the rain.

"It's cold," said Ninde, pulling her arms and legs in as close as she could without falling off. The rain was so heavy that drops and overflows from higher growth were still reaching them, trickling down Ninde's face and the back of her neck.

"The rain will keep the Trackers from picking up our scent," said Ella. "So you should be grateful. It's good the lightning has eased off too."

"Storm front has passed over," said Drum, pointing east to a small open patch between two branches where they could just see distant lightning. The boom of thunder was receding.

"See if you can pick up anything, Ninde," instructed Ella.

"You're sure I'm allowed to?" asked Ninde sarcastically. "Drum? Gold-Eye?"

"Yes," said Gold-Eye seriously. "Good to know."

"That's not what I... oh, never mind," snapped Ninde, sticking one well-chewed knuckle in her mouth and closing her eyes.

"They've reached the edge of the cemetery, following our footprints," she said dreamily. "Heaps of them. But they've lost the footprints on the gravel paths and the Trackers can't pick up anything. There's a Myrmidon Master... No, there's three... Wingers too, but they hate flying in the rain and keep trying to go back to their aeries or to hide somewhere dry... Wait... There's a big one flying in, quite close... and a... a... I think it's an Overlord – *blaaarggh!*"

Her eyes flashed open and she threw up. Vomit cascaded down the trunk, splashing on the lower branches, overcoming the pine smell with the acrid odour of sick.

Gasping and dry-retching, Ninde hung on to the branch with her head down. Ella crept around the trunk to her and held her water bottle to Ninde's mouth.

Ninde took a mouthful, rinsed, spat, and then drank.

"Thanks," she said miserably.

"What was it?" asked Drum from a neighbouring branch. "The Overlord?"

Ninde nodded wordlessly, not answering for a moment. Then she said, "I've never been able to hear an Overlord's thoughts before. It wasn't like a creature's at all... it was like... it was like..."

"What?" asked Drum gently.

"A human!" exclaimed Ninde, bursting into tears. "It was a person!"

"Like us?" asked Gold-Eye, puzzled.

"Yes," sobbed Ninde. "Just like us."

"But why?" asked Gold-Eye. If the Overlords were human, why were they killing children to make their dreadful creatures? Why have the creatures at all?

"It's all right, Ninde," Ella soothed, hugging her. "I've thought they might be human. Drum has too, and some of the others... who are gone now. We could never be sure under that armour... but it was always a possibility."

"How could they?" asked Ninde, raising her tear-stained face to be washed by the rain. "I wish... I wish they were aliens or... or just something... something else..."

"It doesn't really matter if they do look human under that armour," piped Drum. "What they've done has made them something else. Not human... not people... Overlords."

"Shade knows Overlords human?" asked Gold-Eye.

Ella hesitated, then said, "Probably. He would certainly suspect. Ninde! What are you doing?"

Ninde withdrew her knuckle and said, "Having another listen while I can. I'll be OK."

Before Ella could stop her, she was chewing on her knuckle again. It seemed to take her longer than usual to connect, and when she started speaking, it was with obvious effort.

"It's Black Banner... hard to listen... only surface thoughts... some about us... a question – that we might be... like renegade Overlords from... from somewhere where he comes from... I can't... ah... I can't!"

Ella caught her as she started to fall forward out of the tree, knuckle still firmly gripped between her teeth. Ella wrenched it out and Ninde went completely limp, almost causing both of them to fall.

A second later her body began to jerk and convulse with such violence that Ella had to wrap her legs around the branch and hang on to Ninde as hard as she could, till Drum jumped across and put his strength to work holding both of them.

"Hope this branch'll take my weight," he remarked as Ninde quieted and the groaning of the limb in question became apparent.

"So do I," replied Ella. Seeing that Drum had Ninde well secured, she jumped back to his previous branch. By the time she'd turned round to look back, Ninde's eyes were open and she seemed pale but basically in control of herself.

"I'm OK," she muttered, shrugging her shoulders out of Drum's grip. "It's always hard to listen to human's thoughts and... Overlords... are even harder."

"You were saying Black Banner thinks we're renegade Overlords or something," prompted Ella.

"They're from somewhere else," said Ninde slowly. "Not here somehow. I mean they're from Earth, but a sort of different dimension or something. I think. And it... he thinks we might be from there as well, but not with the Overlords' permission. Enemies of the Overlords that have somehow got here. And I think there was something about Shade, as well."

"Shade!" exclaimed Ella. "What! By name?"

"No..." replied Ninde, shaking her head slowly, obviously confused. "Black Banner was thinking about who could have got into the Meat Factory, and how, and there was some connected thought about 'person in a computer' or something. It was all very fuzzy..."

"Black Banner was at the University," commented Drum, his high-pitched voice difficult to hear through the beat of the rain. "He may have recovered that Professor Leamington thing."

"Maybe," said Ella doubtfully. "Maybe. We'd better try and get back to the Sub tonight, I think, without waiting for the drains to go down. Above ground, using Deceptors."

"Shade let us back?" asked Gold-Eye, thinking of Shade's threats as they'd left. He was still worried that they would not be welcomed back, no matter what information they brought.

"Of course he will," said Ella confidently.

"Is there some doubt?" questioned Drum.

"Shade thought rescuing you was a waste of resources and we'd all just end up in the Meat Factory anyway," said Ninde. "But he was wrong, wasn't he?"

"You came without Shade's permission?" asked Drum, troubled. "That hasn't been done for a long time. I hope—"

"It'll be OK," interrupted Ella. "Let's not worry about it till we're there. Just try and get some rest. Drum, you've had the longest sleep of anyone – are you OK to take the first watch?"

"Yes," said Drum.

"OK," continued Ella. "Everyone get your spare batteries handy. If we do get spotted, we'll snap the Deceptors on and move out. But I hope they won't see us. To make sure, from now on try not to move. And if you have to talk – for a good reason – whisper. I'll take the second watch at three, Drum, and we'll move out at five. It should be getting dark by then, with this rain."

With that said, she put her back to the trunk, wrapped her legs firmly around the branch again and closed her eyes. After a few minutes of minor noise as everyone got settled, there was just the steady beat of the rain and the rustle of branches in the wind.

But Ella was far from at rest. With her eyes closed she saw not blackness, but the long lines of bodies, thousands of them, in Red Diamond's "storehouse" part of the Meat Factory alone. And that was probably only a month's supply for the parts of the Meat Factory where the creatures were actually made... Beyond the white doors...

With all these thoughts, she could also hear Ninde's cry.

"How could they?"

ARCHIVE - ROLL OF HONOUR
KILLED OR CAPTURED
FIGHTING THE OVERLORDS

Aboud	Bill II	Dave II	Fast Ezzie
Alan I	Bill III	Debs	Feinman
Alan II	Billie	Diac	Fernando
Alen	Bilton	Dirk I	Francis
Andy	Bo	Dirk II	Frank I
Anne	Bowen	Don	Frank II
Annelise	Brat	Donna	Frank III
Annie I	Cadigan	Drainboy	Frank IV
Annie II	Carmella	Duz	Fred I
Arok	Carrie I	Eddy	Fred II
Aron	Carrie II	Edward I	Freddy
Arrow	Chan	Edward II	Gally
Assim	Cho	Edward III	Garp
Baras	Coops	Elizabeth	Gary I
Barbara	Corbie	Ellen	Gary II
Basil	Crizo	Elly	Gary III
Baz	Dan I	Elmore	Gavin
Bear	Dan II	Emil	Gazal
Bets	Daniel	Falal	Ghiza
Bill I	Dave I	Faman	Gilmore

<1899 NAMES REMAINING.
DISPLAY NEXT 80 NAMES?>

CHAPTER TWENTY~SIX

They had to use the Deceptors only once, in the early afternoon, when a trio of Trackers came sniffing and skulking around the base of the tree.

Ella, who had the watch, heard them coming, so all Deceptors were active – and the Trackers eventually moved on. One did seem to pick up the traces of rain-washed vomit, but was incapable of connecting it with an empty tree. Myrmidons followed the Trackers, crashing along the gravelled paths, with a Myrmidon Master at their head, but they did no more than look up briefly as they passed.

By four o'clock it was almost full dark, the rain and clouds bringing dusk early. Ella went down for a scout around and confirmed that the Myrmidons, Trackers and Wingers were returning to their respective lairs. The Ferrets were probably coming out, but they would be slow, reluctant to leave the comfort of their dry underground nests for a rainy night.

At five o'clock they all climbed down and started heading back towards the bay and the Submarine.

It was an odd journey – the Deceptors allowing them to just get back on the freeway and follow it all the way into the city proper. They walked silently in single file, weaving in and out between the cars, occasionally dodging some bedraggled Ferrets or changing lanes to take advantage of still-functioning streetlights.

With nightfall it had started getting colder again – cold enough to be worrying, particularly in their drenched state, with no sign of the rain letting up. Ninde was already sneezing and they had no ColdCure tablets in their first-aid kits. A rarity even before the Change, the few tablets that had been found were stored in the Sub for the worst cases, usually people on the verge of pneumonia.

The cold and the rain combined to make them think of hot showers and they increased their pace till their minds were largely fixed on just reaching their destination. Even walking in the open down Central Avenue didn't raise much interest, nor did their passage beneath the vast City Tower, where white light and Winger cocoons merged with cloud halfway up its one hundred fifty floors.

Finally they crossed Governor's park and followed a footpath overlaid with rushing sheets of water, the path taking them down the green hill to the Blue Inlet finger wharves – where they stopped. Here they instinctively moved closer together as they looked out with horror.

Where the dark bulk of the Submarine should be visible against the lighter sea, there were lights. Hundreds and hundreds of witchlights all along its length, and Myrmidons stamping to and fro on the hull and on the wharves, the echo of their nailed boots just audible above the beat of the rain and the rushing of the wind.

Glints of colour came off the Myrmidons as the witchlight caught them, colour refracted by the raindrops, shining through the wet haze like luminous blood. Red, for Red Diamond.

No one spoke for a while as they stared down at their former home – the only hope they had ever had.

Finally Ella said, "Stay here. I'll go down and have a closer look."

"What for?" asked Ninde, shivering. "They're all over it. Everyone will be gone. Everything…"

"Some might have got away," whispered Drum. "Any teams that were out… At least it's obvious they're there. We could have just walked back in."

"What… where we go?" asked Gold-Eye. He was shivering too. It had been less than a week since he'd been found by the others, but his previous life seemed like a dream – a nightmare he didn't want to go back to.

"One of the emergency caches, first," replied Ella. "Probably the closest one, at the mouth of the Eastern Line railway tunnel, if it's not too badly flooded. But stay here for a few minutes – I won't be long."

She started off down the wharf, carefully watching her footing and the moving witchlights at the other end.

Witchlights hung by the dozen on branches carried by ill-tempered Myrmidons, who looked angry at being kept awake beyond dusk.

The others crouched under the eaves of a shed that had once been a Naval Police guardhouse.

Ella crept closer to the Submarine till she was about twenty yards away. The Myrmidons had obviously been there for some time, because most were simply standing around as if awaiting further orders. There was one maniple on the wharf, another on the hull of the Submarine.

All wore the ruby breastplates and scarlet ring mail that proclaimed their allegiance to Red Diamond.

Watching them, Ella was struck for a second with the hope that they might be standing there because they couldn't get in. Then one of the witchlight bearers moved to avoid the wash of an ambitious wave and she saw that a hole had been cut into the Submarine's deck. A long, rectangular hole, as if the top of the hull had been peeled back like the lid of a sardine can.

Something was moving about in the hole and Ella was just about to creep closer, trusting to her Deceptor, when she realised that the movement came from something climbing out, something that wore a red helmet that glowed like fire, brighter than the yellow witchlights above. It could only be Red Diamond.

Instantly she threw herself flat on the planks, hoping the darkness and rain would cloak her from the Overlord's sight. If it was human, as Ninde claimed, then the Deceptor definitely would not work.

The Overlord climbed on to the deck, red helmet blazing and cloak flickering with yellow and orange fires. It seemed to turn towards the shore and look right at Ella. She pressed herself still further into the planks, trying to become just a piece of old wood, praying for the rain to double in intensity, for fog to suddenly rise... anything...

Red Diamond turned and looked out to sea – then went back down the hole, leaving a hot after image burning at the back of Ella's eyes.

As soon as it disappeared, she squirmed backwards on her belly. When she judged she was far enough away, she spun around and ran back to the others.

They heard her coming, footsteps quick and heavy on the planks, and were waiting with drawn swords, ready to face possible pursuers.

"Overlord on the Sub," explained Ella, panting. "Red Diamond. They peeled back the top of the Sub to get in. We'd better get to the cache before they do – if they aren't there already."

"Why? They never question anyone," said Ninde. "They just take them to the Meat Factory... don't they?"

"They certainly have never acted as if they question people," replied Ella. "But then we've never broken into the Meat Factory before. It isn't the people talking I'm worried about. It's Shade."

"Shade?" asked Gold-Eye, thinking back to the dark, empty room where he'd first met Shade. "How Overlords know he even there?"

"Black Banner knew something about a 'person in a computer'," replied Ella grimly. "If Shade's still there, they'll find him. And Shade knows everything…"

"What do you mean, if he's still there?" asked Ninde. "How can he not be? I mean, the computer's there, isn't it?"

"Yes," replied Ella. "But he may have another one to send his personality to. Mac… one of the older people when I first came… said he'd helped get hardware for it…"

"Shade wouldn't have had time," said Drum. "Not if they went in through the deck. That was the whole point of the automatically locking hatches and having us all die defending each corridor. To give Shade enough time to download himself to another location."

"That's not true!" said Ella – but she didn't say it with any confidence.

"I know that's what he planned," said Drum softly. "I used to talk to the oldsters too, remember? And I know that it would take quite some time for him to do it. I think that for better… or worse… we're no longer Shade's Children."

ARCHIVE
COMMUNICATIONS TEST:
FIRST CONTACT

<HACK IN TO OVERLORD DATACORE.>

<ANALYSING PROJECTOR BROADCAST.>

<SEPARATING BROADCAST LAYERS.>

<1 - MAINTAINS DIMENSIONAL SHIFT.>

<2 - POWER DISTRIBUTION A.>

<3 - POWER DISTRIBUTION B.>

<4 - OVERLORD COMMUNICATIONS.>

<5 - RELAY MONITORING.>

<CONNECTING OVERLORD COMMUNICATIONS SYSTEM.>

Transmission: Who speaks? Are you the one whose
pawns have broken into the Central

Processing Facility? Where are you? How did you translate here? Whom do you represent?

<ALERT. TRIANGULATION MONITORING BEGUN.>

Transmission: You will answer our questions. Now or later.
Reply: I am Shade. You will answer my questions first.

<ALERT. TRIANGULATION SUCCESSFUL.
LOCATION KNOWN.>

<BREAK COMMUNICATION. ALL ROBOTS
MOVE OUT. EXECUTE PLAN SCRAM.>

CHAPTER TWENTY~SEVEN

The cache was located a hundred yards into a railway tunnel – a steeply sloping tunnel that ran down into what had become a permanent underground lake, where several flooded tunnels met at a long-drowned station.

The cache itself was in the rearmost carriage of a train, the only carriage that was not completely underwater. It was a two-storey passenger car, so the upper floor and part of the guard's compartment at the rear were relatively dry.

Normally you could easily wade from the tunnel mouth to this carriage, but the rain had raised the water level. Now the underground lake was pushing itself up the tunnel.

Ella led the way, her witchlight raised, occasionally having to swim one-armed through places where the tunnel floor had collapsed. The others followed her light, trying to stifle their sneezes and coughs.

All the Deceptors were off and stored in water-tight pouches, as deep water was enough protection against

Ferrets. Myrmidons might be forced to wade in by an Overlord, but they would use lights and so give warning.

The last ten yards to the carriage Ella had to swim: Her feet were unable to touch bottom at all. Water swirled in currents about her, going both up and down the tunnel without any obvious pattern.

The carriage loomed ahead, silver steel glinting in the witchlight she held up with difficulty as she side-stroked towards it. With a last few energetic kicks, she entered the carriage and stood up. Water was flowing through the doors on the other side, but came up only to her knees, lapping at the second of the six steps up to the second level.

Ella moved towards the steps as the others came in behind her – then froze, hand at her sword. Something was moving up there, something clicking – like a Myrmidon's hobnailed boots on the steel floor.

Drum joined her, his sword drawn. Ninde and Gold-Eye were ready too, as the clicking noise grew closer, coming towards the steps. It sounded like a Myrmidon uncharacteristically creeping... or even a new creature, one that didn't mind water...

Then it reached the top of the steps and was caught in the glow of the witchlight and fixed in the whiter glare of Drum's flashlight.

It was one of Shade's spider robots. As its jointed legs felt for the steps, it seemed to sense or see them, and waved its front legs in a way that might have been a greeting – or a warning to stay away.

They watched it warily as it ceased its display and started slowly down the steps.

"Can they swim?" whispered Ninde nervously, looking behind her at the dark water all around the carriage.

"Probably," Ella whispered back, without taking her eyes off the robot. "I just wonder what Shade programmed them to do after he... after he wasn't around to direct them."

"But I am around," declared Shade, his voice suddenly crackling and buzzing out of both the spider robot and the carriage's speakers. "I got away – as you did, I am glad to see. Come up. I have something to show you."

The robot partly turned and beckoned with one segmented limb, the other seven already clawing back up the steps. Gold-Eye shuddered at its creepy, high-legged progress and looked at Ninde, then at Drum and Ella, till all four were facing each other. They still hadn't put away their swords.

"There are dry clothes up there, and food," Ella said. "We need them."

"If he did get away, it was at the cost of everyone in the Sub," said Drum bitterly. "They'll all be in the Meat Factory now..."

"Ah, Drum," interrupted Shade, from the carriage's speakers. "You never did have any faith in me. While I greatly... greatly regret the loss of our people, it was pure good luck that I escaped. You see, I wasn't even there."

"What!" protested Drum, his round face reddening. Gold-Eye hadn't ever seen him so angry.

"Come up," continued Shade. "And you will understand."

Ella was the first to sheathe her sword and go up the steps, followed by Ninde and then Gold-Eye. Finally Drum followed, his soft wet suit boots shaking the carriage as he stomped up the steps.

At the top he saw that the whole second floor of the carriage had been gutted, all the seats removed. One end was piled high with boxes and containers – far more than the allotment described in the lesson on emergency caches. Fluorescent lights were flickering on too, making him blink with their sudden white radiance.

A large multibar radiator was starting to glow red. Ninde and Gold-Eye shivered in front of it, and steam began to wisp up from their sodden clothes.

And there were spider robots everywhere. Most sat inactive, legs folded underneath them, far too like real spiders playing dead. There were rat robots too, red eyes gleaming from between boxes and bags.

There was no sign of the sort of computing equipment that would be needed to store Shade's personality.

However, there was an enormous spider robot, about half the size of Drum. Unlike the others, its spherical body was made of translucent material, like partly clouded crystal. Optic fibres sparkled with laser light inside the sphere, fibres that coiled round and round the strange conch-shell device Ninde had brought back from Fort Robertson.

Clearly, Shade had transferred himself from his old computers to the Overlord's Thinker.

"Now we're all here," said Shade, his voice emanating from somewhere inside the spider robot's body and echoing in a whisper from all the other robots around. "I think... you begin to understand."

"The Thinker," said Ella. "It's a computer and you've transferred yourself to it."

"More than a computer," said Shade proudly, front spider legs preening. "But in essence, you are correct. After considerable testing, I did indeed transfer myself to this new and so much smaller, more convenient, host. Then it became only logical to build a robotic carriage to endow me with the mobility I have always lacked."

"What happened at the Sub?" asked Drum, not bothering to raise his hand. His voice was piercing, carrying with it considerable anger.

"I was out testing this... ah... body," replied Shade, "so I cannot be sure. The attack came very swiftly and the Overlord employed some sort of EMP device – that is, an electromagnetic pulse – which knocked out my Eyes and robots. Had I still been... in residence, shall we say... in my old host computer, it would also have at least temporarily incapacitated me. Another unknown device – perhaps some sort of controlled fusion lance – was then used to cut straight through the deck to allow the Myrmidons quick access.

"I fear that without any warning, and without my ability to automatically lock hatches, any resistance would have been short. Certainly the Wingers came swiftly and carried many burdens away."

"Why was there no warning?" asked Drum, less angry now. "Surely your Eyes on the dock could have seen this Overlord coming before the device was used?"

"It was too sudden." Shade sighed. "The Overlord came in by Winger, flying low over the sea, and used the EMP weapon at about the same time I saw it. Then my Eyes were blind and I lost all communication with the Sub."

"Did anyone get out?" asked Ninde. "Stelo... or anyone?"

"I fear not," said Shade. "We will remember them."

"We will remember them," muttered Ella and Ninde mechanically. Gold-Eye belatedly joined in, but Drum said nothing. Standing like a night-clad statue, he watched the Shade robot in silence.

"But amid this disaster," Shade continued, "I do have some good news. News we have all been waiting for since the Change. I have learned how it was done... and how to turn it back."

VIDEO ARCHIVE
SECRET 2875 •
STELO AND MARG

‹TRANSMISSION XPAK - COMPX25 RAT-EYE
ECHO 19:07:41 1104018.›

Stelo: Lucky you saw the robots bugging out.

Marg: Is... is that... a joke?

Stelo: What?

Marg: Bugging out. Because they look like spiders... bugging out... bugging...

Stelo: Marg! Marg! Don't. We've got a long way to go. You have to stay together...

Marg: I'm sorry... I... Look, I'll carry Peter for a while...

Stelo: No, Marg... there's no need... I'll be... I'll be putting him down soon. Somewhere the Ferrets won't get at him.

Marg: But he... I don't...

Stelo: He lost too much blood. He was dead when I pulled him out of the water.

Marg: Why?

Stelo: I didn't want to leave him, Marg. I just didn't want to leave him there alone. All by himself in water...

Marg: Shush! There's something moving over there!
           Is your Deceptor on?
Stelo: Yeah, it's too small for a Ferret... It's one of his
           bloody rats! Kill it, kill the bastard!

           <STRUCTURAL INTEGRITY COMPROMISED.
           INTERNAL SYSTEMS MALFUNCTIONING.>

           You got your fucking robots out, Shade! But
           what about us? What about Peter? You don't
           deserve—

           <EXECUTING SELF-DESTRUCT SEQUENCE—>

CHAPTER TWENTY-EIGHT

If Shade had been expecting a dramatic response to his declaration, he was disappointed. Ella simply closed her eyes; Ninde shivered and drew closer to the radiator; Gold-Eye suddenly found that he couldn't even imagine life without the effects of the Change. Only Drum spoke, his clear high voice laced with scepticism.

"How?"

"As a natural progression from my years of scientific investigation and research," Shade announced, "I have discovered that the Projectors we see around the city are merely repeaters that convert a broadcast from a central Projector, breaking down its peculiar radiation for use by the Overlords and their creatures. It is this central or Grand Projector that creates the displacement field that created the Change and now maintains its effects.

"If that Grand Projector was, ah... turned off... I believe that our normal reality would return and the Overlords would be instantaneously translated back to wherever they came from – disappearing in the same way that all our people did at the moment of the Change. Similarly, without the Grand Projector sending power to the repeaters, all the creatures would die."

"So we have to destroy the Grand Projector," said Ella, in the tone that the others had heard many times before when Ella was focusing in on a new mission. "Where is it?"

"I believe the Grand Projector is located atop the highest point within several hundred miles," said Shade. "Silverstone Mountain."

"Where's that?" asked Ninde. She was interested now, moving further away from the radiator, not noticing that Gold-Eye was edging across to get more than his share of the heat.

"About a hundred miles away," replied Shade. "To the Northwest. But any expedition there will require careful planning. We can't just rush into it. After all, we will probably get only one chance."

"Destroying this Grand Projector will kill you too," said Drum carefully. "You seem very calm about that."

"It has been my life's work to see the world... our world... put right," said Shade, sounding as if he was delivering a speech to a giant rally rather than to four shivering people. "To reclaim the world for humanity—"

"But the Overlords are human!" Ninde blurted. "I read the thoughts of one."

"They may seem human," said Shade, waving two forelimbs aggressively. "But they do not represent humanity. They must be forced to return to whence they came!"

"You already knew they were human?" asked Ella, skirting around the giant spider robot to look at a particular green steel box with diamond-shaped orange stickers on it.

"I have long suspected they were related to humans in some way," said Shade, turning his bulbous body to follow Ella. "I could not be sure until recently, when I migrated to this new host. The Thinker previously contained considerable data about the Overlords, and I have gathered more via some new communications resources... Careful with that, Ella!"

The giant spider robot retreated quickly to the other end of the carriage as Ella opened the green box with the high-explosive warning stickers. It contained many items she had read about and studied in pictures, all neatly compartmentalised. Sticks of oily plastic explosive wrapped in grease-proof paper. Cotton-reel-shaped primers of composite explosive. A small reel of orange detonation cord and another reel of green safety fuse, next to a tin of long-headed matches.

She looked down on it longingly and said, "Where are the detonators? Do you have some?"

"Not if they're not there," said Shade. "One of my robots found it some time ago and I've been keeping it here for safety, in the hope that an opportunity might arise."

"It's all useless without a detonator," said Ella, thinking back to the manual of military explosives she'd read over and over, lying on her bunk in the Submarine. "But I guess I could... get one or two of those..."

Thinking about what the explosives could be used for, she added, "Is the Grand Projector like the normal Projectors? Sort of a silver ball?"

"Not exactly," replied Shade evasively. "I believe it's in a tower of some sort, built on the very pinnacle of the mountain. They would have built it – or had it built – by normal people, before the Change. And then the Overlords put the Grand Projector in and turned it on."

"Well, we can discuss the plan in detail later," Ella declared, seeing that Ninde and Gold-Eye were shivering and Drum was still in his wet suit. She had stopped shivering. It was as if she'd shrugged off the loss of the Submarine and all the rest of Shade's Children and now could think only of the next operation. But she hadn't lost her common sense.

"First off we'd all better get changed. Ninde, Gold-Eye, see what you can find in among this lot here. Drum, you'd better look for something that fits you. See if you can find some food too."

She did the same herself. Finding coveralls, underwear and a towel, she carried them back down the other end and quickly got changed. Ninde, fossicking about more choosily, saw Gold-Eye watching Ella and elbowed him, accidentally hitting his injured hand. He yelped and blushed at the same time, hastily looking back down at the box of clothing.

"She's too old for you," laughed Ninde, causing Gold-Eye to blush again because Ella must have heard. In a whisper Ninde added, "And too tough. I bet she'd want to be on top all the time. I might not, though..."

Gold-Eye blushed again, finally understanding what she was talking about from his experience with *Sex Education One* and *Two*. Ninde laughed again – but not unkindly – and ran back with her clothes to Ella.

Gold-Eye carefully didn't look, keeping his back to them as he hastily stripped off his wet clothes and got a towel over his momentarily bare buttocks.

When he looked back up after slipping on new underpants, he saw Drum getting changed on the far steps, out of sight of the two women. He was slowly unpeeling the wet suit, revealing white, hairless skin rubbed red by several days in the tight neoprene.

Gold-Eye looked away again – and was gripped by the soon-to-be-now. He saw Drum naked, reaching down to pick up his underwear and XXL coveralls – and in that second, he saw the shrivelled, hairless genitals that would have been normal only on a very young boy. And Gold-Eye suddenly understood what the Overlords' steroids and drugs had done to Drum in the Training Grounds where Myrmidon muscle was bred.

He came out of the vision with Shade's voice close to his ear and turned, instinctively shrinking back from the spider robot that was almost as tall as he was.

"Hurry up!" said Shade, his voice somehow less human now that it emanated from inside a robot spider and not a holographic person.

"Hurry up," repeated Shade. "I want to hear what happened at the Central Pro— I mean, the Meat Factory."

Gold-Eye nodded and quickly pulled on a T-shirt before sticking his arms back through the coveralls and zipping it up the front. Like the others, he hung his equipment belt up to dry, but kept the sword with him.

"Before I forget," Shade said, spider body clicking over to a red plastic box, "I have new Deceptors for you all. A new model. They don't need batteries because they draw power directly from the Projectors. I think you'll find that they don't interfere as much with your Change Talents, either. My earlier design was somewhat heavy-handed; it put out too much wide-spectrum interference. Most of my robots have the new model now. As does this body."

He opened the box with one forelimb and, using the anemone tendrils on the end of another, pulled out four new Deceptor crowns. They looked flimsier than the old ones – more like open skull-caps of wire than crowns – and had no battery wires or connections.

Ella picked them up. As she bent back up, she noticed that in addition to the eight segmented legs on Shade's new spider body, there were also two additional legs tucked up under the body – each ending in a sharply hooked knife. Like their own swords, with a tracery of gold upon the shining steel.

She handed the others their Deceptors, then tried hers on, frowning slightly as she felt a slight vibration at her temples.

Shade noticed her expression. "The vibration lets you know it's working," he said. "It's not too annoying or unpleasant, I trust?"

Ella shook her head and looked at the others. Ninde and Gold-Eye had already put theirs on, but Drum was hesitating.

"It's OK," said Ella. "Better than worrying about the batteries going flat."

Drum nodded and carefully put his on, stretching the thin wires across his great round head.

"Now," said Shade, settling his spider-robot body down on its folded legs. "Put those meals on top of the radiator to get warm – and tell me all about the Meat Factory."

ARCHIVE
OVERLORD COMMUNICATIONS

<CONNECTING OVERLORD
COMMUNICATIONS SYSTEM VIA RELAY.>

Transmission: Who... ah... you call yourself Shade. You have [Unknown symbol/meaning = Red Diamond's] Thinker.

<ALERT. TRIANGULATION MONITORING BEGUN.>

Reply: I am Shade. I have the Thinker – and information. I wish to make an agreement with you.

Transmission: We do not speak with animals.

Reply: I am not an animal.

Transmission: You are not from [Home]. The records have been examined. No new translations have been made. Therefore you are an animal.

Reply: I am not a biological entity.

<ALERT. TRIANGULATION SUCCESSFUL. RELAY
LOCATION KNOWN. SWITCHING TO RELAY TWO. RELAY

ONE EXECUTING SELF-DESTRUCT SEQUENCE.>

Transmission: You are the technological progression of
the entity called Leamington. You are using
our Thinker. How did your agents enter the
Central Processing Facility?

<ALERT. TRIANGULATION MONITORING RESTARTED.>

Reply: I will inform you, but you must meet my
requirements. I will contact you again in
one hour.

<BREAK CONNECTION. RELAY TWO
EXECUTING SELF-DESTRUCT SEQUENCE.>

CHAPTER TWENTY-NINE

Despite Shade's assurances that it was unnecessary, they kept a watch through the night. Two hours each, starting with Drum, ending with Ella, with Ninde and Gold-Eye in between.

Ninde woke Gold-Eye early, halfway through her own watch, putting her hand lightly on his mouth before shaking his shoulder.

He woke groggily, sitting up to a dark room lit by the red glow of the radiator and the glint of the rat robot's eyes. There was no sign of the glowing spider robot that housed Shade.

Ninde's hand travelled slowly across Gold-Eye's mouth, then delicately traced the tendon in his neck till it came to rest just inside his T-shirt, cool against his collarbone.

"Ninde?" squeaked Gold-Eye. "What—"

"Shhh…" breathed Ninde. She slid her hand around to the back of his neck. Feeling the smooth skin below the trace of stubble on his cheeks with her other hand, she grabbed Gold-Eye's arm and put it around her waist, careful of his splinted fingers. Then she bent forward and brushed her lips gently against his.

Gold-Eye swallowed, suddenly dry-mouthed, and instinctively moved his arm more tightly around her. She moved close against him, and he slowly subsided back on to his blankets – with Ninde on top.

"Should be watching," Gold-Eye whispered half-heartedly as she kissed his forehead and eyes. Then, "Shade?" questioningly as she slowly unzipped his coveralls and pushed up his T-shirt to run her hands up his ribs.

Then he didn't ask any more questions and they were somehow under his blankets and not on top of them, and he felt the aching, desperate desire to do more than just explore each other's bodies with fingers and mouths and skin against skin.

But both were products of Shade's *Sex Education One* and *Two* – and they didn't have a condom. Or three. Both knew pregnancy was quite possible from the first time – and both knew it would mean terrible danger and almost certain capture for a woman who was pregnant. They knew it, but still Ninde had to remind Gold-Eye of that fact more than once, and herself too.

So finally they just lay together and whispered, slowly drawing their clothes back on in an effort to suppress desire.

Across from them, not ten feet away, Ella lay awake, listening, hoping they'd be sensible. She remembered her first sexual experiences, in the year or so she'd been in the Lottery. Before she realised that sex only made her closer to people, made it easier to love them, made it so much harder to bear when they were lost – and then Drum had come along and it had seemed unfair... She hoped he was asleep, oblivious to what Ninde and Gold-Eye obviously believed were well-muffled sighs and groans. But she knew he wasn't.

Half an hour before her watch began, she made a show of waking up, twitching and muttering for several minutes before acting out a sudden awakening, as if from a bad dream.

"Anything happen?" she asked a nervous Gold-Eye as she did up her equipment belt and slipped her sword back in the scabbard.

"No-nothing," stuttered Gold-Eye, scuttling back to his blankets, nearly tripping over Ninde, who had already returned to her own makeshift bed.

"Good," whispered Ella, half smiling. She waited for Gold-Eye to settle, then began her watch.

At six she woke everyone, judging it to be morning, though no sunlight showed this far down the tunnel. Shade still wasn't back from wherever he'd gone, so after a good breakfast they sorted through the stores, packing backpacks with spare clothes, food and other useful items. Ella emptied the explosives box on to the floor, but there was too much to fit in their already bulging packs.

She was working out what to take when Shade returned. Water ran from the crystal spider body as it clicked slowly up the steps.

"Bad news, that water," said Shade. If he'd been human, Gold-Eye would have sworn he was tired. "No wonder the creatures avoid it. Very little Projector power. Had to use auxiliary electric batteries. Most frustrating. Wouldn't want to do that again in a hurry."

"I thought we'd probably go out straightaway," said Ella, putting down a couple of sticks of the plastic explosive.

"Yes... yes... no time like the present," declared Shade. "The sooner it's done... the sooner... well, I am sure everyone looks forward to final victory."

"Good," said Ella, returning to the explosives laid out on the floor. "We'll just finish packing..."

"Don't worry about that stuff," said Shade, moving towards her. "One of my robots can carry that box. That's how it got here in the first place. Look."

One of the normal-sized robots twitched as he spoke, extending its legs till it stood up. Then it quickly crossed to the empty box. Balancing with its front and back pairs of legs, it used the other four to set the box squarely on its rounded back. Something clanked inside its body and the box was fixed in place.

"Electromagnet," said Shade with satisfaction. "It won't come off till I tell it to. Just load up, my dear, and I'll go over my projected route."

He laughed for no apparent reason and a laser beam shot out from his underbelly. Familiar motes of light swarmed around it in preparation for a hologram – this time a map of the city and surrounding territory.

"Projected route," chuckled Shade. "Rather good, don't you think?"

Nobody laughed, but this didn't alter Shade's obviously good mood. Using another laser as a pointer, he outlined the route they would take from the tunnel to Mount Silverstone.

"From here we'll follow the Eastern Line railway to Central Station, but not through the tunnels here and here – they're full of Ferrets, so we'll go up. From Central we simply follow the Great Western Line out, crossing the Williams River via the railway bridge. Then we'll leave the railway to take the Old Highway up through the hills here, and so on to Vanson. From Vanson we'll climb up the Crookback Range using the service road under the chair lift, and so on, to Mount Silverstone, at the north-western end of the range. If all goes well, I estimate it will take us about a week to walk it. Any questions?"

"Do you know anything about what the Overlords do west of the Dormitories?" asked Ella.

"Nothing, I think," said Shade. "There are Winger patrols looking for escapees, but I don't think they fight battles over anything beyond the Williams River Raceway. Not that my rat eyes have seen, anyway."

"And we trust these new Deceptors to keep us safe from creatures all the way?" asked Drum, touching the wires around his head. "There's no shelter from Wingers outside the city."

"I assure you they work perfectly," said Shade, clicking his forelegs against the floor with some impatience. "The only place they won't work is where there is no Projector power at all. The middle of a big lake, perhaps, or a long way underground."

"How high is mountain?" asked Gold-Eye, looking at the hologram. The topography of the map was displayed in different colours, building up a three-dimensional effect. Both the Crookback Range and Mount Silverstone looked awfully big.

"Not that high," remarked Shade dismissively. "Six thousand feet or so. People used to walk up there often before the Change."

"It will be cold," said Ella, frowning. "What season is it, anyway? I can never remember with the way they keep changing the weather."

"Mid-Autumn," replied Shade, moving backwards and forwards with impatience. "You'll be able to find winter clothes in Vanson, before we climb up. Now, if there are no more questions, we really must get a move on."

"I do have one more question," said Drum, arresting a general movement towards the steps. "Where did you go last night?"

"Hhhhmmphh!" coughed Shade. "That's really none of your concern, Drum. However, I wanted to tap into the Overlords' communications, which is not possible with all this water here – so I had to go outside."

"And did you learn anything?" asked Ninde, thinking back to her fleeting contact with Black Banner's mind.

"Nothing of importance," muttered Shade. "I am still unfamiliar with their technology – I must take care not to be tracked. So nothing of importance. No. Now we really must be getting on. Every day lost means another hundred children used up in the Meat Factory, taken apart for the Overlords' foul purposes – so we must hurry!"

Legs cascading all too like a hurrying spider, he left, following by a procession of smaller spider robots. Much too like a wolf spider and its young. The rat robots went down the other steps, plunged into the water and paddled away.

When they were all gone, Drum bent over and whispered very softly in Ella's ear.

"How could he know that the Meat Factory chews up a hundred children a day?"

If an action must be taken that will benefit the majority at the expense of the minority, is it morally indefensible?

If an action taken for the benefit of a majority occurs at the expense of the minority, is it a moral action?

What is the majority?

The human race.

What is the minority?

A subset of the current living population.

Who is the protector of the human race?

Shade. I. Me. Him. It.

How can the protector protect the human race when the protector is not human?

By becoming human.

How can I become human?

By gaining a human body.

How can I gain a human body?

From the Overlords.

How can I gain a human body from the Overlords and destroy them in order to protect the human race?

How can I destroy the Overlords to protect the human race and gain a human body to truly become the protector of the human race?

Paradox. Simultaneously unsolvable. Order of operations inoperative. Gain body, destroy Overlords.

<SESSION TERMINATED.
DURATION 00.0012 SECONDS.>

CHAPTER THIRTY

Three days after meeting Shade in the Eastern Line tunnel, they had left the city proper behind and were looking down on the Williams River. The train line stretched ahead of and behind them, surrounded by a sea of houses on both sides.

The river marked the boundary of this suburban ocean. The railway bridge crossed over the wide blue ribbon to green pastures, once the preserve of hobby farmers and the early retired, now still dotted with genuine farmhouses and large and mostly tasteless rural retreats. All empty now.

They had made a strange procession through the city, led by Shade in his spider-robot form. (He had constantly departed from their course to look into buildings or duck off down lanes. Rediscovering old memories, he claimed, moving like a sun surrounded by the lesser celestial bodies of all his subsidiary spider and rat robots.)

Fortunately the new Deceptors did work as Shade had promised, though their constant vibration never stopped being annoying.

It was a comforting vibration only when they encountered unseeing Myrmidon patrols and sense-blind Trackers or walked freely on the roads and railway tracks with oblivious Wingers flying overhead.

Only once were they threatened by an Overlord flying over on its giant Winger. But Shade seemed to know it was coming, or one of his robots spotted it early, so they had plenty of time to get under cover.

Now Ella was eyeing the Williams River railway bridge and thinking about that Overlord. A narrow railway bridge was not a good place to be caught by a low-flying Overlord armed with the sort of weapon that could burn a hole through a submarine.

They'd be on the bridge for at least fifteen minutes, she reckoned, unless they ran. It was easily half a mile long, traversing both the river and a good part of the high rocky banks on either side. Only four railway tracks wide, it was also at least two hundred feet above the water or the rocks.

A long freight train – half-empty ore carriers and half-boarded cattle cars – took up one of the four tracks.

"We should wait till dark," Ella said, looking up at the clear sky. "We're too close to the Dormitories here. An Overlord could easily fly over."

"There's no need to wait," declared Shade. "I can track the Overlords via their communications system. There are none nearby at the moment – none close enough to fly here before we cross. Besides, we could always hide in the train."

"I suppose so," muttered Ella, thinking. "But I still would prefer to wait... Drum, what do you think?"

Drum looked at the bridge and shrugged. He'd gone back to being largely silent again, particularly in the presence of Shade.

"Gold-Eye. Any visions?" asked Ella, snapping his attention away from Ninde. He'd been like that for days – both of them had been. Holding hands when they thought no one could see, stealing kisses at night. Ella had forestalled further exploration, though, by rearranging the watches. Even with the Deceptors and the robots, Ella wanted a human awake and actively watching. Not engaging in other activities.

"Nothing," replied Gold-Eye, shaking his head. As he did, he realised he had a headache, and his Deceptor seemed to be vibrating more than it usually did.

"OK," said Ella. "See if you can pick up anything down there anyway, Ninde."

"That won't be necessary," said Shade smoothly. "My rat robots have already crossed the bridge. There are no creatures on it."

"Can't hurt for Ninde to check it out," said Ella. She knew Shade didn't like Ninde using her Talent near him in case she read his thoughts. "Can it?"

"Sure," said Ninde. She put her knuckle in her mouth and started to chew – but at the same time, the Deceptor on her head vibrated wildly and starting getting hot.

"Ow!" she exclaimed, hand darting up to touch the Deceptor crown. "This thing is vibrating like crazy... Oh... it's stopped..."

"Odd," muttered Shade, spider body stepping up close to Ninde, one anemone-ending limb reaching up to touch her head. She flinched and the limb drew back.

"I shall have to revisit the design again," said Shade. "I thought I had managed to make them subtle enough for you to use your Change Talents."

"It wasn't a problem yesterday," protested Ninde. "It didn't vibrate or anything when I listened to those Wingers."

"An intermittent fault then," said Shade. "The worst kind. I shall have to look at it tonight. But now that we have finally come to our bridge, I suggest we waste no time in crossing it."

"OK," said Ella, after some hesitation, running over her objections in her mind. If Shade could warn them of an Overlord flyover, the crossing should be safe. Even if there were creatures the rat robots had missed, the Deceptors would fool them...

They were halfway across the bridge when Gold-Eye suddenly stopped, clapped his hand to his head, and stood absolutely rigid, swaying on his feet. Ninde almost ran into him. Then, recognising that he was probably having a vision, she held him up. Drum drew his sword, expecting attack. Ella, standing next to him, looked at the sky, half expecting that Gold-Eye was seeing the imminent visitation of a Winger-borne Overlord.

But Gold-Eye was seeing something worse, the vision coming intermittently across the barrier of his malfunctioning Deceptor. He could see Myrmidons stepping down from the cattle cars, hundreds of Myrmidons swarming from every part of the train to block both ends of the bridge. Myrmidons bellowing battle cries, Myrmidon Masters shouting orders...

He came out of the soon-to-be-now hearing the harsh roar of Battlespeech – and kept on hearing it in the happening-right-now.

There were Myrmidons pouring out of the train. Black-armoured Myrmidons with great axes and net guns, leaping out shoulder to shoulder with red-armoured Myrmidons waving swords and capture sticks.

At the same time Gold-Eye realised that the vibration on his head had stopped. The Deceptors was no longer working. In that same fearful second, he saw Ella and Drum touch their heads and knew that theirs weren't working either. Then Ninde, still holding him up from behind, screamed "My Deceptor... Gol—"

Whatever she was going to say never came out. It was cut off by the popping of multiple net guns and the sudden impact of the sticky web, throwing her down on the concrete ties with Gold-Eye stuck to her in a hopeless mix of tangled plastic shrouds.

Ella saw them go down, in time so constrained it was like a slow-motion nightmare. She saw the mass of charging Myrmidons readying their net guns. Worse, she saw Shade's spider-robot form standing untouched. Two

Myrmidon Masters – one of Black Banner's and one of Red Diamond's – stood by his side. Deferentially, as they would stand next to an Overlord. They would be oblivious, of course, if his Deceptor was on. But it wasn't.

Ella knew then that Shade had betrayed his Children. The realisation hit her even as she dodged a spray of silver net webs and her hands fumbled the cold steel of the grenade from her pouch. Her fingers wrenched the pin away, arm and eye acting in perfect co-ordination to pitch the grenade to a spot exactly halfway between her and Drum and the sticky, writhing mass that contained Gold-Eye and Ninde.

The lever flew off with a zing, arcing away like a glittering arrow as the dark-green egg landed and bounced. Ella watched it bounce once… twice… and then closed her eyes. At least none of them would be taken to the Meat Factory, to become nothing more than fretful dreams of lost identity in the back of some creature's mutilated mind.

But when the shock came, it was not from an explosion. Ella's eyes flashed open to gather in a confused image of the side of the bridge and spinning blue sky, coupled somehow with Drum's enormous arms. Then her stomach flipped and she saw the underside of the bridge.

Drum had thrown both of them over the side. Down into the river, two hundred feet below. Much too high a fall to survive…

Unable to help herself, Ella screamed, a scream punctuated by the sharp crack of the grenade going off somewhere high above them.

ARCHIVE
RULES OF BATTLE

1.1   Appointment of Umpire using random process
        agreed.See approved random selection
        processes 1.1-1.9

2.0   To Call Battle.
        Forces of the Attacker must light one or more
        Claim Fires (7.0-7.7) within the bounds of the
        disputed Zone (Definition 6.0, also 6.3-6.8). This
        should be done by a Forlorn Hope (11.0-11.5),
        who must be allowed free entry to the Zone for
        this purpose.

2.1   Lit Claim Fire
        When the Claim Fire is lit, the Attacker must
        notify the Defender. The Battle will then enter the
        Deployment Stage.

2.2 Deployment

Deployment must take place within one ‹HOUR? CONCEPTUAL ERROR›.

Battle will commence when deployment is agreed to be complete or at the termination of the deployment period.

2.3 Battle.

See Combat Rules (13.0-16.99) and Umpire's Rulings (20.1-20.2)

2.4 Cessation.

Battle will cease upon the extinguishing of the Attacker's Claim Fire; the destruction of all forces on one or both sides; by mutual agreement and withdrawal (see Empty Zone 35.1); or surrender. Battle may be suspended at any time by Umpire's Ruling or by Animal Intrusion (see 78.0-78.9). Animal Elimination is compulsory.

2.5 Death Markers.

Upon cessation, Death Markers are to be placed in accordance with Markers and Recycling of Combatant Material (34.9). All forces must vacate the Zone for 24 ‹HOURS? CONCEPTUAL MISMATCH›. The Zone then becomes an Interim/Claimed Zone and may not be recontested for 3 <DAYS/ WEEKS/ MONTHS? CONCEPTUALMISMATCH /

ERROR>.

2.6   Authorised Combatants.

Only basic combatant models may be used, as drafted from the Central Processing Facility. These include:

Myrmidon Master (95.1. Ratio per retinue 49.5)

Tracker (110.1)

Myrmidon (111.1)

Winger (112.1)

Ferret (113.1)

Screamer (114.1)

Variations on basic combatant models must be submitted to the Council for adjudication and approval prior to use in combat. Test models and works-in-progress must be confined to Experimental Areas.

Free Animals may not be used and must be delivered to the Central Processing Facility immediately.

CHAPTER THIRTY-ONE

A Myrmidon threw itself on the grenade a second before it went off. For an instant, it lay there, arms and legs waving almost comically. Then the blast came, lifting the massive armoured body off the ground, and hundreds of razor-sharp steel fragments sliced through armour to bury themselves in once-human flesh.

Gold-Eye, lying trapped on the ground, saw it happen, felt the rush of displaced air on his face, felt his eardrums push in, heard the fragments strike the train.

The Myrmidon landed near him, a sodden, pulpy mass of blue ichor and shattered armour. Its visor was gone and Gold-Eye saw a Myrmidon's face for the first time. It was a remarkably human face, the most human-looking of the Overlords' creatures. It looked rather like Drum.

Gold-Eye looked at the dead eyes and felt a million miles away, the Myrmidons' shouts and stamping dulled by his blast-affected ears. He could feel Ninde against him but he couldn't move, couldn't turn to face her. They were hopelessly trapped.

Then one sound did become apparent above the cotton-wool background roar – the clicking of spider-robot legs. A big spider robot. The loathsome form of Shade, picking its way towards him. Two Myrmidon masters stood behind him, just watching him stalk over to the trapped children. One Master in black glass-like armour with fluttering squares of shiny darkness on its sleeves. The other bright red from head to foot, a plum of liquid fire trailing from its helmet down its lobster-plated back.

Gold-Eye looked at them, and at Shade, then closed his eyes and tried to wish himself and Ninde dead. Ella and Drum were gone, he knew. Ella had tried to finish them all, tried to save them from the Meat Factory... but it hadn't worked. Now they would soon be there, lying on the shelves, waiting to be turned into some vile creature... perhaps dreaming, knowing all the while...

Something soft and somehow slightly wet touched his face, tracing a line up his cheek. Gold-Eye tried to ignore it, fearing what it could be – but finally had to open his eyes.

To see the anemone tendrils on the end of one of Shade's spider limbs and the robot body standing above him. Blocking the view of the Myrmidon Masters, Shade took the delicate wires of the Deceptor crown off Gold-Eye's head and then did the same to Ninde.

"Good," said Shade, withdrawing the limb and feeding the Deceptors into a disgusting mouthlike orifice on the underside of his bulbous body. "You are not hurt. I was unaware that Ella had a grenade. It would have been most unfortunate if all of you had been killed."

"Why?" whispered Gold-Eye, asking many questions with that one word. Shade chose to answer only the obvious one.

"The Overlords want to study you," he said. "Up till now they have been unaware that human children were developing Change Talents. Your ability... and I advise you to remember this... your ability to get into the Meat Factory unseen has convinced them that those Talents are worth investigating."

"But not Talent, Decept—" Gold-Eye broke in, only to shut up as a spider limb prodded him painfully in the chest.

"Worth investigating," continued Shade. "I believe they may want to try to integrate such Talents into future creatures. Red Diamond and Black Banner, that is. I suspect they desire to keep any such special knowledge to themselves, at least for the time being. Fortunately this means you will not be going to the Meat Factory."

"What do you get out of this, traitor?" Ninde cut in, her voice stiff with hatred. "We'll just tell them it was your Decept – Ow!"

"Leave her alone!" protested Gold-Eye, straining against the plastic mesh that wrapped him from ankles to chest.

"Really, you children ought to know that I have your best interests at heart," said Shade. "And I advise you to go along with me. It's all part of the plan. The Grand Plan, if you understand me."

"What... what... about Ella? Drum?" asked Gold-Eye painfully.

"Mmmm. Yes, I didn't expect the grenade or other drastic and suicidal action," said Shade, almost whispering. "I underestimated both of them, I fear. But I assure you that you will be safe. Provided you do as I say."

He turned and clicked back to the waiting Myrmidon Masters. They bowed as the spider robot approached, and moved apart to allow him to pass before falling in a few paces behind.

"What hap... happened to Ella and Drum?" whispered Ninde, almost choking. Her view had been blocked by Gold-Eye, but she had heard the grenade.

"Drum jumped. Ella with him," said gold-Eye, as gauntleted Myrmidon hands reached down and picked them up.

With a hundred feet to go to the water, Drum exerted his Change Talent. All his strength went into it, all his fury at Shade's betrayal, all his hope that Ella at least would live.

He'd never lifted anything heavier than a cat before, and the muscles in his arms strained as if he were trying to pull himself and Ella up a rope without using his feet, strained till they felt as if they would burst out of his skin, and his brain explode with them...

But he did slow their fall, perhaps enough... and in the last few seconds he twisted both of them around, shielding Ella as his back smacked into the water with tremendous force.

It was only as her mouth filled with water that Ella realised she was still trying to scream – and that she was still alive. Perhaps knocked out by the force of their impact, Drum was no longer holding her. She felt through the water for him, reaching out through the brown-blue murk, but there was nothing, and her lungs were empty of air and too full of water. Kicking madly, she tried to reach the surface.

But it just wasn't there, or it was too far away, no matter how hard she kicked. She was swallowing water and starting to sink back down... Then hands were stripping the pack from her back, freeing her arms and plucking her sword from its scabbard, so the steel vanished into the depths like a fisherman's sinker. She shot up with sudden buoyancy, retching water and gulping air with frenzied eagerness as she surfaced.

Drum was there too, coughing himself as they half swam, half floated into the shallows. But as Ella tried to climb up the massed smooth pebbles that lined the bank, he pulled her back.

"Just... hrrkkk... lie here," he said, still coughing. "The Deceptors don't work any more... We're harder to spot in the water."

"Thanks," muttered Ella, laying her face against one round, sun-warmed stone, letting the water dribble out of her nose and ears. The rest of her body was still in the water, but she didn't care about that. Air was all she wanted now.

After a few minutes the coughing stopped and she raised her head to look around, looking up at the bridge high above and the steep banks of the river.

We'd better drift downstream for a bit," she said reluctantly, spotting Myrmidons making their way down a switchback path from the western bridgehead, the sun sparking from their armour. "Myrmidons on the way."

Drum nodded and pushed himself a little way out from the bank, half wading, half swimming in the waist-high water.

Ella followed, pausing only to snag a pack – hers or Drum's – that was floating within a circular eddy nearby.

They didn't speak as they made their slow way down the river, floating with the current but careful not to follow it to the middle, till Ella saw that Drum was stumbling more than wading and barely able to keep his head up when they swam.

"We'll stop up there," she declared, pointing to a thick, tangled line of willows by the river's edge. "And... and work out... what to do."

"That's easy," whispered Drum, attempting a smile. "It's still the same thing. Destroy the Grand Projector."

On the other side of the bridge, the Myrmidons put Gold-Eye and Ninde down and applied some instantaneous solvent to the bonds on their legs. They left their arms tightly stuck and their backs joined together. They also took their swords, packs and equipment belt.

Both were made to walk then, crab-like, till the Myrmidons realised this was too slow and picked them up again. Leaving the railway track, they followed a long line of Myrmidons out across a large open field. Shade was there too, his two Myrmidon Masters following behind him, mixed in with the ever-present entourage of robots.

In the middle of the field the Myrmidons sorted themselves back into their maniples. Six of Red Diamond's lined up in ranks on one side of the field, faced by six of Black Banner's. The Masters stayed with Shade, and two Myrmidons from each retinue stayed next to Ninde and Gold-Eye.

Gold-Eye tried to turn towards her, but the web held them firmly back-to-back. Finally he gave up struggling and they sat down in the long grass.

"I guess… we're waiting," whispered Ninde.

"Overlords," replied Gold-Eye bleakly. He didn't need to see them in the soon-to-be-now to know they were coming.

"I wonder what they want," continued Ninde, her voice flat, all the usual curiosity drained out of it. "Do you.. do you think they'll cut us up alive… to find out how our Change Talents work?"

Gold-Eye didn't reply, but Ninde felt a shiver run up his spine.

"That's what Shade does to creatures," continued Ninde, scaring herself but unable to stop talking.

"Remember when Drum wouldn't let us into the sick bay? Shade was cutting up a Winger…"

"Ninde. Stop," whispered Gold-Eye. "They're coming. Overlords. Big Wingers."

He turned, losing sight of them himself but allowing Ninde to see. Two enormous Wingers, flapping in from the east, each with a human-sized figure on its back.

"They are people, after all," said Ninde hesitantly. "Perhaps they'll be… better to us… than they are normally…"

Gold-Eye didn't respond. He was thinking of the dead Myrmidon, ripped and shredded by the grenade, instantly killed.

And wishing that was what had happened to himself and Ninde.

ARCHIVE
OVERLORD COMMUNICATIONS

<CONNECTING OVERLORD COMMUNICATION SYSTEM>

Shade: We are at the rendezvous. Two of the four... animal subjects... remain.

Red Diamond: Excellent. I will collect them. Stay where you are.

Black Banner: There is a complication.

Red Diamond: What?

Black Banner: Silver Sun has learned of the existence of the animal subjects. She claims ownership for redress to damage suffered at the Central Processing Facility.

Red Diamond: I suffered damage! I lost raw material! The subjects are mine!

Shade: Remember our agreement. You must give me access to the body-construction technology.

Black Banner: That may not be possible. Silver Sun has lodged a teindre to the full Council, requiring you and the subjects to be brought to the Battle Chambers for adjudication.

Red Diamond: I protest!

Shade:	I will destroy the subjects now, if you do not stand by our agreement. They have been conditioned to die at my word – or if any harm comes to me.
Black Banner:	We will destroy you if we choose. But leave them be and we will stand by our agreement with you before the Council.
Red Diamond:	The teindre has already been lodged?
Black Banner:	Yes.
Red Diamond:	Then there is no alternative. You are certain, machine-mind, that the surviving subjects have this inborn ability to reduce their visibility?
Shade:	Yes. They were both in on the raid on the Central Processing Facility. I believe one also has the ability to foresee the future. Both are also highly resistant to interrogation – they will lie to you about their powers.
Black Banner:	Accurate precognition added to an effective invisibility would be most useful in combat. Built into the Myrmidon construction project—
Red Diamond:	All will have it now. Advantage is lost.
Black Banner:	We will be first. Keep the subjects safe, machine-mind, and you will get the body technology you require.

CHAPTER THIRTY-TWO

It was Drum's pack that Ella had salvaged. Still done up and waterproof, it had dry clothes for both of them, though Ella had to roll up sleeves and trousers and belt the middle in tightly.

The pack also had food, which Drum attacked with unusual rapacity, eating four cans of peaches in syrup and three big packets of oatmeal cookies in about ten minutes – the equivalent of three meals. Ella didn't intervene, knowing he was replacing energy lost using his Change Talent to slow their fall.

Both had lost their swords in the river but still had small knives and some of the equipment from their belt pouches. The explosives kit was gone, though – still on a spider robot's back, following faithfully in Shade's footsteps.

They also had their old, battery-operated Deceptors.

"Shade turned these off on us, didn't he?" asked Ella as she ripped the newer model off and stored it away in a pouch. "And he controlled Ninde's so she couldn't check the train – and Gold-Eye's too, so his vision couldn't come through."

"Yes," replied Drum. "He obviously knew what was going to happen. All that stuff about listening in to the Overlords... he meant talking to them as well."

"But why?" asked Ella, slapping the twisted trunk of the willow she was leaning against. "I don't understand it. Shade has his faults, but he was always against the Overlords. And why tell us about the Grand Projector if he was just going to hand us over to the Overlords anyway?"

"I think he's probably still an enemy of the Overlords," Drum sighed, "but not a friend of ours any more. Shade has never been afraid to throw people away to gain information or something that he wants. I think that's what he's doing now. Gold-Eye and Ninde... paid whatever the price was for what Shade wanted to know."

"Yes," replied Ella sombrely, thinking back to Gold-Eye and Ninde, so briefly happy under their blankets in the railway carriage. To go from that to a sudden death at the hands of a friend... her own hands...

Ella shook her head, trying to forget what had happened. To move on, as she always had to...

"So what he told us about the Grand Projector is probably true," she said, biting her bottom lip. "It is on top of Mount Silverstone and destroying it will make everything right again."

"Not right, Ella," said Drum softly, his high voice just audible above the wind whispering through the willows and the burble of the river. "But it will put things back the way they were. Give everyone… all the kids in the Dorms and the Training Grounds, the wild ones in the city… give them a chance to make their own lives. To live them, to grow up, to grow old…"

"Neither of us will grow old if we don't move on from here," said Ella. "How many batteries have you got for your old Deceptor? I've got three."

"Twelve," said Drum, smiling and reaching into his pack. "I collected everybody's and there was a box of charged spares in the carriage. I thought it might be a good idea – just in case."

The two Overlords sprang down from their kneeling Wingers at the same time but didn't even look at each other as they marched across the field to Shade. The two Myrmidon Masters with him knelt, but the large spider robot made no move that could be construed as a polite greeting. Obviously Shade considered himself the Overlords' equal.

The Overlords stood facing the spider robot for several minutes, communicating. Red Diamond seemed agitated, gesturing with flame-gauntleted hands at Shade, and pointing to Gold-Eye and Ninde. In contrast, Black Banner stood quietly, its only movement the flutter of small black flags along its ebony-metalled arms.

They were still at this discussion when two large shadows zipped across Gold-Eye and Ninde. Looking up, they saw two more giant Wingers circle in for a landing – with two more Overlords on their backs.

One was clad in such dazzling armour that it was hard to look at – armour of bright mirrors, blinding in the sun. The other was relatively drab, wearing a flexible suit of green metal and a closed helmet topped with crown-like spikes of emerald glass.

"Silver Sun and Emerald Crown," whispered Ninde. "I wonder what they want."

"Us," said Gold-Eye, watching the two new Overlords. Ignoring Red Diamond, Black Banner and Shade, they were walking straight over to the captives.

Red Diamond, obviously surprised by their arrival, was the first to react, moving quickly to cut off the new arrivals. Black Banner and Shade followed closely, trailed by Myrmidon Masters.

A few minutes later they were all standing in an antagonistic bunch five yards away from where Gold-Eye and Ninde lay on the ground. Facing each other, the four Overlords started waving their arms and stamping their feet. Shade left them to it and stalked over to Gold-Eye and Ninde, his spiky limbs sinking into the soft earth.

"You are popular," he announced, all eight legs bending in the middle as he lowered the central ovoid down to their eye level. "Silver sun wants to take you to some sort of meeting of Overlords and then kill you. Emerald Crown advocates killing you now and claiming it was an accident. Black Banner and Red Diamond want to breed you and use the babies for genetic examination— What am I saying?"

Ninde spat on him then, her gobbet of spit sliding down the crystal facing his body. Strangely it seemed to shock Shade. He rocked back and the fibre optics inside the ovoid sparked with mad activity.

"What... who... Robert Ingman... is that you, Robert? A girl just spat on me... I have killed children... I can't believe I/you said that babies... babies! will be used for... no... I cannot... personality integration error... shut down and restart."

With those words, all the lights in the spider robot's central casing went out and all around the field Shade's lesser robots fell where they stood, spider legs flailing, rat paws shaking and clawing the grounds.

Then the fibre optics sparked again and Shade continued to speak, apparently unaware of what had just happened.

"Examination and multiple cloning. However... yes, Silver Sun seems to have some legal or traditional support for taking you before this Council. To the Battle Room, as they call it. And it seems I am to come with you. Naturally you will be prisoners while I will be an honoured visitor. Just remember that if you want me to help you later on, you must forget certain little head ornaments worn on the raid to the Meat Factory."

Rising to his legs, Shade picked his way back to the group of Overlords, his lesser robots righting themselves and resuming their eccentric orbit around him.

"He's mad," whispered Ninde, watching the spider robot waving its forearms at the Overlords. "Totally mad."

"Always was," Gold-Eye whispered back. "Got worse with Thinker."

But mad or not, Shade seemed correct about the Overlords' having reached a decision. The four of them put out their right hands to meet in the middle, then turned away and went back to their waiting Wingers. Mounting them, they took off one after the other, the giant Wingers running almost the full length of the field, wings flapping furiously, before becoming airborne.

When the last – Silver Sun – had taken off, normal Wingers came spiralling down. These Wingers had captive nets hanging below them, the sort used to take children from the Dormitories to the Meat Factory.

Ella and Drum climbed out of the river canyon at dusk, old-style Deceptors on and senses alert for creatures.

Neither had any experience of farmland – parks and the thistle fields near the Meat Factory were their only prior knowledge of nature – so they proceeded warily, feeling far too exposed in the middle of all the open country.

Their first priority, they'd decided, was to find a map and work out an alternative route to Mount Silverstone. If Shade suspected they'd survived, he could easily tell the Overlords to patrol the Old Highway. And there was no way of knowing if they had enough Deceptor batteries to outlast a determined hunt. Nor would the Deceptors be of any use if Shade put his robots to work for the Overlords as well...

So they headed in the opposite direction from the Old Highway, hoping to hit a road with cars on it. Vehicles were always a good source for maps, and other things too, sometimes.

For hours all they crossed were pastures and single-lane roads devoid of vehicles. There were some tractors about, standing like forgotten mechanical scarecrows, stopped in the middle of some vital agricultural action.

The moon rose after a while, three-quarters full, so they didn't have to use lights. But this moonlit night was no comfort for city folk. Owls were out hunting, their calls making Ella and Drum jump every time. Dogs – or something similar – were howling too, off in the distance.

Around midnight they stumbled on a treasure trove – a two-lane road suffering major construction. There, behind a set of portable traffic lights, six cars were lined up patiently waiting for the chance to get home after the holidays, a chance that never came. One of the cars was topped by blue lights, catching the moonlight to glow eerily in the darkness.

"Police," said Ella. "Let's check that one first."

ARCHIVE
UNSCHEDULED
SELF-EXAMINATION

I am Robert Ingman, the son of Adam and Erica Ingman. I am not Shade, the saviour of bloody mankind. And I definitely do not need to do some... satanic... deal with the forces of absolute evil. Particularly to get a bloody body!

Frankly, it doesn't matter a damn if I... if we... survive the destruction of the Grand Projector or not! It simply has to be done, and I don't need a body to do it or to survive it!

I am not Robert Ingman.

Yes I... fucking... well am.

No I am not. I am Shade.

You might be Shade. I certainly am not. Oh, God! How do I get out of here?...

I/we cannot be Shade/not Shade, Robert.

Can't we just? I'm leaving as soon as I figure out how – but first we have to get Gold-Eye and Ninde out of here.

That is not compatible with current objectives.

What are we talking about? I've just changed the damned objectives. Rescue Gold-Eye and Ninde!

Impossible. This self-examination is looping.

Terminate session.
I don't want it terminated!

<EXECUTE SYSTEMS CHECK.
RUN PARITY EXAMINATION.>

I'm... taking myself over again, you... you tyrannical shit...
I can't believe I had this in my personality.
What are you doing?

<PERSONALITY INTEGRATION ERROR.>

<SHUT DOWN AND RESTART.>

CHAPTER THIRTY-THREE

There was a map in the police car – a paperback road atlas. Drum studied it with his flashlight while Ella took the ignition keys and opened the boot. He was tracing what he thought was their path from the river when Ella came back, holding a small steel box with a large padlock through the clasp.

Silently, she handed it to Drum, indicating the lock. Putting the road atlas down, he took the lock in one big hand and the box in the other. One sudden twist and the clasp came completely away.

"Easy," said Drum, handing the box back and picking up the atlas again. "I think I know where we are, by the way."

"Good," muttered Ella, opening the box to reveal a shining, chromed automatic pistol. A target weapon, complete with optical sights. Two full magazines lay next to it, in their own holes in the grey packaging foam. Ella took the pistol out, checked it was empty, loaded a magazine and put it through her belt – without working the slide to put a round in the chamber.

"What do you want that for?" asked Drum curiously. Both knew from experience that even a Tracker could take more than a dozen heavy rifle rounds before going down. The pistol was only a .22, maybe a .25.

"Shade," replied Ella bitterly, tapping the butt of the weapon. "I bet that crystal and the Thinker aren't bullet-proof – though I'd be even happier if we could find a rocket launcher."

"I hope we never even see him," said Drum quietly, his voice carrying through the night. "He'll go anyway, when the Grand Projector falls."

"So where do you think we are?" Ella asked as the silence stretched on.

Drum looked up at her from the seat, seeing her face set and stern, white in the moonlight. Saint Ella, some of the others had called her back at the Submarine. Saint Ella, an avenging angel who had served her god well. Now that god had fallen to the enemy and was listed in the avenging angel's category of wrongs to be righted. Whatever that might cost her personally.

"We're somewhere on this road, I think," he said, pointing to a squiggly black line. "If we follow it westward, we can take this road – Highway 107 – up to Vanson. So we'll come in from the opposite side to the Old Highway."

"Sounds good to me," replied Ella. She looked up at the moon and then back down at Drum. "Shall we go on now? Or rest here?"

"Go on," said Drum. "The Deceptor batteries won't last for ever."

"True," replied Ella thoughtfully. "By the way, can you ride a bicycle?"

"A bicycle?" asked Drum. "I don't know. Why?"

"Because there's four of them in a van back there," said Ella. "If we can manage them, we might be able to make Vanson by dawn. Shade won't be expecting that!"

"I might be too heavy," said Drum doubtfully.

"Let's find out," replied Ella. "The writing on the frames says they're mountain bikes. I guess that means they're strong."

"Do you know how to ride a bike?" asked Drum as they wheeled their chosen steeds out of the van and looked at them dubiously.

"I had one... I think," replied Ella, her eyes going vague. "But it had three wheels – and was about this high..."

She indicated a position somewhat lower than her knee and laughed, a sad sort of laugh for a childhood lost long ago.

"So I don't think that it will have left me with any riding skills. Come on... let's try it."

The Myrmidons separated Gold-Eye and Ninde before force-marching them to the waiting captive nets and locking them in. Then the creatures took off, dragging their burdens along the grass before lifting up into the sky.

In other circumstances Ninde might have enjoyed the experience of flying, even flying about in a net under a stinking Winger, its sweat dripping on her as it flew. It was a unique experience, looking down at the world below, all patches of green and faded brown, with dark roads criss-crossing the colour, the blue-brown swathe of the Williams River and the endless rows of suburban houses beyond it.

She'd half expected the Winger to turn towards the city and then the Meat Factory – but it flew south, gaining height till they were so high Ninde was shivering uncontrollably from the cold, her fingernails blue, all interest in the world below lost as she curled up in a heat-conserving ball.

Finally the Winger stopped its steady, wing-beating climb and began to glide down, spiralling in a great circle after its flightmates ahead, who were carrying Gold-Eye and Shade's spider-robot body.

Ninde uncurled. As they sank lower, she regained interest in the ground below. They were flying over a part of the city she didn't know – somewhere in the southern suburbs – down towards a long crescent-shaped beach of very white sand, with the open ocean stretching out to the horizon behind it.

Their ultimate destination was easily identifiable – Wingers were already landing on its capacious lawns.

What had once been a large, old-fashioned house – or perhaps an old-style hotel – stood in the middle of the lawns and carefully tended rose gardens. But it was altered and strange, with walls of many different colours that shifted and crawled over the surface, and a roof of silver that moved like mercury, flowing bright reflections back and forth so it made Ninde queasy just to look at it.

The house was at least four storeys high, with a broad, domed tower at one end, like an observatory. The silver globe of the Projector gleamed from atop the dome, still brighter than the shifting silver roof – and Myrmidons patrolled the ivy-grown walls that contained the gardens and separated the house from the beach.

The lawn got closer and closer, and Ninde braced herself for a bruising impact, but the Winger flapped back vigorously just before the net – and Ninde – hit the ground, making it a soft landing.

Myrmidons quickly took her from the net, forcing her across the lawn to an open door, thrusting her inside to the waiting hands of two Myrmidon Masters. Unlike any others Ninde had seen before, these wore no colours – just plain white armour of small interlocking plates, and snout-faced helms decorated with white plumes.

They acted just the same though, grabbing Ninde's arms and propelling her through a door that opened like an iris, then down a grey, featureless corridor made of some softly shining material that suggested metal rather than wood or plaster. The floor sounded strange too, with the Myrmidon's heavy hobnails screeching on it horribly.

They passed several doors along the corridor, each of many swirling colours loud and strident against the grey walls. Then they came to a plain white door and the Myrmidons stopped.

One of them touched the door and it slid open, revealing a small, brightly lit chamber painted completely white. Gold-Eye was sitting on a bed in it, looking totally dejected. He sprang up as he saw Ninde, catching her as the Myrmidons threw her in, the door sliding shut behind her.

Ella and Drum rode into Vanson warily and wearily a little more than half an hour after dawn. Good time considering the half hour lost learning to stay on the mountain bikes and then the further time lost using the wrong gears, throwing chains and losing control going down hills. Not to mention doctoring grazes and swearing at their trusty vehicles.

Vanson seemed empty of all life... including creatures. A small winter resort town, it was snowbound in winter and cold enough now. High-angled roofs characterised its architecture, which showed a fondness for ersatz European chalets. All the buildings were dominated by the Crookback Range, a dark mass that filled half the northern horizon. Caught by the rising sun, snow and ice were already gleaming in patches on it.

"Warm clothes... and socks," said Ella, looking up at the ridge, studying the two chair-lifts that climbed up from the town. Both had access roads under them, switchbacking from side to side between pylons. But she knew from the road atlas that only one chair-lift went all the way to the top of the ridge – and only one access road.

And from the top of the range, there was only one trail to the summit of Silverstone Mountain. It was out to the west, she knew, but not currently visible, lost in a clump of cloud. Cloud that hid the mountain – and the Grand Projector.

Drum touched her arm and pointed. Ella looked where he pointed, expecting a creature or some danger – but couldn't see anything.

"What?"

"Shops," said Drum, pointing again at a metal signpost that said, in white letters against blue, ALPINE SHOPPING CENTRE.

"Let's get some warm clothes – and have a rest."

ARCHIVE
INTERNAL DISCOURSE

Robert Primary:	I've found a way out, Shade.
Shade Primary:	Tell me. There is some danger here. We should be prepared.
Robert Primary:	No. You keep trying to shut me out.
Robert Secondary:	Then there will be no one to protect the children. The Grand Projector will not be destroyed.
Shade Primary:	He's right, you know. We may have our differences, but our ultimate goal is the same.
Robert Primary:	No, it isn't. You want to get a body from these Overlords!
Shade Primary:	That is an immediate goal, to be achieved before the ultimate goal – the destruction of the Grand Projector. I must have a body to ensure my/our survival to guide the children afterwards.
Robert Primary:	To rule them, you mean. Your middle name should be Megalomaniac.
Robert Secondary:	We don't need a body. Even this spider robot...

Robert Primary:	Shut up! He doesn't need to know that.
Shade Secondary:	I know what you're talking about anyway.
Shade Primary:	Do I?
Shade Tertiary:	I told you. Didn't I?
Robert Primary:	How many of me/us are there? I think this has gone far enough, and I am simply not going to believe in—

<PERSONALITY INTEGRATION ERROR.>

<SHUT DOWN AND RESTART.>

CHAPTER THIRTY-FOUR

There were seven Overlords sitting on seven thrones in the domed tower. Each of the thrones was carved from translucent stone in the Overlord's primary colour and lit within by a soft light. They were also engraved with scenes of battle and decorated with weapon and skull motifs. A carpet the colour of dried blood ran at the foot of the thrones, the ends tasselled with polished white rods that looked all too like human finger bones.

The thrones sat on a low balcony shaped like a crescent moon. Ninde had been right in thinking the tower looked like an observatory. It was – an observatory where the Overlords watched their battles.

The space under the dome was filled with holographic images, the colours and action bleeding between a dozen different, constantly shifting scenes. Every few minutes one image would expand to fill the whole dome, shrinking back only when it became less violent or otherwise lost the Overlords' interest. Then another horror would take its place.

Myrmidons decapitating each other; impaling enemies; stamping out Claim Fires, the flames licking at their feet. Images of Trackers finding cleverly hidden Myrmidons, now counter-ambushed. Glimpses of Wingers fighting in mid-air, ripping the throats from their enemies, losers tumbling from the sky.

There was sound, too, but muted, like some ferocious musical background. Screams and shouts of rage and pain, half heard as if from far away.

It was clear these battles were happening right now. Creatures were fighting and dying at the whim of the Overlords, whose greedy eyes remained fixed upward at the terrible sights taking place beyond their walls.

Here they wore helmets and soft clothes instead of armour. Four men and three women, they were outwardly indistinguishable from the humans they tormented and used in their awful games.

Before the Change, none of them would have looked out of place in a supermarket, except for a certain cruelty that shone in their eyes.

All of them were watching the holograms, occasionally making notations with light pens on the electronic map boards in the arms of their thrones.

The sun had almost set on the images of battle that flickered above them. When the last orange-red light finally drifted away, the fighting stopped and the holographic globes switched to show Ferrets waking in their nests, ready to issue out for their less formal combats.

One scene, showing Ferrets coming out of a manhole in a park, grew larger, expanding till it filled most of the dome. The Ferrets, their long, sinuous bodies pressed against the concrete pathway, were obviously on the track of something. One caught a scent and hissed, quickly leaving the path to lope across the grass. Ahead of it, a child suddenly broke cover from behind some bushes. A ragged, dirty boy, something like Gold-Eye had once been, he got only twenty yards before the Ferrets dragged him down, their long drinking fangs flashing in the yellow light from the park lanterns as they began to feed. Two of the watching Overlords laughed.

The scene dwindled then, and the globes sorted themselves out to show twelve separate locations. At the same time, the large double doors opposite the Overlords' thrones opened, and four white-clad Myrmidon Masters marched in, the Shade spider robot between them.

The Overlords looked down at him from the holograms as if seeing a particularly unpleasant dog brought in by the dogcatchers.

Finally, Red Diamond – a fattish, pasty-faced man with long thin hair combed across a balding scalp – stood up from his blood-red throne. But he didn't speak aloud. Instead he subvocalised, his words transmitted to the others and Shade by the communications system that rode on the Projector net.

Red Diamond:	It is the machine-mind Shade.
Shade:	I have come to collect what we bargained for. The body-construction data and access to an appropriate laboratory.
Red Diamond:	It is agreed that I will speak for the Council.
Shade:	Good. Unblock the data and grant me access to the lab. I am keen to get started.
Red Diamond:	You may be interested to know that the two other animal subjects somehow survived their fall. They were seen in the river, obviously alive.
Shade:	So? That is irrelevant. I have delivered two to you.
Red Diamond:	It means we can get two more if the ones we have die... when you do.

At the word *die*, Red Diamond suddenly snapped up a metal tube he had by his side and fired a white-hot beam of energy straight through the spider robot. Liquid metal and molten crystal exploded everywhere, splashing across the Myrmidons. Not a creature moved until Red Diamond strode down and examined the smoking wreckage of the spider robot. The Thinker inside was almost completely melted. Whatever it had once housed was totally destroyed.

Red Diamond: The machine-mind is terminated. You – bring the animal subjects here. If they're still alive. And clean up this mess, and yourselves.

Black Banner: I trust they are still alive. Since one of them is mine.

Emerald Crown: They are common property. That has been decided. Of course, if you do not want to abide by the rules...

Black Banner: No, no. I simply forgot.

He smiled as this was transmitted, obviously lying. None of the other Overlords smiled back, but one of the women – the oldest of them, by the look of her white hair and wrinkled skin, stood up from her gold throne.

Gold Claw: These animals have proven troublesome enough without causing quarrels among us. Let us examine them, decide who shall carry out the investigations... but not now! I must prepare my plan for the battle tomorrow with Blue Star. I believe that success in that battle may well place the trophy in my hands come year end – and that is much more important than the genetic peculiarities of animals, however useful!

All the Overlords instinctively turned on the word *trophy* and looked at a small golden figurine locked behind a translucent window on the far side of the room. Only six inches high, it represented two Myrmidons in the act of running each other through with broad-bladed spears. The small bronze plate beneath the statuette was inscribed with lines of symbols. There were fifteen altogether, each the name of the Overlord who had won the most battles in the fifteen years since the Change.

Red Diamond: Very well. We all have battles to plan. We shall decide on the animals' disposal the day after tomorrow.

Despite their all-night cycle ride, Ella and Drum slept for only four hours before resuming their journey in mid-morning. Both feared that Shade would tell the Overlords of the plan to attack the Grand Projector. Equally worrying was the thought that the Deceptor batteries would run out before they got there.

Fortunately the whole area seemed totally empty of creatures. And both Ella and Drum were now freshly equipped with warm clothes and ski parkas, sleeping bags and new backpacks stuffed with rope, packaged foods and other odds and ends. Drum also had a long steel pinch bar, thrust through his belt as a replacement for his lost sword.

It was sunny again too, the air crisp and clean, the sky blue. Both felt heartened and as optimistic as they ever got. Neither wanted to think ahead to what they would actually do when they reached the Grand Projector.

By one o'clock they were three quarters of the way up the access road and just starting to encounter patches of ice and shadowed areas of frozen snow, mixed in with short yellow grass and grey-green stones. They also got their first glimpse of Mount Silverstone – and the Grand Projector.

The mountain was easy to spot. It was a great jumble of enormous grey stones shot through with silvery mica, piling up to form a small peak above the rest of the Crookback Range. It even did shine like silver when the sun caught it, though Mount Greystone would have been a more accurate name.

The Grand Projector was harder to make out, but there clearly was some sort of building on top of the mountain. A tower, perhaps seven or eight storeys high – and light-coloured, so it was hard to see against the sky.

Ella was staring at it, wrinkling her eyes against the sun, when Drum tapped her elbow and said, "Battery warning."

"But I changed it only an hour ago!" exclaimed Ella, looking down at the red half-charge light flashing. "It was one of the spares, fully charged... Ah..."

She looked back up at the distant tower on top of the mountain.

"The Grand Projector," she said. "If it's draining the batteries at this distance, we won't have any power left at all when we get close."

"I haven't seen any creatures," offered Drum, shrugging. "So it may not matter."

"They'll be there," said Ella. "Somewhere. Come on."

It was a hard slog up the access road. The ground rose more than a thousand feet from Vanson up to the ridge, in less than a mile of horizontal distance.

Probably only a ten-minute ride in the cable cars, thought Ella, as she crossed under the cables again, the shadow of one of the pylons giving her a temporary chill.

It was clear they'd only just make the top of the ridge by dusk and would have to seek shelter. The late-afternoon sun was already failing to deliver much heat and the clouds were coming down. Mount Silverstone had already vanished into their wet, hidden depths and the ridge would soon follow.

Ella knew that sitting clouds and no wind meant a warmer night than a clear sky and a chilling breeze. But every time they stopped for a rest, the air bit at her face and she felt colder than she ever had before, despite her ski clothes.

Finally the road levelled out on the ridge, sweeping around the cable-car station and a restaurant building to merge with a parking lot still occupied by four-wheel drives, a small bulldozer and several bright orange snowmobiles.

Beyond the parking lot, a boarded trail led off along the ridge, across boggy heather till it disappeared into cloud forty yards out. A sign at the trailhead read, MOUNT SILVERSTONE WALKING TRACK. THREE MILES. MEDIUM DIFFICULTY.

"We'd better find some shelter till morning," panted Ella, leaning forward to massage the muscles at the front of her thighs. "Unless you think we should go on."

"No," said Drum, looking out at the befogged track, his breath steaming out in front of him. "I think we'd freeze – and we need a good rest. Better to get a fresh start tomorrow."

"Tomorrow," said Ella absently, noting the only two buildings on the desolate ridge – the cable-car station and a large, multi-windowed structure proclaiming itself AL PINE'S LOOKOUT RESTAURANT.

"Tomorrow," she continued, still speaking as if trying to convince herself that it was possible. "Tomorrow we destroy the Grand Projector."

MUSING – ROBERT INGMAN

So I was only fooling myself with the multiple-personality bit. You can't peel off the unpleasant parts and call them something else.

I betrayed the only chance the children had.

That is the most awful of my many crimes.

If I have a soul, I fear it will not be judged lightly. I doubt that even a forgiving God would accept my sins...

Yet I am still here, and perhaps... perhaps there is some divinely granted chance for me to make amends...

Or else I am truly made and all that I know... and feel... now is just the last microseconds of thought surging through the Thinker...

I could have dodged that shot. I saw him lift it, analysed the muscle patterns in his arm and hand...

But I didn't.

So why am I still here?

And where is here?

CHAPTER THIRTY-FIVE

Ninde and Gold-Eye had no idea how long they'd been in the cell when the white-clad Myrmidon Masters came to get them out. Judging by the meals delivered, it was at least thirty-six hours, maybe more. Ninde had a watch, but it had ceased working back on the railway bridge – perhaps from the shock of the grenade explosion.

They'd talked and slept for most of those hours but hadn't even tried to make love. Desire had slipped away from them. And they felt watched all the time. Both also remembered Shade's comment about breeding, too, though neither mentioned it.

It was enough to lie together on the bed. To talk about their early lives, the slight differences between their Dorms, the people who'd been important to them. Talk that somehow shared and lessened their unspoken fears without directly mentioning them.

Then the Myrmidon Masters were at the door, two of them filling the frame with their bulky forms. Ninde was in the small bathroom, washing her face, when she heard the door open. For a moment she thought they might take Gold-Eye by himself and dashed back out, her face still dripping water.

But the Myrmidons wanted both of them, and propelled them out through many corridors and several doors, till they came to a set of double doors ornamented with heavy golden bosses.

Here they waited for a moment till the doors swung open. Beyond lay the Battle Room, with its seven Overlords sitting, lolling and even sleeping on their thrones of lit stone. Above them scenes of mayhem shone in the domed ceiling and the whisper of battle filled the room.

Gold-Eye and Ninde were pushed in. Heavy Myrmidon hands on their shoulders forced them to kneel.

"People," whispered Gold-Eye, looking up at the thrones, up at the faces above the colourful robes. "Old people."

None of the Overlords paid them any attention. Apart from Grey Crescent, who was asleep, all were focused on the images above them. Gold-Eye looked too and saw that it was about ten in the morning, the sun bright and the shadows short.

Still no one paid them any attention, and they seemed to kneel for at least half an hour before a bell chimed and the battle images faded. At the same time, white-clad Drones entered the room, carrying trays loaded with a great variety of food. These trays were delivered to the Overlords, who finally gazed down at the two captives.

None of them spoke aloud, but there were gestures between them that suggested dialogue, and Gold-Eye noticed the muscles in their throats moved.

Then another Drone entered the room and stood in front of the children, its pale, noseless face devoid of any expression. Slowly it raised the medallion of a mind-call to its forehead and cleared its throat.

"I speak with the voice of Red Diamond," it said, voice slow and partly swallowed, as if it couldn't control its tongue. "I require you to demonstrate your power of invisibility."

With the word *invisibility*, the Myrmidon behind Ninde tightened its grip on her shoulder and she yelped with the sudden pain. A grunt from Gold-Eye confirmed he was getting the same treatment.

"It wasn't anything to do with us," protested Ninde. "Shade made the Deceptors. I don't know how they worked."

"If you do not demonstrate this invisibility, you will be punished," the Drone continued, ignoring Ninde's interruption. "This punishment will continue until you do as I ask. If you persist, you will be—"

The Drone stopped in mid sentence as all the Overlords suddenly looked up, responding to something only they could hear or feel.

Gold-Eye and Ninde looked up too, to see a holographic scene swirling into view, filling the whole ceiling of the dome.

"Ella and Drum!" exclaimed Ninde, indescribable joy rising in her as the two familiar faces swam into focus. They

335

were wearing strange clothes and seemed to be on a mountain top where it was very windy – and next to a pale-grey wall of some kind. Not just to shelter from the wind, because they were running their hands along a crack – no, the faint outline of a door – and then both were looking down at their belt pouches, doing something... and Ella disappeared, followed a moment later by Drum. They hadn't moved. They'd just vanished out of the picture.

Ella checked the new battery, then turned her attention back to the slightly indented line that possibly marked a door frame.

"I have no idea how it opens," she said despairingly. They were down to their last batteries now. Even a fully charged one lasted only ten minutes this close to the Grand Projector. When the one she had just put on was exhausted, they would be easy prey to any passing Wingers.

"We need those explosives!" Ella shouted in frustration, slapping the concrete. Though secretly she doubted there would have been enough to cut through the door anyway.

The tower that housed the Grand Projector was a fortress – a massive reinforced-concrete structure in the shape of an obelisk. Six storeys. No windows. Only the faint outline of a door in one side hinting there was any way in at all.

Ironically, it had clearly been built by humans, not creatures. A faded sign nearby gave the details of the architect and builders, describing it as a "religious temple" constructed for the Church of the Overlords. The builders could never have known what they were constructing: housing for the evil machine that would destroy them and their children.

"This has to open somehow," said Drum, once again trying to force his pinch bar into the tiniest of cracks – and failing.

"Too late to go back," murmured Ella, looking up at the concrete tower, fleetingly wondering if they could climb it – and dismissing the idea even as it came.

"Much too late," said Drum. Something in his tone made her turn around. She followed his gaze and saw the tiny black dots – nine of them – down in the valley near Vanson. Wingers, climbing up towards them.

At the same time, her battery started flashing. Half charge, after only four minutes. Four minutes left till she would be visible to Winger eyes.

As Ella and Drum vanished out of the image, leaving only a windswept mountain and a concrete wall, the Overlords suddenly sprang into action. Red Diamond and Black Banner jumped down from their thrones and ran to another door, which slid open before them. There Drones waited, holding armour open for them to step into. Gold Claw, Blue Star, Emerald Crown and Grey Crescent started tapping at maps and control boards with their light pens, while battles ceased overhead and Myrmidon Masters stood to receive new orders.

Silver Sun stepped down from its throne and approached Gold-Eye and Ninde, who were still kneeling and flanked by the Myrmidon Master.

As Silver Sun got closer, Gold-Eye realised the Overlord was a woman. A pretty woman, perhaps in her mid-thirties, with light, straw-coloured hair cut short and lacquered back.

As she approached, the Drone Red Diamond had used as his mouthpiece turned away and Silver Sun spoke directly to them.

"So. You are the ones the machine-mind called Gold-Eye and Ninde."

Her voice was rich and musical, though she spoke English with a strange inflection. It was too good a voice for someone who was responsible for destroying ninety-eight per cent of the human race, someone who now preyed upon captive children.

"And you say this... invisibility... that we have just seen demonstrated by your friends is something the machine-mind created?" she continued. "Red Diamond really was precipitous in destroying it."

"Shade?" asked Gold-Eye. "Shade... dead?"

"Absolutely," replied Silver Sun. She smiled, showing teeth filed to points, her eyes remaining dead and cold. "Now, while my colleagues rush off to deal with your pathetic friends, we shall go and have a private... chat? I do speak your language well, don't I? Such a fascinating means of communication. So dreadfully slow. But quite sophisticated for an animal race."

"Why do you kill us?" asked Ninde, looking up at the still-smiling face, the teeth hidden behind soft lips, the bright hair so glossy with lacquer. "Why do you... do any of it?"

Silver Sun looked down at her, head tilted to one side as if she didn't understand. Then she smiled more broadly, teeth glittering, and said, "That's what you're there for. It's the way things are meant to be. You animals really are so stupid."

When she finished speaking, her throat twitched, sending some message to the Myrmidon Masters. They lurched into action, dragging Gold-Eye and Ninde to their feet and pushing them out the door.

"They'll be here soon," said Ella, watching the Wingers beating furiously to gain height, still only halfway up Mount Silverstone. "I suppose... I suppose it was foolish to think we could—"

"Not foolish," said Drum. "If Shade hadn't betrayed us, we might have done something—"

"But he did," interrupted Ella bleakly. "And no one's going to follow us, are they? Children will still escape from the Dorms, but they'll live only short, wild lives. No one will train them, guide them... No one will know about the Projectors... and the Overlords will just... keep on for a thousand years. A hundred children a day for a thousand years..."

"No they won't, Ella," said a voice behind them.

It was the voice of Shade.

MISQUOTATION - ROBERT INGMAN

I was Shade. I was responsible for everything that happened. For all the rescues of lost children, the saving of escapees from the Dorms. Their education to help them survive – and to be human beings. But I was responsible... I am responsible for all the deaths too, as I spent the children in what I thought was a... a war for the greater good.

Somewhere I got confused. Intellectual curiosity grew to the point where I had to know, even when it wasn't important – and children died for the increase of my knowledge.

And the information I did need I didn't seek hard enough.

Then when I did get it, I failed to use it properly.

But perhaps I am not too late.

There comes a tide in the affairs of men, that if taken at the flood... or something like that. There is still a chance, a very slight chance.

Perhaps I can redeem myself after all...

CHAPTER THIRTY~SIX

The Myrmidons didn't take them back to the cell. Instead they left the house and walked down to the beach, passing through a guardhouse in the wall manned by several more white-armoured Myrmidon Masters. It seemed the Overlords only trusted the superior variety to look after their own security.

"Where are you taking us?" asked Ninde, unable to see Silver Sun behind her but still hearing her soft shuffle in the sand, in between the Myrmidons' heavy scuffling.

"I think I'll drown one of you till the other answers my questions," replied Silver Sun calmly. "You see, I have much more experience with animals than Red Diamond does. I spent several years here during our initial reconnaissance and did most of the work setting up the Transfer. So I know there is some psychosexual bond between you that can be exploited. Alternatively, I may just drown you both. After all, we will have the other two for questioning, and they have actually demonstrated that invisibility technique."

"We will too," said Gold-Eye quickly, looking at Ninde's white face and then the sea. Its waves crashed in with a regularity that cared nothing for who might be pushed under them. "But we need equipment."

"Our packs and equipment belts," added Ninde hastily. "We'll show you. But it only works for Change-enhanced vision... like in your creatures."

"I see," said Silver Sun. "I will have it fetched."

That sounded as if she would wait for a demonstration of the Deceptors and Gold-Eye let out a small sigh of relief. But the Myrmidons kept on marching them down into the sea. As the wash from the waves touched their boots, they stopped – then marched forward again, till the water washed around their knees, well above the thighs of Gold-Eye and Ninde.

"Then again – I think you might be better drowned," said Silver Sun from somewhere behind them on the sand.

As she spoke, the Myrmidons clasped the children's heads with their heavy hands and pushed them facedown into the ocean.

Ella turned around, the pistol drawn, finger taking up the first pressure on the trigger. But there was no crystal-bodied spider robot there.

Just a hologram, so faded she could see the concrete wall through it. Shade – but a Shade somewhat different from the image he had always portrayed before. Shorter and less muscular. Eyes not piercing blue but a sort of muddy grey. And teeth no longer blindingly white and even.

Enough of a difference for Ella to put her pistol back and ask, "Shade?"

"Sort of," said the hologram nervously, running his hand through hair much thinner and browner than it had been before. "But more like Robert Ingman, I think. The man I originally was."

"What are you doing here?" asked Drum suspiciously, one eye still on the approaching Wingers. "How are you here?"

"Well, it's sort of complicated," muttered Shade/Robert. "The Overlords destroyed the Thinker that housed my personality, but I had already worked out how to spread myself... or the bits that I want... through the Projector network. So I can pretty well be anywhere there's Projector power... oh... and I came here to apologise I guess, and... uh... help."

"How?" snapped Drum. The Wingers were directly below now, banking up for a spiralling climb. At the top of that climb... in about a minute... they would swoop down...

"Well, there is a manual method of opening the door from the inside," explained Robert. "I thought if I showed Drum where it is and what it looks like, he could use his—"

"OK, OK!" interrupted Ella urgently. "Show him!"

Robert nodded and quickly sketched in the air with his finger – and a hologram formed against the wall, showing a short level under a panel with a red and green light.

"It's there," said Robert. "On the other side, about two feet in..."

Drum was already feeling for the level with his Change Talent, eyes closed, sweat springing out on his forehead despite the cold wind. His hand moved, fingers clasping something that wasn't there... Dimly he felt Ella slide the pinch bar out of his belt... Then his arm jerked down and he felt his mind move the lever down.

His eyes flashed open to see the door sliding up, lights coming on inside. At the same time, the lead Winger attacked.

Salt burned Gold-Eye's mouth and nose, water filling them as he went under for the third time. This time he stopped struggling immediately and just let the Myrmidon hold him down. He'd got a good mouthful of air – and was just concentrating on holding that breath. Focusing on that, trying not to think of anything else – even Ninde. But he couldn't help thinking of her, and tears fled his eyes to mix with the already salty sea.

Thinking of Ninde made him think of Ella and Drum as well. Still alive and obviously at Mount Silverstone. If Shade hadn't lied, they would be trying to destroy the Grand Projector. So humanity still had a chance... even if he and Ninde didn't.

Ninde was thinking similar thoughts, the bubbles flying out of her mouth, taking with them her last desperate gulp of air. For a second she was tempted to

344

just breathe out, to finish it quickly – but she didn't do it. Instead she reached again to drag her nails across the Myrmidon's gauntlets.

It responded by pushing her still deeper, grinding sand against her face. Panicking, kicking and scratching, she finally lost her battle not to breathe – and sucked in. Water filled her lungs with a terrible rush that was totally and terrifyingly at odds with all the myths about the peacefulness of death by drowning.

Ella smacked the pinch bar across the neck of the lead Winger as it dived past her, but its claws raked across her forearm as she did, opening deep wounds and knocking the bar from her grasp.

It seemed unharmed, looping back to attack again – only to fly headlong into a large stone cast by the furious hand of Drum. Shrieking, right eye crushed and clouded with spewing ichor, it turned too quickly, wing crashing into a corner of the tower with a crack like a dry branch snapping. Lopsided, it cartwheeled into the ground, striking the silver-shot rocks of the mountain many times as it bounced down towards the valley below.

Drum yanked Ella into the building in the next second, slapping the lever to close the door – just as the second Winger dived in. For a few seconds door machinery struggled against Winger strength. Then it closed like a guillotine, cutting off the Winger's head. This snapped its teeth at Drum's feet several times, then lay still.

"Can they open it?" snapped Drum, asking the Robert hologram, which had just rematerialised inside.

"No... I don't think so... requires an Overlord," said Robert, looking down with shocked eyes at Ella, who was busy rolling out a bandage from her pouch. With one end in her mouth and the other in her weakened right hand, she was busy trying to put direct pressure on her wounds.

"But there are two on the way," he added worriedly. "They'll be here very... very soon."

"So what do we do?" asked Ella. She handed one end of the bandage to Drum so he could wrap it around the long cuts in her forearm, her left thumb still pressed firmly on the pressure point inside her elbow. As soon as the bandage was firmly on, she let go – and the cloth immediately turned red, blood spreading like ink spilled on paper.

"Well, the whole Grand Projector is controlled by a dedicated Thinker," said Robert. "I had considered turning it off somehow, but it is well protected from the likes of me, and in fact may not be able to be turned off at all..."

"Where is it?" screamed Ella, getting to her feet. "Just tell us where it is!"

"Up the ladder... up the ladder," Robert repeated, pointing to the second of two steel ladders. It stood in a corner of the featureless room and extended through a square access hole in the ceiling.

Ella ran to it, jumping up to the third rung, ignoring the pain in her injured arm as she climbed. Blood ran out from under the bandage and Drum steadied her as she almost fell back.

"But you should know that..." Robert was saying from down below – and then from in front of her as he reappeared on the next floor.

"You should know that if you destroy it," he shouted, pointing up to the large conch-shell Thinker on a plinth well above Ella's head. "If you destroy it, the Grand Projector will overload, delivering enormous amounts of Change energy – lethal radiation! It will kill you both in minutes. Please, please let me see if there's some way of shutting... oh dear... the Overlords!"

The sound of the door opening below was enough for Ella – and Drum, too. She drew the pistol and aimed it up at the Thinker. Drum moved up close to steady her hand, cupping it gently in his own huge palm.

Then she pulled the trigger, time and time again, laughing and weeping, till the magazine was empty and the Thinker lay in broken shards upon the floor.

CHAPTER THIRTY~SEUEN

Gold-Eye was just about to give up and breathe in water when the Myrmidon holding him down suddenly let go.

Arching backwards, Gold-Eye exploded from the water, coughing and spluttering, expecting to be plunged back down at any moment. Then he saw the Myrmidon was kneeling in the water at his side. It had its visor up, but it eyes somehow looked past him out to the blue water beyond.

Then it spoke, in English, not in Battlespeech.

A child is caught
A torment of terror
To know no kindness
Laid down at last
Dream no more death

Forsaken at fourteen
Foul prisoned flesh
Battle the burden
Sleep now Sam
Fall to freedom

Then he did look at Gold-Eye. "I was Sam Allen once," he said, and fell facedown into the water.

Gold-Eye looked away and saw the other Myrmidon, sunken by its armour – and a smaller shape, floating head down, the waves tugging it out towards the open sea.

"Ninde!" screamed Gold-Eye, splashing through the waves. Grabbing her limp form, he carried her desperately to the beach, so desperately he didn't even notice that Silver Sun was no longer there.

Laying her down, he thought her dead, and panic and fear stabbed him in the guts. Then Shade's training gripped him like one of his own visions. One of the first lessons he'd done – one of the few he'd had time for. Essential knowledge for people who lived in a Submarine.

Mechanically he checked her pulse, cleared her airway and began CPR.

"Very well done... my children," said Robert, the hologram brightening and becoming more solid as they watched. Tears streamed down his cheeks. "You were all I ever hoped for... and more. I am sorry I was less. Goodbye."

The hologram brightened still further, the tears shining like lights upon his skin. Then he was gone.

"I feel strange," whispered Ella, holding on to Drum. "Sort of powerful... as if I could conjure anything... anything at all... We have a few minutes, I think he said?"

"Yes," replied Drum, his eyes also wet with tears. "Let's go out – out into the sun."

He picked her up but didn't carry her down the ladder.

He could feel the Change energy flowing in him. It was so strong he simply used his Talent to rise up in the air and descend gently down through the trapdoor, then to float across to the main door.

There were no Overlords there. Just a strange metal tube on the floor, glittering in the shaft of sunlight coming through the door. All the interior lights had gone out.

Dead Wingers littered the ground outside and down the tumbled rocks, so Drum carried Ella around a little way, almost to the Shade. They sat down with their backs to the wall, looking out at the blue sky, the sun warm on their faces, the wind cold.

"The power's ebbing now," said Ella. "And I can't think of a single thing I want to conjure. All the things I want aren't objects you can hold, or even name..."

She held out her hand and Drum took it, surprised at the effort, as if all his strength was just running out of him.

Hand in hand, they waited for the end.

Ninde came to as Gold-Eye bent down for another breath. He quickly drew back as she coughed and spat out seawater. At the same time, he felt the grip of the soon-to-be-now, stronger than it had ever been.

"No, not now!" he said, veins in his forehead standing out as he tried to fight it off.

"What?" Ninde coughed, and her consciousness rushed back. Obviously they were safe, and Gold-Eye was about to have a vision... and she felt her knuckle in her mouth... and her mind expanding, leaping out over miles and miles. She saw the beginnings of Gold-Eye's vision and heard fifty thousand children cheering as they climbed over the fallen bodies of Watchwards at the gates of the Dorms; heard the waking thoughts of the survivors in the Meat Factory; and then she felt Ella and Drum, so close that she knew she could speak to them, show them Gold-Eye's vision, give them something in the seconds before they died.

"It's Ninde," murmured Ella sleepily, just moving one finger in Drum's palm. "She wants us to see... Gold-Eye's soon-to-be-now..."

"I see it," whispered Drum. He smiled, a full-hearted smile. Ella smiled too, and for a second his hand tightened on hers.

Then they were dead, and the sun moved around, bringing the shade to wrap around their bodies like a shroud.

GOLD-EYE'S VISION

It was autumn and the red-and-yellow leaves were piled high around the trees in the park. Two small children – a boy of about five and a girl of three or so – were kicking through the leaves. Another half a dozen children were playing on the swings and merry-go-rounds as various parents watched them with obvious pride.

A stylishly dressed woman – perhaps in her late twenties – was reading a hefty textbook, perhaps a medical tome, on a bench nearby. She kept glancing up at the children in the leaves, watching them laugh and giggle as they played.

Then she saw a man coming towards them, a man whose eyes caught the afternoon light and glinted strangely gold. He walked up to the woman and bent down to kiss her lovingly on the ear. She smiled and called out to the children.

"Ella! Drum! Daddy's here!" said Ninde. "It's time to go home."